This is a novel about
search for the true
family. She grew up in Bronxville
and lives on the Upper West Side

I Am Alex Locus
A Novel

When she begins her quest.

This is a contemporary novel.
I have also written novels set
in New York City in the 1870s, at
the dawn of the Gilded Age.
My books can be found at
DermodyHouse.com / books

Joseph P. Garland

DERMODY
HOUSE
PUBLISHING

If you enjoy this book, please
DermodyHouse.com
share

A Warning

This is the story of a family, though it is entirely fictional. In the course of discovering the truth about her family, Alexandra Locus will come upon some uncomfortable truths. Particularly in regard to the relationship between her mother and her father. This includes, she will learn, abuse and **rape**, all of which is discussed as happening in general terms, i.e., there are no explicit scenes, in the past, well before the story begins.

Insofar as you as a reader will be overly troubled—I use "overly" because I assume most readers will be troubled, please consider *not* reading this novel.

To my sister Patty.
Without whom none of the
Garlands would be who we are.

PROLOGUE

At 3:18 p.m. on August 8, 2008, a New York City 9-1-1 dispatcher efficiently processed a call. A woman had collapsed in apartment 3F at 34 West 94th Street in Manhattan. Within fifteen minutes, the patient was on the way to St. Luke's Hospital, never regaining consciousness. Upon arrival, she was placed in a medically induced coma as doctors tried to come up with a course of treatment. The damage from the woman's stroke, however, was beyond repair and at 2:22 p.m. on August 11, 2008, she was removed from life support, and she died, surrounded by her husband Steven, her fourteen-year-old-daughter Alexandra, her parents, and her mother- and father-in-law. Her name was Emily Locus. She was thirty-eight years old.

1.

My name is Alexandra Locus. This is the story of who I am and, more importantly, who my mother was and how I came about learning that.

It started on a Thursday night in mid-September 2017. I was twenty-three and living in a one-bedroom apartment on the third floor of a brownstone on West 85th Street in Manhattan. Near Central Park. My job was deadly boring and mind-numbing, in the back office of a mega-bank in midtown. Thursday nights were my chance to get out. Getting out usually meant meeting my childhood friend Kate Winslow at a not-too-grungy/not-too-upscale bar on Broadway, Columbus, or Amsterdam and sometimes hooking up with some guy with the same kind of empty life as mine.

Actually, the hooking up rarely happened, and when it did it was usually with a sweet-enough guy from some other bank or law firm or maybe ad agency or publishing house. None of them went anywhere.

On this particular Thursday, Kate was working late at her PR firm. "*I can only get there at nine,*" she texted at about 5:30, and I texted back "*Fine. See you then at Teddy's,*" a favorite spot nearby, on Amsterdam.

There were usually book readings on Thursday nights at the Barnes & Noble on Broadway and 82nd Street. It goes up half a block and was, swear to God, the model for Fox Books in *You've Got Mail*. So that'd help me kill time, and if this one was boring, I could bail and wander around and do some magazine scanning before meeting Kate.

It was warm for September 14, and after work, I changed into something flirty but casual—nice black pants, a dark red blouse buttoned to the neck (with burgundy lingerie beneath), and black flats. With plenty of time, I put my hair up and dabbed some you-never-know perfume behind my ears and in a few other strategic spots.

A quick walk and I was through the revolving doors into the B&N. A poster set up to the right of the main escalator said that at eight a Karen Adams would be reading from her collection of stories. From her photo, she looked to be about my age. It was five of or so. I hurried up the long escalator to get a seat and found one on the righthand side near the back.

There were maybe fifteen people in the rows of chairs, and in front was a table on which the author's books were stacked, and a poster for the book—entitled *Lonesome*—draped nearly to the floor. She was there with a B&N staffer and an older—though not old—woman, who I took to be her mother.

Ms. Adams wore a standard-issue suit like I wear to work. It was blue and the blouse was beige, and she had sensible low-heeled black pumps. She'd wrapped a Hermès scarf around her neck, which brought out her rather attractive if narrow face, and her hair looked to have been done, I was guessing, at lunchtime.

I'd been to these readings before and the usual podium with the Barnes & Noble logo and a microphone was off to one side, and after about half the seats were taken, a little past eight, the staffer welcomed us and introduced Karen Adams. Her book was in her right hand, and she opened it as she got to the podium. After looking out across us and covering her mouth with a fist for a brief cough, she started. She thanked us for coming. She stopped. With a shake of the head, a sip of water, and a deep breath, she tried again.

"I am going to go with the beginning of a story that is one of my favorites, though I know I'm not supposed to say that." A few people chuckled. "It came to me when I was thinking back on summer vacations I took in Vermont, and I wrote it when I was in college. It's about...Well, it's called *Lonesome*, and here's how it begins."

Her hand shook as she tried to keep the book open but after a sentence or two, her voice and her hand relaxed. The murmur of people passing off to the side vanished as her words began to flow.

It was the story of two women, a pair of married New Yorkers. They're in Western Massachusetts with their kids and husbands at a house the two families shared each August. It's the Thursday of a week the husbands are working in the city. The kids are at camp, and as they often do the two women are out on a rowboat lolling around a small lake. Others are out too, particularly other wives whose husbands are in town.

These two women are particularly far from the beach when a lowering sky comes across the hills to the west, and they're slow in noticing the clouds. As things darken more, the others are all safely ashore and these two, laughing as they try to coordinate their rowing, are still far away when a curtain of water overwhelms them.

Their friends on the shore are waving their arms and calling to them in the thickening air, but the little boat begins to rock as their now desperate rowing flails and suddenly it nearly capsizes and one of the two is in the water. Neither has a lifejacket on—there was no forecast of storms—and, besides, they would never be far from shore and they are both good swimmers.

Once. Twice. Three times the first woman's head surfaces and her arms flail as the rain pours down. Her friend reaches for her, but she's just too far away.

Cruelly, this was where Karen Adams stopped.

Pausing only a moment, she turned to a later page.

"This next story is not about me." She then launched about a bunch of Tufts students wandering around Boston on a Saturday night in the fall. It's actually early Sunday morning, and the competing factions in the gang are arguing in increasingly irate tones about how they're to get back to campus as they move from bar to bar.

Again, she stopped. The B&N woman jumped up.

"Now you didn't expect she'd give everything away, did you?" She took the book from the author and held it up to us. "We have plenty of copies for you to purchase, given how I know you are all interested in how these and other stories end."

There was applause in the crowd. I checked my watch. About eight-forty. I'd wait for the Q&A and buy a copy to support a struggling artist and have plenty of time to meet Kate.

"Now," the staffer said, "I'd like to introduce American Book Award finalist Nancy Penchant for a few words about her protégé."

The older woman rose and walked to the microphone. This older woman, the famous author and apparently not the mother, was far more stylish in black pants and a raspberry blouse. She had a string of pearls around her neck, which looked to be some sort of heirloom, and her black hair hung loosely a few inches below her shoulders. I think she was slim, and I guessed of average height but wore three-inch heels that I saw were Louboutins when she sat and dangled her left leg over her right knee. She could have been about my mom's age, which would put her late-forties, early-fifties, and the only concession to her age was a pair of tortoiseshell reading glasses that dangled from her neck.

She leaned into the microphone and placed her hands on the sides of the podium.

"I'm so honored to be here with you tonight. I take some credit for Karen's book. Not what's in it, but what led her to give her writing the attention it deserved. She was a sophomore at Dartmouth and wrote a short story for its literary magazine. I don't know how, but I saw it, and it spoke to me. I know that's quaint, but it did."

She reached to her right and lifted a bottle of water with a B&N label and took a quick sip before putting it back.

"I was thinking at the time of an old friend, who passed too young. That friend had some secrets, and one was that she wrote. And she wrote well but made no effort to have others see her words. I may have been the only person who read any of it. I decided to create an award with a small stipend named for her, to encourage writers, and Karen was the first recipient of the Emily Locus Award."

The what? Did I hear that right?

That's what shot through my brain like a laser beam. But what did she say before mentioning my mom's name?—yes, Emily Locus was my dead mother. I know what it was now but sitting there back then I couldn't recall. Something about writing and not telling anyone and secrets.

What I do remember is getting up and rushing down a short, yellow hallway to the ladies' as a bit of light applause rose from the crowd. It was empty and blue and dreary, and I locked the door behind me.

Maybe it's not my mom.

Be serious. How many Emily Locuses can there be?

This was what I was thinking: I could wait it out or slip around and be gone. *No one'd know.*

Except me, of course.

My mom died when I was fourteen. I didn't really know her, and I'd come to regret that. This was a woman, this older writer, who may have known my mom and not in the context of some village social or school thing. In the big, wide world.

As I was trying to make sense of whatever was happening, someone knocked. "I'll be right out," I said. I turned the water on and put some on my face and dried it with a paper towel. A woman was bounding back and forth as I opened the door, and I let her in and headed down the hall.

The Q&A was just wrapping up, and there was more light applause. I reached the reading area, and seven or eight people were lined up to get Karen Adams to sign her book. She sat at the table and the B&N staffer and this Nancy woman stood behind chatting with one another and with the customers.

I tried to recall what this woman said before she mentioned the award, which may or may not be named for my dead mother but seeing as there can't be all too many Emily Locuses I thought odds were that this author knew my mom and that they might very well have been important to each other—though *my* Emily Locus was a simple suburban housewife, unlike *her* Emily Locus who was some kind of writer and friends with this real writer.

I debated approaching her. *What good could that do even if it was my mother?* She was long gone and buried and everyone who knew her had moved on. No, I decided, best to leave it. Then they—the young and the old authors—were heading to the escalator. I walked along a separate aisle that intersected theirs and stopped just before it did. They passed, and the younger one got on. Nancy Whatever was about to, her hand already on the rubber railing and her foot on the step, when I said a bit loudly to be heard over the din, "I am Alex Locus."

I had no idea whether "Alex Locus" would get a reaction. It did. She almost tripped on the moving step as her head shot around and she locked on me all the way down. At some point, she waved to me as I stood watching, with the younger woman oblivious to what was going on behind her.

Since I made this leap, I had to say *something* to her, so I got on. There were now two or three people between us. She pulled the other writer to the side at the bottom and was saying something to her as I went down.

I got to them, and she pulled me out of the way and then said, "Did you say you're *Alex* Locus? *Alexandra Locus*?"

It was a little uncomfortable, the intensity of her stare and of her grip on my arm, but I confirmed that I was, in fact, Alexandra Locus.

"Your mother was Emily?"

I nodded. Before I knew it, she'd pulled me close, so hard that I nearly bounced off her. I looked over her shoulder and the younger writer was completely clueless about what was happening.

The stranger's arms were around me and she whispered, "I so miss your mother," before pushing away, using the back of her right wrist to dab away a tear that started down her cheek.

She was back to holding my upper arms, which were dangling at my sides, as she apologized for her outburst. She took a deep breath.

"Karen and I are going to dinner. Please come."

At a loss and completely bewildered, I backed away.

"Another time, maybe," and before I knew it, I was out on Broadway amid the pedestrians and heading over to the bar to meet Kate. After almost getting picked off by a cab as I crossed 79th—my mind was a blur, and I didn't notice that the light had changed—I reached the bar in what they used to call "a state." (Me, not the bar.)

Teddy's was typically loud with bass-heavy music and a crowd's rumble as I got close. The front door was open and the tables on the sidewalk were full. Kate and I usually tried to find a spot off to the right at one of the small, tall round tables that have a couple of high stools at them. After adjusting to the general darkness and the bright lights behind the bar, I spotted her at one before she saw me.

The music was always too loud here, but lots of cute guys hung out there, and though it smelled like a bar it didn't *reek* like a bar and didn't have too many Goldman-types in their expensive suits and ties loosened below the collars of their white shirts, so we went there often. She saw me and gave me a salute with her wine glass.

"I need one of those," I said by way of my abrupt greeting, and Sally, a waitress who knew me, took my Pinot Grigio order and was gone by the time I was on the stool across the table from Kate.

"You are not going to fucking believe what just happened to me." It was loud, but not quite so loud off to the side where we were, even with the window open.

As I say, Kate's my oldest and best friend and she knew my mom well. Anyway, she was like *What?*

"I went to a book reading at Barnes & Noble to kill time before meeting you."

"I'm sorry but I did have to work late." She was still in her office attire, though where she worked things were a lot less formal than at my bank.

Anyway, I said, "So I'm at the reading by some girl about our age. She's reading from some short stories and there's this older, very classy looking woman with her. Upper West Side type. I assumed it was her mother."

"And it wasn't?"

Just then, Sally moved my glass from her small tray to the table, and Kate said she was fine with what she had.

I took a long sip. A gulp, really.

"No, it wasn't her mother. She was some sort of mentor for the young one. A big deal author. The girl finishes, and this woman gets up and says some things about getting to know her and that she was the first recipient of the…'Emily Locus Award.'"

"The what?"

"That's what I thought. The Emily Locus Award. No doubt that's what she said. It hit me like a brick, and I got up and went to the bathroom and I was, like, did she say, 'Emily Locus' and if she did could it be my mom?"

"What else did she say?"

"I was leaving, to get a handle on it, but something about this 'Emily Locus' being a writer who never did anything with it."

"Did your mother write?"

"I don't remember, frankly, though I kind of recall her doing it while we were on vacation at her folks' place upstate. But it gets weirder. Someone needed to use the bathroom and so I left and I went down the hallway and they were just finishing up on the Q&A and a few people are lined up to buy the book and get her to sign it.

"I didn't know what to do. I thought of just disappearing. But what if it *was* my mom? So, I went to that long escalator they have and watched them and just as they reached it and the younger one was going down, I told the other that I was Alex Locus. That's all I said. 'I am Alex Locus.'"

"And?"

"She almost falls down the escalator and is staring at me and waving for me to come down. What was I to do? I started this. So, I go down and she pulls me off to the side and it's clear that this other, younger writer has no idea what the fuck is going on but the older one literally pulls me to her. She asks if I said I was Alexandra Locus and when I say I am, she whispers 'I miss your mother so much.'"

"So, her Emily Locus was your mom?"

"I think so. She asked me to go to dinner with her and the other writer, but I said I had to go and raced here to see you. What am I supposed to do?"

"Can she track you down?"

"Who knows? How many Alex Locuses can there be?"

This all exhausted me, and I took a long slug of my Pinot.

"I need to think," I said. Somehow, I finished the glass and grabbed a twenty from my bag and threw it on the tall, small round table and rushed out.

I barely made it a block before a breathless Kate tapped my shoulder and then was next to me.

"You can't just go. Let's be logical here."

We both slowed for the seven or eight blocks to my place and on the way, we agreed to go online and find out what was going on.

My place. I was lucky to get it, and it was only because there was a lawyer in my father's firm who represented the landlord who let me have it. It was nothing great, not like you see in the movies. You walked in and you were in the living room. This once was a larger room, and there was simple molding on its high ceiling, but a wall was placed between the left and the center of the three windows that looked out onto the street to create the bedroom.

All the walls were painted in a standard New York off-white. There was a closet in the living room and one in the bedroom. The latter was small, and my bed—just a mattress and box spring on a metal frame—was along one wall. My three-drawer dresser was next to it, along that same wall, and a decent-sized horizontal mirror was over that. I had framed art-deco posters along the opposite wall, and a small table with a lamp and clock next to the bed, near the window. And that was pretty much it for the bedroom.

The living room was twice as big. It had a sofa along the wall to the left—the wall between the two rooms—and a bookcase near the windows. A coffee table was in front of the sofa, and two armchairs were opposite the sofa. They were a matching cream-colored set my father got for me when I moved in. A high-quality if old-fashioned sideboard I got my dad to let me take from home was along the opposite wall, and my TV was on it. To its right, beside the closet, was a table that had two leafs and that was round when the leafs were up. Usually, though, they were down and at most I lifted one for eating or for my laptop, and a couple of wooden chairs were tucked beside it.

The kitchen was tiny, and a door opened to an equally small bathroom with just a toilet, sink, and shower. It sounds depressing, but it was very near the park, and it was my home and I loved it.

Kate was its most frequent visitor, and on the Thursday night I'm talking about, she went straight to the kitchen when we were inside where she opened the fridge for a bottle of Pinot and grabbed a can of mixed nuts from a cabinet and she carried them to my little coffee table before returning with a couple of glasses, which she three-quartered filled.

By then I was on the sofa searching on my laptop and she was quickly backseat driving me. I started with the B&N site for the Broadway store. There was an announcement of tonight's reading and Karen Adams. There was a photo.

"She's kind of cute," Kate said. "Check out the award."

Emily Locus Award went into Google, and there it was.

"Shit."

"That's her," I said, pointing to a photo on the homepage. "That's the older woman. Nancy Penchant."

Kate leaned in as I clicked the "About" tab.

"Impressive," she said, and it was. Her novel *Scream* was an American Book Award finalist. She had several other novels and a collection of short stories with links to literary publications.

I went back. On the front page was an explanation:

Emily told me she had many stories she wrote. One of the purposes of this award is to give someone who discloses who she is in her writings and ends up stuffing it all into boxes never to be seen by anyone else can come forward and have those stories shared with others and, perhaps thanks in part to this little stipend, with the world.

We both leaned back.

"Did your mom write?" Kate asked again.

"I have no idea if she did it seriously. Just stuff when we were away and she was bored. There may be some boxes in the attic in Bronxville."—our hometown—"It was years ago."

As I scrolled down the page, I found a picture of my mom. With Nancy Penchant. So that was that. In Central Park. They were standing. Nancy had an arm around my mom's waist. They were in jeans and polo shirts and wearing sneakers, their heads tilted slightly towards one another.

My mom was smiling, though she was never much of a smiler.

"Your mom may not have been who we thought she was," Kate said, and I thought she might be right. I grabbed my wine and stared at the photo.

2.

I t was a while since my mom died, and I didn't really think of her much though there were times when I felt a gap where she was supposed to be, and suddenly—BOOM!— she was all I could think about. She was kind of there while I grew up and overprotective more than anything. My dad would roll his eyes and say, "Just let Mom be Mom."

Then one August day I was walking through town—it's an upscale suburb I'll describe shortly—with Kate and some other friends when I got a call from my dad that something terrible had happened with my mom and he'd have a car bring me to a hospital in the city. Kate offered to go with me, but I told her it'd be best if I did whatever it was just with my dad.

The car took me near Columbia. At the hospital, the security desk paged a nurse who met me and took me to an elevator. The elevator was very big and smelled like a hospital. The fourth floor smelled worse, and the hallway lights were almost blindingly bright.

The nurse didn't say anything beyond asking me how I was, and I was afraid to ask what was going on. She led me to a large room with beds lined up on either side of an aisle. It was not nearly as bright or smelly as the hall. Beeping was happening everywhere. There were four or five beds with curtains on rods, some open, some closed, on either side. My dad was by the last one on the right. I didn't look at the other patients. Just my dad.

Things are a bit blurry from that point. She was lying there with something attached to her nose and an IV in her arm. Monitors were blinking and showing what I guess was her heartbeat, which looked steady.

She didn't move, and my dad had his arm around me and took me to the hallway. He asked if I wanted something to eat, and before I could say anything he led me to a vending machine near the elevators. He got some chocolate candy for me, and then I followed him to a row of orange plastic chairs that were in an opening. There were a couple of other rows, but they were empty—except for one woman sitting near us and staring ahead as she rocked front and back. She must have known someone in the ICU. Sure, I felt bad for her, but my issue was my mom.

My dad simply said she was visiting a friend when she had some kind of medical "episode" and they got her to the hospital very fast, but the doctors were, he said, "not optimistic."

"She's on life support. They say she'll be a vegetable if she even survives. They said we should think about pulling the plug."

I'd just seen her that morning, happy as could be. It was Friday so she'd be going into the city to meet friends as she almost always did. I told my dad it couldn't have happened. "She was fine this morning."

"She was just walking with the friend, and it hit her. A stroke."

He and I spoke about the options, but it was clear that there was only one. After we got her parents down from upstate and my dad's came from outside Philadelphia—I am an only child—on the Monday, my dad nodded to a doctor who turned off the machines. We stood there. My dad held my left hand and my grandma (my mom's mom) held my right. We waited. It wasn't long before the doctor leaned in and put her fingers to my mom's neck. It didn't take long for her to look up at my dad and shake her head. She was gone, and somehow I kept from wailing as my dad put his arm around my waist and led me out. By then, the others had already left.

I hadn't thought of those days in a while. My life turned to shit when she was gone and I nearly flunked out of school—I did enough damage that I couldn't get into the colleges I wanted to get into and was nearly thrown off my field-hockey team—and it took some mandated anti-bullying counseling to get through it all—and the sight of this author woman at the bookstore that night reminded me of that visit to the hospital on Amsterdam not two miles due north of where I sat.

Now here my mom was in this photo with this woman's arm around her.

"What do I do?" I asked in some kind of stupor.

Kate got closer. "We'll figure it out, baby girl," and she put an arm around me and gave me a shake. "We'll figure it out."

After a minute, I said, "I should probably speak to my dad about it, but it's, I don't know, a bit weird."

"If it's what it might be, it could be a problem to just bring it up with him. What about those boxes?"

"In the attic? I don't even know if they're still there, but you have a point. I can just ask to come up and see them and maybe get a hint about whether something was really going on between my mom and this—" I looked at the photo and read the name—"Nancy Penchant."

I leaned my head on Kate's shoulder. "That's what I'll do."

"Do you want me to come with you?"

I pulled up, keeping my eyes on the photo.

"Thanks. But just now I think it has to be me going up there alone. I'll play it cool, or at least try to, till I understand it a bit better."

She stood and looked down at me.

"Will you go up on Saturday?"

I nodded.

"I'll be around. Give me a call if you need anything."

Then Kate was gone, with me still sitting on the sofa scrolling for a few minutes until I grabbed my phone.

3.

It was nearing ten-thirty but not too late to call. My dad answered after the second or third ring.

"Hey, baby. What's up?"

"Sorry to call so late, but I was wondering whether Mom used to write stories."

"Write stories? Where does this come from?"

Having brought up writing, I found myself saying more than I planned. "I went to a reading at a bookstore and the author won something called the Emily Locus Award. I looked it up. I think it's Mom"—I didn't want to overcommit—"and it said that she wrote stories she never did anything with, so I was just wondering whether Mom did and whether they're somewhere in the house."

He paused. "There's an Emily Locus Award?"

"Yes."

"How do you know it's her?"

I paused, but not for long.

"I saw this author for maybe five seconds and when I told her my name, she said she knew Mom from years back, when you were in the city."

It was his turn to wait.

"Dad?"

"I'm sorry. An author?"

"Yes."

"I think I know who you mean. I think your mother may have mentioned an author friend she met before you were born who she saw sometimes when she visited the city after we moved up here. I don't know anything more. And you spoke to her just briefly? Nothing more than, 'Hello'?"

"Pretty much. So are there papers?"

"Sorry. Yeah. I think they're in the attic. Been there for years. Just taking up space. I sometimes think of tossing them. But, yeah, there were stories. You want to see them?"

"Can I come up on Saturday?"

"Saturday? You just found out about them. What's the rush?"

"It's just that having found out that they exist, I'd like to see them."

He said he was fine with it, and I told him I'd walk from the station and see him in the late morning.

4.

I didn't get much sleep. No surprise there. I wasn't in the mood for a Friday schlep to the subway to get to work and, more, being stuck with a bunch of strangers that particular morning and was up in plenty of time to walk through the park—it was quite a nice morning—and to my office on 44th Street, a bit over two miles and quite pleasant if it's not hot and humid and it wasn't.

Fortunately, work moved quickly, and it was noon before I knew it. I grabbed a salad and water near Bryant Park. Though it was crowded, I found a chair close enough to the fountain by Sixth Avenue to hear its gurgling. Instead of going through *The Times* on my Kindle, I checked for Karen Adams's book. I downloaded a sample.

The first story was the one with the boat. *Lonesome*. It was the title story for the book and the one that brought her to the attention of Nancy Penchant. The sample, though, only got to around where she stopped the night before, with the one woman struggling to at least grasp the side of the boat until the initial rush of the storm passed. I bought and downloaded the collection and was soon sitting on a hard, metal forest-green chair in Bryant Park on a beautiful day with people passing oblivious to what was happening on that lake in the Berkshires. The woman in the water—Audrey—tries to hold on and the other—Michelle—tries to grab her wrist. But it keeps slipping away and Michelle panics that the boat will capsize and hurries to the other side until the boat calms.

The rain will not ease. Audrey is drifting away from the boat, now away too far to touch it. Michelle throws out an oar, hoping it will do. Audrey can't get a grip on it. My heart was beating as I exhort her to grab it, grab it. Then she goes down a final time without a trace, the crust of the lake still violent with the rain.

It's not long before a lifeguard gets close on a board but it's too late when he arrives and it's too late when the storm's fury is spent. Her friend sits in the boat, begging them not to pull it in. "She's here, she's here," Michelle repeats until she must admit Audrey is gone and her boat is towed in by another and an ambulance is waiting on the beach.

It went like that, and I lost track of time as I fell into the story of the kids and the husbands and how calm the lake becomes not ten minutes after the drowning when the firemen paddle out to begin the search for the body. I wanted to throw my Kindle away in each of the trash bins I passed on my way back to my office. How could such a seemingly nice girl write something so...dark?

I went to the ladies' room in my office and looked in the mirror and I couldn't stop thinking of these two women. Michelle and Audrey. Strangers to me. But I had to stop thinking of these two fictional women and was glad the pace of the afternoon's work matched the morning's so before I knew it, it was five-thirty on a Friday afternoon.

I walked home. It was another of the September days that I live for in the city. My mind was a bit of a mush the whole way. I had the remains of the dinner from the night before— the takeout from the bodega that I seemed to have started eating in a different lifetime—and threw it into the microwave.

I thought about opening a bottle of wine, but that was not a good idea, and I had a glass of milk. I set up my laptop on the leaf of that little table in my living room and scrolled while I ate.

The "Readings" link on the Broadway Barnes & Noble page gets me to Karen Adams.

Before she graduated from Dartmouth College in Hanover, New Hampshire, in 2016, Karen noodled about writing fiction. An economics major, she found it an outlet. With the serendipitous intervention of American

Book Award finalist Nancy Penchant, she was able to connect with an editor and get her collection of stories published.

Karen lives on the Upper West Side of Manhattan, not far from the store, and is currently at work on her first novel. We are proud to be the host for her first public reading.

I clicked the link to Nancy Penchant. It took me to her publisher and her author's page with the gushing blurbs she'd gotten from other authors. A Barnard grad who worked through the publishing world until getting stories published in *The New Yorker* and a publishing contract from one of the major houses. After one kindly reviewed but lightly selling novel, she hit upon *Scream*, which got not only good reviews but also solid sales and ultimately to an ABA finalist slot.

She was "happily single but never alone."

I didn't know what to make of that peculiar phrase and suddenly I thought of Kate saying my mom might not have been who I thought she was.

The photo of Nancy Penchant from the page was more recent than the one with my mom. She was pretty with a narrow face, a slightly pointy nose, and a small mouth plus good dark brown hair and a legitimate number of wrinkles. She spent more time at the beach than she should have but if there was one way to describe her from the photo and more from actually seeing her in person it'd be as a, well, classy MILF.

It was still early, and I pulled up Karen's collection on my Kindle. I was almost afraid to go deeper into it, but what she read from that second story about the Tufts kids made it sound like the whole thing wasn't a lot of *Sturm und Drang*. And the next story I picked out, almost at random, was far lighter and as well written.

That done, it was still early, and I thought of looking at Nancy Penchant's novel. I could download it, but the bookstore was only a few blocks away.

It was quiet, being a Friday night. I found the paperback with its sedate cover and "American Book Award Finalist" plastered on the lower right side and read a few pages. I found a comfy chair and fell into both the chair and the novel. Before I knew it, I was several chapters in and it was getting late. I had to be up for the trip to my dad's, so I headed to the escalator, the one where I'd followed her down the night before, and on the ground floor bought her novel.

I called Kate when I was through my door. We spoke a couple of times during the day, to replay the call to my father more than anything. She again offered to come to town with me when I went to check out those boxes, but I begged off and was back on my sofa reading *Scream*.

I started with: "To Emily Locus. A Too-Soon-Departed Friend." Which I stared at it before returning to where I'd stopped at the bookstore.

Scream tells the story of a woman whose husband dies at thirty-five after suffering a heart attack while they were having sex. (It was *quite* more descriptive and detailed than "having sex," of course, but that was its gist.) The sudden widow was Catholic, and her dead husband was Jewish and after the funeral she was left completely outside her husband's family and was left, childless, to wander. The *Scream* was a reference both to her reaction to his collapsing on top of her and to the frustration she felt every day because he left her alone. A fair number of men were attracted to the young widow, her finances bolstered by a tidy insurance payment. She dates occasionally at the behest of neighbors and work colleagues, but nothing comes of any of it other than the occasional hook-up (including one torrid but brief one with another woman).

The story covered four years, and one never learned whether the wife got past losing her husband. I was pulled through it, finishing a little after one.

I couldn't fall asleep, unable to get thoughts of that widow and her loneliness and desperation out of my brain. I was too tired, though, to get up. I heard the sounds of the city at two in the morning, mostly the buses rolling up and down Central Park West. A couple's conversation, echoing in the quiet and somewhat drunken, floated up as they headed away from Columbus was the last thing I remember.

5.

It's important to my story, so let me say something about my hometown, Bronxville, New York. Though I was born in Manhattan and lived on its Upper West Side when I was a baby and for a few years, we moved up when I was small.

It's a square-mile patch built around a train station that sits just about fifteen miles north of Grand Central and grew around commuting bankers and lawyers and businessmen. The houses are big, but the lots are small. And very expensive. It has just a few blocks of stores spread along two business streets. A movie theater, two or three liquor stores, the last remaining Womrath Bookshop, Starbucks and non-Starbucks coffee places, restaurants, and a mishmash of other stores. A population of about six thousand and well-regarded schools (from which, as I say, I was nearly expelled).

Our house was in the area north and east of the train station. It was on a slight hill and its streets—some maintained in old cobblestones—meander around. There's little need for sidewalks. As I say, the houses are big and of a variety of architectures, nearly all pre-dating World War II.

Rich as it is, ostentatiousness is positively frowned upon. You won't see a Ferrari in a Bronxville driveway but you're unlikely to see many cars or SUVs that are more than a few years old either, unless the owner is a contrarian fond of old Volvo or Mercedes wagons.

My father remarried, Maggie Daniels, a few years after my mom passed, and thanks to her I have a three-year-old half-brother named TimTim—Timothy Allen Locus.

It was where I was going on Saturday.

I was up early and after a five-mile run in the park and a bit of post-shower moping around, I walked to Harlem/125th Street for the train north. It was another great

September day, but I didn't want to get there too early. *"Be up at about 10"* I texted my dad when I got back from the run.

Kate knew my plan. I texted her from the train platform:

{Alex:} Heading to B'ville. Wish me luck!!

She responded quickly:

{Kate:} Good luck. I'm here and waiting.

The train was largely empty. It rolled into Bronxville a little early, and I walked to the house, nodding at the two or three women walking their dogs along the way, though I didn't recognize any of them.

Passing the brushed-steel Range Rover and black Mercedes huddled at the top of the driveway, I went around to the back and in through the kitchen. This was my stepmom's pride and joy (other than TimTim, of course). It was large and open with an AGA stove and Sub-Zero fridge. It had a large island and opened to the dining room. When I grew up, a wall separated the two, but it was long gone, and I was used to the open feel. On the island, Maggie'd set up a plate with bagels, butter, and cream cheese.

"I'm here," I called out. Suddenly steps were bounding down the stairs, and TimTim rushed to crash into me.

"Alex! Alex!" He grabbed my leg as he always did.

"Mama got bagels for you," he said. I loaded a Keurig and sliced a cinnamon raisin bagel and slathered on the cream cheese. As the coffee machine worked its magic, Maggie joined us. She was in tennis whites, and we exchanged air kisses and shared a slight hug.

My relationship with Maggie was, well, complicated. She was barely ten years older than me. She was a lawyer who was an associate at my dad's firm but left when told she wouldn't make partner. She went to work for the legal department of a big bank (not mine) in midtown, where she still was. The official line was that she didn't begin to date my father until she was long gone from the firm and that they "ran into each other on Park Avenue one Thursday at lunchtime and it was magic," and I had no reason to doubt that. I was at Villanova during this courtship and first met her when I was home for spring break my sophomore year.

Maggie was not my mom. No matter how hard she tried, we both knew she never would be. Of course, she fit the Bronxville profile, with long (natural) blonde hair and a petite figure, usually in some sort of Lululemon tights and Nike trainers, in contrast to my mom's red hair and roundness.

TimTim was a lifesaver for all of us and even my cold heart softened to Maggie a bit when he popped out and when I got to be his godmother. I would like to say I see bits of myself in him, but he was the epitome of cute and sweet. I never was and never will be.

"I hear you're doing some detective work," Maggie said, nibbling on the corner of an unsliced plain bagel as I added milk and sugar to my coffee and took my first sip.

"It's just that I heard some things I want to follow up on."

"Your dad will be down in a minute," she said, and we sat across from each other on the island. TimTim was off to show me his latest toy.

"I didn't know your mom, of course. But are you sure you want to do this?"

I swallowed the bite of my bagel and dabbed my mouth with a paper towel and looked across. She was hard to read, and I didn't know whether she was thinking of protecting me or my dad. Or even her. *What does she know that I don't?*

I was honest.

"I really thought about it. I've asked myself that question a thousand times. But I always answer that I *need* to know. I was a pretty shitty daughter and now that she's gone, I think I owe it to her."

It was probably unfair of me to say this about myself. Over the years, I may have thought more of the difficult times I had with her, the brattiness of an only child (which exploded when she died). Perhaps I hoped that knowing more about her now that *I* was a woman would remind me of those special times we had as mother-and-daughter. In some respects, then, I think I may have owed it more to myself to discover the truth about her.

Maggie reached over, and I moved my hand across the top so she could tap it. "You know I am always here for you, Alex," she said, "even if we don't see eye to eye and even though I will never be your mother."

"I appreciate that. But I don't know if I'm ready for the friendship thing with you, okay?"

She nibbled a bit more on her bagel, and I was pissed for having said what I did.

"I'm just here to help." This said with a slight degree of pout. She cheered and stepped away, her ponytail giving a quick flip. "Your dad should be right down."

As if on cue, he came in, also in his tennis whites, and Maggie moved to intercept TimTim, who was holding and waving some sort of colorful robot with flashing green eyes and a bit of a rumble in his right hand as his mom took him to get ready to leave.

I got from my stool for a hug from my dad.

"You sure you're up to this?"

"You make it sound like some Indiana Jones thing. Is there something you're not telling me?"

"Not as far as I'm aware," he said. "We're going to the club for a few hours. We'll have lunch there. Give us a call if you need anything. I pulled two boxes down from the attic. They're in the living room."

"We're dropping TimTim off with friends," Maggie said as she left, pushing him in front of her and him calling "Bye, Alex."

"So, you have the house to yourself. There's lunch stuff in the fridge."

With that, and me calling "Bye, TimTim," they were off.

I walked into the living room with my coffee mug. This room, too, was largely Maggie's work. She didn't make major changes but brightened it up and, again, I give her full points for how it turned out. A couple of times a year I went up to a party, and the living room was the center of everything. It was bright while my mom was alive, but Maggie made it more welcoming. It was two steps down from the front foyer. Two sides were lined with tall windows facing south and west. It wasn't the best of views since the neighbors were close, but I always found it peaceful.

An ebony Steinway was near the windows. They bought it when I was nine or ten hoping I'd take to music but I couldn't bear the practicing and knowing my imperfect scales would waft over the town and so it sat unused except when my folks (or, later, my dad and Maggie) held a party. When that happened, a tuner would come in the day before and work it into shape and they'd hire a kid from Sarah Lawrence to play for a few hours. Maggie, though, started taking lessons and I bet TimTim banged on it whenever he got the chance.

The walls of the room were yellow, and a very large (and expensive) oriental rug covered most of the floor. Some feet from the stone fireplace were a pair of couches facing one another across a broad, square mahogany coffee table. The table had a glass top. Quality paintings—landscapes mostly—hung along the walls and the furniture was a dark color no longer in fashion but perfect for this room and this house and this town.

A pair of bankers' boxes sat side-by-side on the coffee table. I put my mug on a side table and stood over them. I went from one to the other and ran my right hand along their lids, and for a moment it felt, not for the last time, like I was touching a bit of Emily Locus.

I won't describe the process I went through in my initial review. Both boxes were messes. One had mostly legal pads filled edge to edge and often on both sides with my mother's distinct handwriting, distinct because she was left-handed and how she wrote varied by her mood. That box also had bunches of loose papers or five or six pages that were stapled together, and those staples were rusty.

The other box had printed things. Several big groups of pages with big binder clips, which were rusting and left rust stains on the paper. I pulled them out and put each on the coffee table, where I'd made space. Longer pieces. Stories. Some ran over a hundred typed pages. *A Summer Affair. Flying to Paris. The Love of My Life. Pandemonium. Floating Away.* Each had a title and "By Emily Locus" below it, both centered on the cover page.

But this second box also had bunches of legal pads, and as far as I could tell they were drafts of those typed stories or of things that never got past the draft-on-a-legal-pad stage.

"Later for you," I said to the stack of stories and returned to the first box. I took the top pad out. It'd been so long since I'd seen much of my mom's penmanship, and it struck me strangely when I saw it then. There were the lines of her ballpoint pen digging into the pads. I ran my finger across the first page, with its sloppiness and the striking out of a word or two. Near the top, right after the title and the date— 6/12/03. It started: "I was late and the morning was ~~rainy~~ overcast and humid when I reached the street." *Taken for a Ride* was its title, and I flipped over several pages.

Follow the rules, everyone said. The unwritten rules. Keep your head down. Hold your bag close. More than anything, don't stare. Do. Not. Stare. Read the ads if you must but nothing more.

I followed these rules for months and months. I walked down the steps and put my token in the slot and stood back from the platform with my back near but not against the wall waiting for the train. On board, I liked standing, holding onto the pole as the car rocked. At my station, I shuffled up the wide stairs in time with the others, up to Sixth Avenue, holding my bag close to my body.

I never knew why I stared at him that ~~summer~~ late September afternoon.

The story got a little...racy with that banker she stared at, and I put it aside. If I read everything in this first visit, I'd have been there all day. For this one, with the hot sex with a stranger—oh Mother!—I wondered if my father saw it and what else might be in these papers. I dropped it to the floor face down and stared at the remaining things. I needed a plan now that I had a sense of the papers were like *physically*, how seemingly random and disorganized it all was.

I went to the kitchen for coffee, and while I waited for it to brew, I texted Kate.

{Alex:} Just getting started.

There's a lot of stuff. And I mean A LOT of stuff.

Big. Small. In between.

It's complicated.

Kate called a few minutes later and offered to come up or have me go to her place on the way home, but I passed.

"I can't spend all day here. It's too draining. I'll ask my dad if I can take them with me."

"You want me to come by?"

"I may. I may not. Let's play it by ear."

"I'm around," she said.

"I know."

"And Alex. I mean for everything."

"I know that too."

I was back in the living room by the time the call ended. I put my fresh coffee on a side table and got back to my, well, to my quest.

6.

Sitting on the sofa and leaning over the coffee table, I resumed with the pads. The first drafts. It dawned on me that there was no point in cloistering myself in the house and brought the stack from the first box, the one with that bit about being afraid to look at someone on the subway, outside to the patio. It was chilly when I got up, but it turned into a nice late summer day. No point in wasting it.

The patio was just off the kitchen and had an outdoor grill and a low stone wall around the irregularly shaped and variously colored tiles on the ground. My dad would pretend to know something about cooking on the grill—in the period between my mom and Maggie, a sweet woman named Helen came in three times a week to clean and prepare dinner for us and though I hadn't seen her in a while, I think she was still doing that. I put cushions from a chest along the wall on the chairs and the lounger and after I got it set up, I plopped myself on the lounger, with my coffee now on the low metal table to my right.

The patio was on the northern side of the house which meant it didn't get much sun. A hint of wind had come up, and the tips of the trees moved and sang slightly in a way I always loved about the house and especially the patio when I was the only one home or only had Kate and maybe a few other friends for company.

With a breath, I reached for the top pad and read. *Starless Nights* was scrawled across the top. It was dated "July 16, 2006." It was about a young wife living in an unnamed city that is clearly New York. She and her husband have a child, a little boy. The boy races between parked cars chasing a ball, and he is struck by a cab. Dead. His blue eyes are dead, open and staring.

Holy shit. I put it down without continuing. Why did I have to start with this? I was afraid of what was to come.

I picked up another. Thank God it was lighter. A holiday in the country for three generations of a family in Chicago. It is a joyful outing, for the participants and the reader, and is bathed in detail. Perhaps too many. I loved this one and got all the way through in no time.

Just as I did, my dad called to check up. With a pad on my lap, I told him it was taking longer than I expected. There was still a lot on the patio, not to mention what was in the living room. Plus, as I told Kate, this was taking more, much more, out of me than I expected, with the ghost of my mom hovering not far from me. I asked if he could take me, and the boxes, into the city.

"I won't get through today. There's a lot here. Can I take them to my place? Can you give me a ride down?"

"Um, sure. When do you want us to get you?"

I said, "Whenever you're ready." I hoped it'd be sooner rather than later.

That was at about two. Before they got back, I'd managed to get through the initial pages of the rest of the pads. Some stories were so short I finished them in a flash. Others were a bit long, and I only got through a few of those.

What I did finish and from the bits and pieces of the others, I saw that her writing ran the gamut. From the tragedy of *Starless Nights* to the joy of the family outing and things in between. I found some erotica. Man-woman. Man-man. Woman-woman. This was a side of my mom I didn't imagine existed.

I looked at several of the items bound by clips. *Floating Away* sounded light enough. I was on my back on the lounger, and I was right about the story. It was a breezy thing about life in the suburbs. Two neighbors were forever trying to one up each other. Keeping up with the Joneses. Car. House. Kitchen. And a joint balloon ride.

I was reading it when the kitchen door slammed and I heard, "Alex! We're home!" from TimTim, soon followed by his throwing himself across my stomach and how heavy he was getting.

"Mommy said we're taking you home and that I can come."

"Of course you can come, buddy," I said, rubbing my hands against the sides of his head and giving his butt a slap.

"How'd you make out?" my dad asked as he came around from the driveway.

"There's a lot of stuff and I think I just scratched the surface. I haven't really read that much. It's been more of a preliminary look to get a handle on what's here."

He reached to the pile of the longer things and lifted the top one.

"*Pandemonium*? What's that about?"

"I haven't looked at it yet. Did you read any of it? When she wrote it?"

Still holding the story, he sat in a chair to the right of the lounger and flipped through the pages while Maggie corralled TimTim, and they disappeared into the kitchen.

"She sometimes showed me something and asked my opinion. But they weren't my thing. More chick-lit than anything so she stopped showing them to me. I didn't realize how much she'd written and how seriously she'd taken it until after she passed."

"What do you mean?"

"Well, you remember the spare bedroom where she kept her stuff? It was always 'her space,' and when she was gone, I went to clean it up. Must have been a few months after she...passed. You remember the chest in there? When I opened it, I found this stuff. I hate to say that I just wanted to get rid of it. I brought some boxes home and filled them and put them in the attic. Where they've been ever since. For years."

"You never looked at them? I mean, you weren't curious?"

"It was still a tough time for me and after they were in the attic, I forgot about them. Then you called. I looked inside one of the boxes but figured they were better meant for you."

He leaned forward and dropped *Pandemonium* on top of the pile. "So, I'm leaving them for you. I honestly don't know what's in them."

7.

We pulled in front of my little brownstone a bit after three. Maggie stayed in the double-parked Benz with TimTim while my dad helped me carry the boxes from the trunk up to my place, one each.

He put his on the floor in my living room and I bent and put mine on top of it. I'd somehow make space against the wall for them later.

"Is it okay that I took them?" I asked as he was at the door, declining my offer of a glass of water. He turned back to me. "They were just sitting in the attic. If there's something you want to learn about your mom, take all the time you need. Are you okay?"

I was a bit shaken by this whole experience, but I smiled and assured him I was fine. He leaned to me and gave me a hug and a moment later he was out the door and I was alone.

With two boxes of my mom's writings.

I thought of calling Kate. Maybe take a short walk with her. But that would be putting it all off. Whatever "it" was. So, I stood there looking at them. The two boxes of my mom's writings.

I spent the next hours plowing through it all. I can't say that I *read* it all, but I read most of the shorter things and had things in better order than they were when I left Bronxville.

It was a little after five, and now I needed to get out. Kate was waiting to hear from me.

"Hey, babe. It's me."

"Yeah, I know. What's up? You want to get a bite to eat."

"You're a mind-reader. It's early and maybe we can get the old farts' early-bird discount at Arnold's."

Arnold's, I should note, was—still is—a good neighborhood place to get comfort food without being overwhelmed by things like noise and too many B&T— bridge and tunnel—types. It may have had early-bird specials decades earlier, but by the time I moved into the neighborhood, it was one of those Upper West Side secrets that always seemed to be crowded with locals.

It wasn't crowded yet when I got there. Kate was outside, rocking back and forth and looking in the direction I'd be coming from when she wasn't looking at her phone.

We don't hug often, but that late afternoon she had her arms around me before I could stop her. It wasn't for long and I almost cried before she pulled back.

"You okay? Really. You can tell me. Are you okay?"

I could have gone either way on this, but I held it together and said, "As well as can be expected," and her expression relaxed and she asked whether I wanted to sit outside—it was, as I say, a nice late summer day—and that's what we did.

8.

Although I glanced at the boxes when I returned from dinner and a stroll on Columbus with Kate, I largely put them out of my mind. The normalcy of my dinner and stroll with her relaxed me more than I could have imagined, and so the things I'd retrieved from Bronxville were, at least for the rest of the night, just a pair of bankers' boxes that happened to be against a wall in my living room.

I spent the evening on my sofa with my laptop on my stomach grazing from random site to random site online, going down clickbait rabbit holes mindlessly, until I found the energy to get up and get my teeth brushed and do whatever else I had to do and get into bed. With all that taken care of, I was asleep, I think, when my head hit the pillow, and it was after eight when I woke up on Sunday.

The boxes were, of course, there. I made coffee in my little French press and had some shredded wheat with fresh strawberries I picked up at the Korean market on Columbus. I sat at my little table with one leaf up as I always did for what passed for my breakfast and went through my email, the requisite social media, and *The Times* on my tablet.

"Alright. I see you," I wanted to tell them but didn't, and I again ignored them as best as I could. I went for a four-mile run in the park and the boxes were there when I returned. While I was under the shower, I committed to dive in, and I knew where.

The Love of My Life. It was one of the printed ones. A first-person romance. It seemed to be a good way to get started, deferring the more serious stories till later.

It began nicely enough. The narrator was looking back. Growing up in a small, fading town in Upstate New York. Being one of the few in her class to get into a top college and working in the dining hall to help pay for it. Loving parents. An only child. The handsome man from a rich family outside

Philadelphia. Somehow capturing his attention and somehow getting his ring.

It was well-written but a bit too predictable a Cinderella story. I enjoyed the words, though, and began to understand it was barely concealed autobiography, and it was nice to read a romance of how my parents got together. I was waiting for what she'd write about me coming along.

Then the wheels came off.

He's off to the office on yet another Saturday and here I am yet again to fend for myself. At times I'm glad he's working so diligently. Down the road, a partnership would set us up for life. Which he keeps telling me.

My work, though. It's boring and getting boringer and boringer and becoming ever more tiring. When he's up and out of the apartment early on Saturdays, I get the chance to lounge around or take walks on my own, something I'm fonder of now that I'm getting larger.

It's harder this time, the carrying, and it's not like I have much of a choice. Still, I shall "gather thy rosebuds while ye may" and so I go to the park for my normal Saturday constitutional, people fleeing left and right as the Blimp heads towards them, wearing a not particularly flattering maternity dress and not-worn-often-enough Nike trainers.

It's hot. More than I expected. The men runners are mostly shirtless and the women are in their sports bras and I tell myself that once I lose the baby fat, I'll get back to doing it again.

Yeah, it's going to be a hot one.

The thick air hits me as I walk on the path near the tennis courts, by the bridle path. I hear the swoosh of the racquets and the ping of the balls and the "out"s and "nice shot"s echoing in the humidity. Sometimes I stand at the fence and watch the players, some of whom even I know are very good. Now, I realize I best get home for a lie-down.

I'm not desperate. Not by any means. I'm just tired and overheating and getting crabby. On a downhill stretch of a path, I feel nauseous. It happens more often now. But it'll pass, and there's a streetlamp to my left and I put my left hand on it for stability.

My OB-GYN told me to use deep-breathing exercises when this happens, and that's what I do.

"Are you alright?"

Fuck. I don't feel like company, thank you very much, and now I'm about to attract a swarm of do-gooders. It's a woman's voice, perhaps a mother herself, so I'm maybe more tolerant than I would be in light of the shitty mood I'm suddenly in. I turn. She's about my age and appears to have a genuine look of concern in her brown eyes.

"Just taking a breather," I say, hoping she'll just leave me be. I can go lamppost to lamppost home on my own, so leave me be. Though I don't say this later bit.

"C'mon," she says. "Let's get you sitting down."

This Samaritan half drags me to a nearby bench. With each step, I realize I'm in worse shape than I thought, though it's not serious. It was like this the first time.

I waddle over with her escorting me like a delicate porcelain figurine, and we sit.

"You looked a bit wobbly there."

"Just a momentary thing. I'll be alright. Thanks."

"Don't be a stubborn cow. You're pale and I'm helping you home. I brook no dissent."

This last is done with mock flair, and I can't help but laugh. She stands, and I get my first real look at her. She is stylishly but comfortably dressed in a light blouse over white pants that drape, I admit, well over her sleek body, and her face is narrow and lit up by a hint of a smile.

"Lead on, handsome prince," I tell her, and she half hoists me to my feet and puts her arm through mine as

we go. Seeing us, a few strangers stop and ask if I'm alright and she assures them that I am. I tell her my address, and as we walk the nausea drains from me, and by the time this stranger and I hit Central Park West I'm myself again. (And a large myself I am, ha, ha.) She won't let me go alone. She has no wedding band.

"Do you have any children?" I ask.

She laughs. "Me? I've never had the mothering instinct. Which allows me to live life without requiring the presence of a man."

This makes me feel...differently about her arm being through mine. It sort of hangs above me as we go. Yet she seems to give her little comment no mind, and she asks about me and my husband—"Michael" I say—and whether I have kids already and other things that complete strangers talk about when they're passing the time while walking arm-in-arm to the apartment of one of them.

"I've frightened you, haven't I?" she observes or asks, I'm not sure which, as we reach my stoop.

"Not at all."

"You're a bad liar. Has anyone ever told you that? I just like to get that out of the way when I meet an attractive woman."

"And is it your practice to pick up heavily pregnant women in Central Park on Saturday mornings?"

"You'd be surprised." She laughs. It's something, laughing, she seems to do a lot. "I'm sorry. I'm not such a predator. Seriously. Though I guess I'd say that if I were. Don't worry. You're not my type."

She turns serious. "I want you to know that I am around if you need anything. As a friend. I'm up on Ninety-First Street. Give me your phone."

She puts her name and number in.

"Natalie Porter," I read back to her.

"Yes. Are you okay making it up to your place?"

"I'm fine now."

She offers to accompany me upstairs, but I decline. "I brook no dissent," I say and for the first time with her I smile and for the second time so does she.

"Natalie Porter" steps down to the sidewalk as I open the outer door to my building, and we share waves as she heads east and back towards the park.

"You're such an ass," I tell myself when I've thrown the keys into the bowl by the door and plop onto the sofa. I find my phone in my bag. I imagine her still walking up Central Park West to 91st.

"You don't know who I am," I say when she answers.

"So, tell me."

And I do and she says she now has my number and I laugh and again say goodbye and think about her for longer than was probably appropriate but when Michael gets home at around five, I return to thoughts of my baby. Where they should be.

The Love of My Life continues along these lines. Like diary entries popping up every few months. I didn't understand her vague references to having been pregnant before, but this baby, a little girl, is born. It goes well and the author is instantly mad about her. Michael, the husband, continues his working too much and too hard. She fights whether to return to work after her maternity leave is over. She has some heated arguments with Michael until they decide he makes enough for her to stay home. But he cannot hide his growing resentment.

She doesn't call Natalie, however often she thinks about doing it. She has few friends in the city, almost all wives or girlfriends of other associates at Michael's firm, all anxious or jealous of the competition for the grail of a partnership. Her parents come down every month or so, and for Christmas, they go to his folks.

The baby is four or five months old and in a stroller when she runs into Natalie. Again, it's in the park, and for a moment she thinks of turning away before she is seen, but too late. Natalie is calling to her by name.

"So, this was the product of your little adventure," Natalie says, as she leans down and gives the baby a touch to the head.

"This is Annie," the mother says. And they walk together, and the meeting and the walking become a routine. Natalie is some type of writer and works from her place so she's usually available when the mother needs a break.

Though Natalie is careful to avoid the subject, the mother begins to feel for her in a way she'd never felt for anyone, even her husband, before. Michael, that husband, is keeping his distance as to intimacy since the birth, and the mother is sometimes glad. She often, too often, thinks of Natalie.

As I read this, I was becoming uncomfortable. So uncomfortable that I put it down. This story was so much more personal than even her erotica. I wasn't sure whether I should have read it. It was too raw. Far different from the lightness I expected from its title and its first chapters. Was *any* of it fiction?

I pulled my laptop over and navigated to the Emily Locus Award page and to the picture.

"Holy fuck." I said it out loud.

While my own fever was raging, I did a series of online searches till I had the phone number for Nancy Penchant in New York, New York. There was only the one.

"Hello?" A somewhat husky voice answered. I couldn't say I recognized it from Thursday night's brief encounter at the bottom of the Barnes & Noble escalator or from her little speech before that. But it was two-thirty on a Sunday afternoon and whoever this was sounded like she just got out of bed.

"This is Alex Locus."

"Who? Oh, fuck."

"Yes. 'Oh fuck.' Can I see you?"

"What? Now?"

"Can I?"

She sounded discombobulated and I tried to sound like I wasn't. She asked where I was and when I told her she said it was just blocks away, so we agreed to meet at a bench on Central Park West. It was about halfway between our two places, and I said I'd be there in twenty minutes. I was there in ten, pacing back and forth on the hexagonal stones that make up the sidewalk outside the park's walls, in front of the designated bench.

I saw her approach from the north. A woman in a light blouse over tight jeans and sneakers and walking hurriedly with a big black leather bag over her right shoulder. As she got close, she waved and though I was tempted to close the distance between us, I decided to simply stand and wait for her without a wave.

"Were you her lover?" I asked before she could do anything.

"What, no 'hello'?"

I reached into my bag.

"You were right. She wrote things. Lots of things. I went up yesterday and got two boxes from Bronxville and brought them home. All sorts of stories. But," and I thrust this one at her, "this one's true, isn't it?"

She sat and swung that expensive bag of hers onto the bench beside her and began reading.

"Page 76," I told her in as flat a voice as I could muster. "You show up, I mean the writer Natalie shows up, there."

She went to page 76.

"How much did you read?" She didn't look up, her eyes focused on and moved down that page and then the one after it.

"I had to stop. When she talks about being sexually interested in this Natalie. I didn't want to know what happened. I assume she had an affair with you." Her head shot up and whatever veil she normally wore was gone.

"Oh, sweetie. You make it sound so bad. 'Affair.'"

"You were fucking her or whatever it is you people do while she was married. What would you call it?"

I regretted the "whatever it is you people do" swipe as I said it and stared at her, but I couldn't help myself. I couldn't tell from her look whether she wanted to kill me or hold me, but it passed quickly. She looked at the pages, which she placed on her lap.

"I don't know if this matters, but I did love her." She looked up at me again, me whose stare hadn't moved from her. "I still do. It sort of happened."

"You picked her up when she was pregnant—with me—and then fucked her."

She had an affair with my mom when I was a baby. She didn't even try to deny it. What else was I supposed to think about it and what she did?

9.

I never did sit on the bench with Nancy Portman or "Natalie Porter" or whatever I was supposed to call her. I just turned south and walked away from the bitch, towards my apartment. I didn't get far. I turned. She was sitting, staring ahead with the story still lying on her lap.

I don't think she noticed that I glanced back. With a shake of my head, I resumed the walk but decided to go to Kate's instead of mine. I sent her a vague text earlier about having some reading and thinking to do and that I'd get back to her when I knew what I wanted to do.

Her apartment wasn't far, and when she let me up, I exploded in tears. I babbled all I'd discovered since we met the night before. We shared a convenient tub of ice cream, or what was left of it. I asked to lie down on her sofa for just a minute and the next thing I recall was the smell of Chinese food.

"Hey, sleepyhead," Kate said from the armchair she was sitting in across the coffee table from me with her legs stretched across its top after putting down one of the trashy, blissfully predictable novels she and I read and liked and shared and laughed about. "You just drifted off there."

"How long?"

"Only a few hours. How do you feel?"

"I feel like shit. How do you expect me to feel?"

"Oh, I haven't seen 'Bitchy Alex' in a while." She was right, and I was embarrassed. I washed up and got myself a few dumplings and some sesame chicken. I told her my mind was jelly. We were side-by-side on the sofa, the plates on our laps and the wine glasses on the coffee table.

"You can't be surprised after you saw the photo."

"It's one thing for there to be hypothetical 'love' but this was an affair. She cheated on my father. Again and again."

"I won't excuse it, whatever 'it' may turn out to be, but I think you owe it to her and to you and maybe even to your dad to figure out what happened."

"I was so much happier last Thursday morning."

She shifted and her arm banged against mine. "Can't change the past, babe."

We were quiet as we ate. My stomach as it was, I switched from wine to water. As I was getting it from the fridge, I heard: "I just thought of something."

I went back into the living room—Kate's apartment was set up much like mine though her living room was a bit darker, being on the south side of the block and thus facing north—and she was staring.

"She died on a Friday visiting someone in the city."

It was my turn to stare. How could I not have seen it? Without thinking, I grab my phone. It was answered on the third ring.

"Was my mom with you when she had her stroke?"

There was a pause, but I said nothing.

"Yes." Finally.

"You fucking bitch," and I hung up.

I turned to Kate. She'd figured it out, but I confirmed it.

"Yeah. She killed her. That fucking dyke killed my mom. She'd be alive...we'd have a normal family if she didn't show up in my mom's life. Fucking dyke."

"I should've stopped you from calling. You were in no—"

"'No shape'? What kind of shape was I supposed to be in? Kate. She killed my mom as sure as if she put a bullet through her head. She should roast in hell."

She grabbed my upper arms. Hard. "Stop it. Just stop it. You're getting too emo—"

"Fuck you, Kate. You didn't just find out—"

"Stop! I mean it." She was shaking me, and I thought she might slap me if I didn't get some control. I took a breath and nodded to her and sat back down on the sofa. I drank some of the water just so I'd have something to do.

"Give me your phone."

"What? What's wrong with yours?"

"Your phone." She extended her hand, and I unlocked it and placed it in her palm. She disappeared into her bedroom. I walked to her window and looked out to the street and the brownstones across from hers and, since this was turning me philosophical, all the simple, uncomplicated lives all these other people led.

They said it might rain in the afternoon, and it hit about twenty minutes earlier. The heavy stuff at the front of the storm was gone, but it was still awful.

She was back in five or maybe ten minutes. I was still by the window, with no sense of how long it was. She pointed to the sofa, and I sat. She joined me and passed my phone back to me.

"I could not let her sit with what you said ringing in her ears. Whatever she did, she knew your mother for years. She loved your mother for years and from everything we know your mother loved her. It's all fucked up, I get that. But you need to get a handle on things before you get all Biblical. Agreed?"

I nodded. Not sure whether I was serious, I said, "I need to get wasted. Maybe go to a bar on Broadway and pick up someone so I can get a Sunday-evening lay."

Kate glared at me the way Serious Kate sometimes did.

"I'm kidding," I promised. I wasn't sure whether the best course wasn't to get drunk and laid, without regard to the order in which they occurred. Still, it was best to do neither, so I told Kate, "I do need to get out. You want to come?"

She found an extra rain jacket and umbrella for me, and we walked into the park. We didn't talk. My arm was through hers and after we were shouted at by a cyclist with rain spraying off his rear tire on the Park Drive, we found ourselves a more hospitable stretch around the Great Lawn. We wound our way south—I don't know who was steering— and reached the boat pond. Notwithstanding what became a mist, there were several boats on it, their owners clustered on the right side in varying degrees of seriousness.

Opposite was a statue of Hans Christian Andersen with a little duck staring at him—you know, the "Ugly Duckling"— and no one was there. Though it was damp bordering on wet, I got Kate to sit on the bench to the right of Hans.

"God, I wish you weren't working late so I didn't go to that reading on Thursday. I was happy."

Kate's arm was quickly around me, and I let her pull me to her. I tilted my head against her shoulder and stared out towards the little boats. Only when I felt her finger cross my cheek did I realize I was crying.

"Tell me what I should do."

"The first thing you should do is get the fuck up. This is very not comfortable."

I lifted my head and looked at her. She flashed her I'll-always-be-your-friend smile before Serious Kate was back, her eyes boring into mine. She did that a lot in that dark period after my mom died. We were both so much younger then, and it embarrassed me that I had disappointed her by doing something selfish and idiotic with the dyke.

This time I was neither a disappointment nor an idiot to her. Just someone who needed the help and support of a friend.

"You can't undo it. So where do you go? I think you have to see this through. I don't see as you have much of a choice."

"Do you know how much I love you?" was my answer.

She pulled me closer, and a pair of her fingers grazed across my lips. She pushed me back.

"Of course, I do. We love each other. Always have. Always will."

"Even when I was such a bitch those years."

"That wasn't you. We knew it. But now, well, I think we have to figure out who your mother was. There's a story here. We have to get a handle on it. Agreed?"

"Aye, aye, captain."

"Fuck you," she laughed. "Let's get home and have a bath and get dry clothes and then we can get drunk."

"And laid?"

"I'm not that kind of girl."

I was going to say something, but we both realized her little joke was getting dangerously close to the sun, and it sobered us up quickly.

We stood.

"I'm sorry, Kate. Things just got more complicated for us."

"They've always been complicated. We just didn't know it."

I nodded. If anything, the rain was getting heavier, and the few intrepid boaters were hurriedly collecting their little yachts from the pond and turning to put them in the storage building near where others were under umbrellas clustered at the small café waiting for the clouds to break with more optimism than was justified by the dark sky and for a moment I thought of the lake and the boats and the rain in that story Karen Adams wrote and a chill shot through me.

Kate hadn't read that story; I'd have to show it to her. But now she and I were heading away, retracing our steps to her apartment. I was too drenched and spent, though, and over her protests, we split up at my building and I went up and she continued to hers.

I was in a bitter battle. About Nancy, who was alternately the instrument of my mom's death or the core of my mom's love. Her existence haunted me and my inability to decide which she was or to accept that she might be both kept me from doing anything.

Kate was right. I had to see this through. I was content enough when I was strolling along the cliff I didn't know existed. Now I'd fallen over the side. I had better damn well follow through or I'd just splat on whatever was at the bottom.

I had this vague notion that my mom had a woman lover she saw regularly beginning shortly before I was born. She cheated on my father. If I sat down with a blank pad, I could come up with tons of questions, but the only one that mattered was: WHY? Why would a young woman, a Cornell grad, with a good if tedious job married to her college sweetheart, a rising lawyer from an Ivy League law school, and pregnant with her...their first child risk throwing it all away for some sexual gratification? It was clearly more than that. Everything came back to that one question:

WHY?

And here I was with clues. I felt like Nancy Drew or Miss Marple. I couldn't unring the bell or whatever it's called. I couldn't pretend with my dad that my mom didn't have a lesbian affair or that she died—I wondered if he knew—in the bed of another woman. A classy but full-of-herself dyke.

10.

You grow up, you make certain assumptions about your parents. Especially a dead one.

The immediate point was that I was falling and had a lot more to learn about my mom. I couldn't speak to my dad about it. Not yet. Whether he knew of the affair didn't matter at that point. I couldn't speak to him.

With him eliminated at least for the time being, the only place I could go was directly to my mom. In her words. I already picked up some themes, but they tended to be found in passing. I was organizing and not studying. I had hints of this and hints of that, and my first job was to flesh them out. Through the stories.

Focus. Focus. Focus.

Of course, I was an idiot and no longer had *The Love of My Life*. That was last seen on a bench on Central Park West between 89th and 90th on the lap of the...on Nancy Penchant's lap. I didn't doubt that she had it or that she'd already pored through it. It'd be some time before I could approach her or have anything to do with her. I wasn't getting it back any time soon.

There were plenty of other things to read, so though it was late afternoon on a Sunday, I set about doing it. I had enough in my fridge to keep me going and decided to ignore the Pinot Grigio on the door.

I remembered earlier glancing at a story that barely registered. I found it in the second pile that I went through. Now I read it. It was a simple story set in east London in the winter of 1940-41. The story was entitled *Alice*, after its protagonist. Alice is a nurse and her husband, Richard, is in the Royal Navy, on convoy duty in the North Atlantic. She works in a hospital and has a five-year-old daughter. The story itself takes place on a single day. Tuesday, February 18,

1941, though unlike *Mrs. Dalloway* we follow just the lone, lonely character in London, the nurse called "Alice."

Richard has been on patrol in his destroyer for four months, and his letters arrive sporadically. Their unnamed daughter was evacuated about a month earlier. At her hospital, Alice is called in by a doctor to help calm a screaming woman, about her age, who's gotten word that her husband was killed. He was an RAF Spitfire pilot, shot down off the coast of Malta. His body was not recovered in the Med. The squadron leader's report said the plane burst into flames on impact. No parachute was seen.

I was in my chair by the window, comfortable with my legs stretched up to the sill and thinking about maybe getting just a half glass of the Pinot. I resisted. I instead turned back to the story, reading it out loud. I can't say whether I sound anything like my mom, but I somehow felt it was her speaking and, sad as the story was, I began to hear the rhythm of her words and her voice.

> *Alice saw it dozens of times. The sudden widow, likely to receive her husband's last letter after she knew he was dead. The sudden fatherless children. Alice, like almost everyone on staff, could just as easily be that woman. She sat by the window, holding the new widow's hand. Listening. Again, it was a story much like her own. Young love. Marriage. A baby. War. Only this one had the sudden appearance of Death.*
>
> *Alice leaves the widow, she hopes, a little better than she was when she was brought into the hospital. She will be sure to visit her on Wednesday. See how she passed this first, long night. Knowing she would not have gotten much sleep, and that what she did get would be hell to her.*

It was a sad story, about the randomness of the pain that war inflicts on the innocent. It was what came next that triggered something about my mom.

Alice went through the door of their small home, one of identical ones on both sides of the block, a little after seven. She made sure that the black-out curtains were in place before she left so she could turn on a light in the foyer when she closed the front door behind her. It was, as always, stuffy but for all its faults, it was home. Maybe only hers at the moment but someday, perhaps, it would again be home for the three of them.

She removed her coat and hat and scarf and hung them on the hat rack by the door and then carried her purse into the small front parlor. She put on a single lamp by the couch and sat. It had been a long day, as all the ones before had been and as would all the ones that followed. Her gaze wandered to the mantel and to the pictures on it. One of her, one of Richard, and one of their daughter. Their wedding photo. And one of the three of them sitting on a bench in Hyde Park on Easter 1939.

Mostly she took in her daughter's photo. She rose to pick it up and returned with it to the couch. She often did this, more often than she'd admit if you were to ask her. Her daughter was four in the photo. This one replaced one of her baby pictures that had pride-of-place for many years. The girl insisted that she was old enough to have a photo that was not her as a baby, and this one was taken when she posed on London Bridge about a week after her fourth birthday.

Her daughter was a tall, somewhat lanky English girl with dark hair. She wore a dress—Alice recalled it was blue and knew that it sat in a box in the attic, saved although her daughter had long outgrown it. Suddenly Alice feared she would not come home. That somehow the Luftwaffe would be able to reach the small town in the Midlands where she was and she would be killed. A random statistic to everyone but her. And, should God willing he survive, Richard.

She had no control over this emotion. It struck her every few months. She knew the Luftwaffe could not reach her daughter. That she was safe. But she was not with Alice and that was enough for Alice to fear that she would never again be with Alice.

Alice had worked hard for her daughter. Her birth was difficult. The pain was indescribable, but when Alice heard her baby's first cry, that pain was forgotten. The euphoria wore off though. Alice convinced herself that she could not be the mother her daughter deserved. That her daughter would be better off were she motherless. That Richard would find someone worthy of raising the child. Richard would marry that woman but could only do so if Alice were dead.

Day after day, Alice thought of how she could help Richard find a new, proper wife and her daughter a new, proper mother. Once she figured that out, she would disappear. It was the only way her daughter would have the mother she deserved.

I stopped. I couldn't bear to read what more my mom said about *Alice*. I recalled *Starless Nights*, that first story, with the child killed chasing the ball, another I couldn't finish. What I read was enough. I started grabbing other stories. If a character was a mother, I read it. Sometimes they were the smallest of items, sketches of a story she thought of telling. Or something she abandoned.

If Alice's was an isolated story, I would have credited my mom's imagination. But it wasn't. The thread of a mother's belief in her inadequacies was repeated again and again. I began systematically reading all her mother stories. Many that seemed innocent when I first quickly went through them became far different on a closer read. Despair and doubt and depression. Some were very hard to get through.

I forced myself to finish each, no matter how uncomfortable that was to do. I read about the wake and the sale of the house in *Nights* and Alice's sweet reunion in an epilogue with a husband and daughter who convinced her of how important she was to them, though that seemed more tacked on to create a happy ending than real.

And I was very upset by it all.

11.

I'm not sure how, but I made it through the workweek. Kate and I spent the following weekend in my apartment organizing my mom's works, taking a long walk on Saturday at lunchtime and having a nice brunch on the East Side on Sunday.

Throughout the week, Kate kept asking me about Nancy. *What was I going to do about Nancy?*

I didn't know. I hoped the call she had with Kate the prior Sunday would relieve some of the stress I put on her with what I threw at her—I kept going back and forth on whether she deserved it—but that'd have to do until I figured out what was going on and until I had some sense of, as I say, why my mom did what she did. My great fear was that Nancy had seduced a vulnerable woman, perhaps going through post-partum issues, and took advantage of her. If that were the case, I would never forgive her and, with luck, I'd never have to deal with her again.

Except, of course, about that copy of *The Love of My Life* she had. That wouldn't have been so bad, but it was the only copy. That'd be dealt with later. For the week and then the weekend, it was about understanding more of my mom. Emily Locus. It was becoming clearer and clearer that she had abandonment issues. Its fingerprints were on nearly everything she wrote.

It was Sunday a little after noon and by then Kate had caught up to me as to what she read. I went through the stack of legal pads that my mom had done the first draft of *The Love of My Life* on and because it was all we had, I had Kate read it too.

It was about four on Sunday afternoon when I thought we'd pretty much read what we could read from the two boxes. Even the seemingly random scrawls.

"Let's go to my place," she said. "It'll do us both good for a change of scenery."

We were sitting at either end of my sofa. The boxes were empty, lying on their sides over towards the (did I mention tiny?) kitchen. The printed things were in an unbalanced stack off to our left, and the others were strewn about on the right side of the coffee table. My original chronological organization was gone. We decided to try to put them in general topics instead and came with five: Stories that were just ideas that revealed nothing about my mom; Sex stories, which revealed perhaps more about her than I wanted to know; her dark thoughts about herself; her dark thoughts about life; and her fantasies about Nancy.

As to the last, "Nancy" appeared in none of them, but as with *The Love of My Life*—and the initial draft was perhaps a truer window into her than the somewhat more polished printed one that was with Nancy Penchant—while there were hints of my mom's vulnerability and need, this was overwhelmed by her, well, "love" for the other woman.

It was something Kate didn't dare bring up, and I didn't want to speak about. But since we were allocating the stories in those five categories, talk of Nancy seeped into our efforts. For a while, that's all it did. Seep.

There we were, though, looking at the loose stacks.

"You should call her." Kate pushed her bare left foot against my thigh from her spot opposite me.

I ignored it.

She kicked me.

"Alex, I mean it, and you know you should. She loved her. Do you think she was taken advantage of?"

No, I didn't. But I couldn't let it go. So, Kate kicked me again.

"You're a mule. Has anyone ever told you that? A fucking mule. You owe it to her. To your mom. And to you to at least talk to her. At least let her know that you don't hate her."

"How do you know I don't?"

I was being, as she said, a "fucking mule." It was *my* mom, and I wasn't ready to forgive the woman who in a true sense killed her. I wasn't.

Kate stood.

"I know that because I know you're not a fool. You began this thing to find the truth. You...we have a long way to go to get there but at this point, you know your mother loved her for good reasons, maybe fairytale reasons. Forgiving your mother for cheating on your father is a different thing, and we'll work on that together. Right now, though, the question is whether you'll help to put the woman your mother loved at least somewhat at ease by simply speaking to her. I don't even know that it matters what you say. You really did a number on her."

She was looking down at me and I up at her, and I saw that she was very, very pissed. At me.

'Give me a minute," I said, rocking slightly back-and-forth on the sofa. Each time I rocked forward I thought of grabbing the phone, but I didn't and rocked back until finally I didn't rock back and just picked the damn thing up and in one motion stood.

"I'm going."

Kate ignored it. I felt her eyes on my back as I strode into my bedroom, slammed the door, and after several more seconds' hesitation I scrolled my call log and hit the number for my adulterous mother's lover.

12.

Much as I didn't want to admit it in my sulkiness, Nancy Penchant had a very nice apartment, especially for an Upper West Side brownstone. She must have been doing alright as an author since her place occupied the entire third floor. I realized at some point between leaving my apartment on 85th and getting to hers on 94th that not only did my mom likely go to bed with her countless times there but that, yes, it was probably where my mom was when she had the stroke that killed her.

Would I ask to see where it happened?
Would she offer to show me if I didn't ask?

I stood on the sidewalk, near the curb, looking up as people enjoying a beautiful day in the park were streaming west. Number 34 was a standard neighborhood brownstone, on the south side of the street. The exterior was a collection of rectangular stones in brown. Steps went up from the sidewalk to the first floor, with an entrance to the ground floor apartment beneath them. A black metal gate ran along the sidewalk, guarding a small tree and a cluster of garbage and recycling cans.

Ten or twelve steps led to the front doors, a pair in a light brown stain with a transom window above it, on which "34" was stenciled in a gold paint. She was on the third floor. It had three windows, a narrow pair to the right and a bigger one to the left, each with a semicircle for its upper reaches. I'd told Kate what I was doing when we canceled our plans to get a bite. She offered to walk with me, but I needed me-space, which she understood.

I took a deep breath, climbed 34's stoop, and headed into...I knew not what.

Nancy buzzed me in, and I climbed the two flights. Unlike the halls in my building, which were bland and hadn't been painted at least since I arrived, hers had wainscoting that angled up the stairs with hunter green paint on the walls. The thick banister had the same type of light-brown stain as the front doors. A series of brushed brass sconces lined the walls, with low wattage narrow, pointy bulbs lighting it.

The staircase was wide to the second floor and then narrowed to the third and above. If you stuck your head over the banister and looked up, you would see a leaded skylight to the roof. At her landing, the door was open, and in I went. She was there, standing by a window, a silhouette really, turning to me as I entered and shut the door.

If the hallways put my building's to shame, that was nothing compared to the apartment itself. The front area, where she stood somewhat frightened, I thought, was one large living room. She still hadn't spoken and since it wasn't my place to begin, I turned to the room itself. It had a large sofa against the wall to the right covered in an off-white pattern. In front of that was a modern, steel coffee table with a glass top on which there was several large Rizzoli picture books of European capitals beside a small, neat stack of *New Yorkers*. Across from the sofa was a pair of armchairs in a fabric that matched the sofa. Several small pillows were spread precisely across the sofa, and each chair had one.

To the left, on the wall opposite the sofa, was a mantelpiece. I couldn't tell whether the fireplace was used, but the mantel was wood in a stain very similar to what was on the banisters. A large oriental rug chiefly in dark blue with an intricate center medallion and cream tassels on the narrow edges covered the floor except for a foot or so of dark wood flooring all around it. A large landscape of a beach scene—two large houses amid some dunes with a slight bit of ocean at the bottom and the slightest flash of red in a window treatment blowing out of an upper-story window of the house to the left—was above the mantel and contrasted with the walls, which were painted in a very light, very summery yellow.

Because the front room faced north, it didn't get much sun. A lone cushioned armchair in yellow and a floral pattern that didn't match the ones across from the sofa was at an angle to the left window. It had a tall floor lamp and a small round table—Karen Adams's *Lonesome* collection sat on it—beside it so the occupant could sit with a book or a *New Yorker* or *The Sunday Times* crossword and put her feet on the windowsill as she read with a nice Merlot within easy reach.

Since I exhausted what else there was to see, I had to turn back to her. She hadn't moved. She stood beside a round table between the sofa and the right window. Her left fingers were touching its top. It matched the other one except it was larger, and a half-full long-stemmed glass of red wine sat like a maroon rose in a narrow crystal vase on it. The glass was to Nancy's left, and for a moment I thought she might grab and drain it before she would say a word.

She left it alone. After I'd done my brief survey, though, she said, "Thanks for coming."

Without thinking, I heard myself say, "Show me." I hadn't planned on it. It just popped out.

I think she too was taken aback.

"Are you sure?"

"Show me."

She took a breath and reached for her glass but pulled her fingers away before they touched that long stem, and she began to move towards me. She made sure not to come close enough to me that she might touch me, even accidentally, and I didn't try to touch her.

There was a hallway painted in a light blue that transitioned perfectly from the yellow of the living room. To its left was a series of black-and-white photos I didn't dare look at too closely. More beach scenes mostly with people, and I didn't want to see whether my mom was among them.

I passed a door for what I assumed was the bathroom. The hall opened to the kitchen, but she stopped before going in.

"You sure?"

I nodded.

She opened the door to the right. Her bedroom.

I don't know what I expected. A bordello, perhaps? But whatever it was, this wasn't it. It was simply a nice, tasteful bedroom. Almost like a spread in one of the lifestyle magazines Maggie liked to display on the coffee table in Bronxville.

But...

"Here?"

She nodded.

"There was nothing unusual about that afternoon. She was—"

She turned away, went into the kitchen, and I followed. She took two glasses from the cupboard and filled one from the tap. She offered it to me and I took it and she poured one for herself. She took a sip, weighing it in both her trembling hands and began to speak, quietly at first. "I've never told anyone. In all these years, I've never told anyone."

She lifted the glass and in one long swallow emptied it and then refilled it. She was looking at the sink, her shoulders slumped, until with some effort she turned. I was still in the kitchen doorway.

"I loved her more than I could have imagined loving anyone."

Before I could move, she threw the glass against the wall opposite the sink. Water splashed and sprinkled throughout the room and the glass shattered into a million pieces that rained onto the floor and onto the lower part of her pants.

"Why did she have to die? Why did she have to fucking die?"

I was frozen. Her back was to the sink and slowly, very slowly, she dropped to the floor before I could warn her about the shards of glass and the pools of water. I doubted it would've mattered to her, the cuts or the dampness or the noise the glass made when it hit on the ceramic tiles between the stove and the exhaust-fan hood.

It was sad, watching this stately woman inch down until she collapsed on the kitchen floor. I froze before leaving her in whatever lonely world she'd fallen into, and backing up, stepping towards *the* bedroom. Without going in, I canvassed it. It had a queen-sized bed with a very simple frame of soft brown wood with a narrow gold trim. A hardwood floor with an aqua-colored oriental.

I took a small step in. Then another. The bed was against the wall straight ahead and a pair of windows with a view south, across to the rears of the brownstones on 93rd Street. The apartment was on a high enough floor that the bedroom would get its fair share of light. The sun was already starting to go down so there were long shadows from the neighboring buildings.

I took another step in. The wall to my right had a dresser in a dark wood between the wall against which the bed was and an opening for the room's door. The dresser had a large, horizontal mirror over it. A traditional mirror, with a nice but not too wide gilded frame. There were two photos on the dresser, also in classic gilded frames. My mom was in both.

One was that picture from the Locus Award website. The other was taken in a gallery that I recognized as at the Met. A Monet of a bridge crossing a lily pond was behind them, and it was clear that it was important that that painting be in the photo. As in the one from the park, my mom looked...happy.

A closet and then a desk were against the wall to my left. A small, pretty woman's desk. A lady's desk, I thought, with a mismatched modern black chair on rollers placed between its two columns of drawers. A laptop was centered on it and a small printer was to the right. A stack of papers, story drafts I assumed, were piled neatly to the left, and envelopes were distributed in a little brass stand against the wall.

Framed *New Yorker* covers were in two columns a few inches from the closet's frame, but they weren't any of the famous ones so I figured they were issues in which one of her stories appeared. Centered above the desk was a large horizontal poster. It was a photo taken at dusk from the northern side of the Great Lawn in the park, looking towards the buildings along Central Park South and behind it. It could almost have been a black-and-white photo except for the colored lights on a sign off to the right and the slightest bit of dark green I could just about make out in the trees.

I turned to the broad window. Beautiful paintings—a superb pair of tall vertical portraits of two women, "fashionable" woman in the Wharton era with porcelain skin and high collars, gazing across to one another—hung in simple gilded frames that flared out at their corners on either side of the narrow blue curtain that framed the window.

"I like to think they were lovers."

I didn't know she left the kitchen, and she startled me. I turned to her. Nancy. She was disheveled with some water stains on her white pants but otherwise seemed recovered and stood at the door, her hand steadying the rest of her on the brass doorknob. She stepped towards me before veering to the right, to the dresser, where she picked up the picture from the museum. She stared at it.

"She loved this Monet. Said she used to bring you there sometimes. Do you remember?"

I hadn't thought of that painting or those outings with my mom in forever. Sometimes she'd be sitting in the kitchen in the morning already dressed to go out, especially in the summer when I was off school.

"We're going into the city," she'd announce, holding a cup of tea. I couldn't believe I'd not thought of those days. For all the shit she put on me and put me through, these outings were special. Sometimes she'd tell me to bring my friends, and Kate and a couple of others would pile in.

But mostly it was the two of us. "Leaving in ten," she'd call to me, and she meant it. A few times, the car'd be in the driveway with her in it and she'd honk the horn. My dad would already be in the city, at work, and it was usually about ten, so we'd miss the heavy traffic.

She let me pick the music on the way down, though I think she wasn't a fan of what I liked, and I'd compromise for her benefit and play something a bit old and more to her taste. She was not the best driver and put the fear of God in me as we drove down the Major Deegan Expressway—I-87—till we got off to cross into Manhattan on the Madison Avenue Bridge and then straight down Fifth Avenue—except for the right-left-right turn around Marcus Garvey Park in Harlem— and she'd park in a garage between Fifth and Madison, and into the Met we went.

And there she was in the photo, smiling with her lover in front of the highlight of the outings I had with her. The Monet bridge. I was sorry that there was no photo of us standing there but there wasn't and never would be. And I wondered whether she smiled as she did in this photo when she stood there with me. Maybe Kate'd remember.

I realized that I again thought of Nancy Penchant as my mom's "lover" but it was not such a vile term. That was no act, the flinging of the glass. The sitting in the damp. The cursing my mom's death. Her studying the photo.

"She said it was special to the two of you, that painting."

This brought me from my past, and she handed the photo to me. I ran my finger across the image, of both women and wondered if my mom had a copy hidden somewhere in the house.

"Did she talk about me much?" I asked, keeping my eyes on the photo.

"You? Sometimes I couldn't shut her up. I may have known more about you than anyone but her. Even your dad. You can't imagine how boring it is to listen to a mother give a weekly status report of everything her ten-year-old daughter had done the prior week."

She laughed. "Still, I loved every word."

I kept looking at my mom's smile.

"Did she...Did she *like* me?"

"She adored you. Though there were times when I don't think she liked you so much. She blamed herself."

Her hands reached for my upper arms and turned me, and I looked up at her.

"It was the one thing I couldn't get through to her about. You. She was always saying she wasn't doing a good job. That she didn't deserve you. Eventually, she would have arranged for us to meet, as 'old friends' of course, but she thought you were still too young and so I never did see you beyond those times when you were a baby. She dreamed of when you'd turn eighteen. When you'd be an adult and she could open up to you."

"You saw me when I was a baby, the times she writes about in the story."

"Yes. Until you all moved to the suburbs. But you wouldn't remember any of that."

"No. I don't."

She left me holding the photo and looked at the bed. Her arms were loosely at her sides, and her hands were clasped just below her waist. She paused before doing it, but there was really nowhere else, and she sat on the side of the bed, far enough toward the foot for me to know she wanted me to sit beside her, and I did.

"It was a normal Friday," she began when I was in place. Her hand reached for mine, and I let her take it and I don't know that she realized how she gripped it. "Absolutely nothing special. It was hot, and we had lunch over on Columbus. It was too hot, though, to sit outside, so we were in the A/C. She said you were at some practice or something."

"Field hockey."

"That'd be it. She said you'd hang out with your friends for the rest of the day, and she wouldn't be missed. She'd get back around six. We strolled back here, it being too hot to walk, and, well, we kissed and undressed and did what we'd done a million times and hoped to do a million more.

"I've never told anyone any of this. She was on top of me and...well, she was on top of me, and she suddenly shook and her eyes got big and she fell hard on me. I shook her and screamed at her, but she was having some type of spasm. I was on to 9-1-1 as soon as I could, and they were here almost immediately."

Her grip grew tighter and tighter on my hand, but she was looking straight ahead, to the brownstones across the way.

"They were here so fast. I'd only had time to throw a robe on. They wouldn't let me come in the ambulance because I wasn't family. I threw a dress on and shoes and ran out to take a cab up to St. Luke's. They wouldn't let me be with her in the ER, though she wasn't conscious.

"A cop and one of the EMTs came to me. I'd grabbed your mom's bag. I told them who I was and who she was. I told them, no, I wasn't her 'partner' and that she was married. I think they—both were men—might have smirked at that but I didn't care. I handed the cop the wallet from her bag, and he opened it.

"'Emily Locus'? he read, and I said that's who she was. He looked but couldn't find next-of-kin information. Her phone was locked so we couldn't get the info there. I said her husband worked at a big law firm. I didn't remember the name completely but that I remembered a 'Murphy' in it and while I stood there, he went off, leaving the EMT with me. The EMT told me to sit and checked me out. While that was going on, a doctor came out and sat beside me and I told her what happened. I said you were the first I told. I didn't count this.

"She—I was glad it was a she—was very kind but she admitted it didn't look good. I remember her hand running up and down my arm as I cried and she whispered that she'd get me in to see her but that I had to be prepared. I nodded and just then the cop came back. He mentioned the full name of the firm, and I recognized it. 'Steven Locus?' he asked, and I said that was it. He said they'd inform him and turned away.

"'When he gets here, will he let you see her?' I was so lucky it was a her and that she understood. Really understood. I shook my head. 'Come on,' she said, and she brought me in. I think the EMT was about to say something, but her glare shut him up.

"It was, as she said, horrible. She just lay there. A sheet covering her body and those monitors blinking and beeping. She nodded to a nurse who was next to the bed, and the nurse stepped back. It was clear that there was nothing they could do. They were just standing there waiting to hear from your father.

"Her arms were above the sheet, and I saw her wedding band—I told her not to take it off when we were together because I was afraid she'd forget to put it back on—as if it were plugged in. I ran my hand across—"

Nancy was having trouble continuing and was beginning to sob again. Now I was gripping her hand. She was looking around for something and when I understood I ran into the bathroom and came back with a box of tissues. I handed a couple to her.

"I'll be okay." This was more optimism than anything.

"I ran my hand across hers," she said. "It was still warm. She was alive and her hand was warm and maybe a bit sweaty. Her eyes were closed and her beautiful head, a Madonna's head, was perfectly still, looking who knows where. 'Can she hear me?' I asked, and the doctor said, 'No one knows, but it can't hurt.' She stepped away.

"I kept my hand on hers and leaned forward. I knew I hadn't said it enough, that I could never have said it enough. I don't know if she believed me when I did, but it was the truest thing I ever said. I told her how much I loved her and always would and though I'm not a religious person I said someday we'd be together. It was pretty clear that she wasn't going to wake up.

"And that was the last thing I said to her. The nurse led me back, and I dragged my fingers over her hand as I backed up."

"Did you, you know, think of doing something crazy?"

She shook her head. "No. Maybe God will put us together again. But I wasn't going to hasten the reunion, much as I sometimes wanted to. I did talk about it with my therapist, though, and that helped."

Saying that seemed to strengthen her, and her back stiffened.

"I had my little vigil. I saw your father rush into the ICU. Him coming out to bring you in about an hour later. He didn't recognize me."

"He knew you?"

"Sweetie, that's enough for now. I'll tell you anything you want to know but I think we both need to step from the ledge."

She suggested dinner, and that's what we did. On the way, she said she was in the hall outside the ICU, that she remembers seeing me and what she assumed were my mom's parents there. But she never saw my mom again.

As we walked down her hallway to go, I stopped at the photos along the wall. She flicked on some halogen lights in the ceiling. A pastiche of professionally shot pictures, mostly of her with one or two others. The obligatory, I assumed, Pride Parade pictures and some with her arm around much younger and very attractive women that looked to have been recently taken.

"I wasn't celibate before your mother, and I haven't been since."

"And during?"

"She knew I had...needs. I think she tolerated it more than anything and I didn't pick up women as often as I had. I never took them here and I always felt like a shit afterward—"

I was so close to again going off on her, for being a cheater on a cheater but that was before seeing her lose it in the kitchen.

"Life's complicated," I said.

She looked at me. "Sweetie, I'm afraid I made it much more complicated for you."

She smiled.

I took another look at her array.

"Why no pictures of my mom here?"

She looked across the display.

"These are just moments in my life," she said. "Your mom was so much more. That's why she's not here," she said.

"But in the bedroom?"

She smiled. "You know I sometimes, but rarely, take someone home with me. It's funny, but when I do, I go in first and look at that photo from the Met and the other one and I say I'm sorry to her and place them face down and tell myself it's alright. The girls I'm with sometimes ask and I just say, 'That's the one that got away' and you know they, most of them, plan on getting away too so it's all good."

She was right. Things were getting complicated.

13.

Before we left her place, I told Nancy I needed to give someone a call, and she went into the bathroom to "freshen up," as she put it.

I reported to Kate that while I still had tons of things to sort out and work through, I was not so anti-Nancy as I had been. I was even going to dinner with her. It just felt like something I should do, whether I really wanted to or not.

She asked if I wanted her to join us. I said I expected they'd meet soon enough. Just not yet. She told me she loved me and was happy that "bitchy Alex" seemed to have been vanquished for the moment.

"Was that the one who called me?" Nancy asked when she left the bathroom after I'd hung up.

"Kate. Yes. I wouldn't be here except for her. We grew up together. I'd be more fucked up than I am without her, and she knew my mom pretty well."

"She mentioned she liked the girls you hung out with. I assume this Kate was one of them?"

"She was."

At the door, I said, "I told her we were going to dinner, and she asked whether I wanted her to come. I told her she'd meet you eventually, but I think this is a one-on-one kind of thing."

"I think you're right. Any particular place you want to be taken where someone else will be picking up the tab?"

"With my stomach in the shape it's in, a fine meal and finer wine would just go to waste."

So, we went to a burger joint we both knew—where we each got simple grilled cheeses with fries—and when we got there, she wondered whether we'd ever been there at the same time.

"Would you have recognized me?" I asked.

"Your mom was always showing me pictures, but that was years before and seeing you now I doubt I would have put two and two together. But *quien sabe?*"

I thought of asking about my dad as we walked to the restaurant. But she asked about how I was getting on since moving to the city. I didn't find a chance to bring it up while we ate as I gave her a bio of my life after my mom was gone. Not the inside stuff but the names/dates/places sort of thing. *I* didn't know some of my inside stuff.

We left the restaurant. She said she'd walk me home, and I gave her the address, though I wondered if that was a mistake before realizing how idiotic I was being.

"You want to know about your father in all this, don't you?"

I admitted I did.

It was getting dark on a Sunday night, but we walked past my building and found a bench along Central Park West not far from that infamous one where I left *The Love of My Life*, which I didn't dare bring up with her just yet. About getting it back.

We were settled on the bench, and she took a deep breath and looked across the avenue. "He found out about us. It was a few years before she passed. He had some private detective follow her a few Fridays. I usually sleep in on Sundays, and one Sunday morning early in the year, it was cold, and my buzzer went off. When I asked who it was, he said, 'It's the husband.'

"I didn't have to think a moment to know what that meant. I let him up. I left the door open, as I did with you and, come to think of it, I stood pretty much where I stood when you came in. He entered and was, well, you know what he looks like. I couldn't tell if he was angry. I really couldn't. Maybe it's his legal training, appearing to be cool under pressure.

"I just stood there in a robe. My back was to the windows, and I heard him come up the stairs and waited for him to come in the apartment. When he did, I didn't know what to do or what would happen. He stopped maybe six feet away, leaving the door open, a little out of breath from the climb. 'I wanted to see what the slut'—that's the word he used—'what the slut who is trying to ruin my marriage looks like. But I swear to you it won't work.'

"He pointed his index finger at me and shook it a little. Then he turned and left. He didn't close the door, and I heard him go down the stairs faster and faster and I didn't dare move till I heard the building door shut. I ran to the window and saw him hurrying down towards Columbus and watched and watched till he was gone. I slammed my door, which I don't think I'd ever done before or since.

"I made it to the sofa, and I collapsed on it and began to shake. That's what I remember. Being in a daze and shaking, not knowing what to do. Had he told your mother? Should I call her? I was paralyzed for I don't know how long."

As she spoke, she became more and more animated, her hands conveying what her words couldn't. She'd long since lost the cool exterior she normally projected. Thank God we weren't in her apartment. On that sofa. As it was, the people passing by on the sidewalk were either oblivious to her distress or sufficiently aware of it to give us plenty of leeway, though I'm sure someone would have stopped had she been alone, as my very pregnant mom was that summer day when she was grasping the lightpole near the tennis courts and what I have to call Fate intervened.

I reached over to connect with this...sad and very lonely woman who only hours before I was afraid would touch me, even incidentally, and who was now clutching my offered hand.

"I knew she wasn't with him, so I called her. 'Yes,' she said, 'he told me he found out. He made me swear not to warn you.' Then there was silence. 'Em?' I asked. After another silence, she said, 'He's making it a condition that I never see you again.'

"'Condition?' I asked her. 'Nancy, he'll throw me out and keep Alex and I can't let that happen.' Then she hung up."

"When was this?" I asked.

"Three or four years before—"

"So, how'd you get back together?"

"I was miserable, of course. Not only didn't I have her anymore and it really hit me how devastating that would be, but I realized I'd jeopardized her relationship with you. He really could have thrown her out and she'd have little chance of getting custody, her having a lesbian affair and all.

"She called on the Thursday. Out of the blue. I couldn't believe it. But there was her '914' number. 'We made a deal,' she said. She said he'd agreed that she could see me once a week but that she had to keep it a secret. She was never to be with a man or any woman but me. In exchange, she was to be the 'good mother' to you and, I'll never forget this, that she'd be the 'good wife' to him."

I didn't understand this last bit, and she turned to me.

"It was horrible, sweetie, but she had no choice. He could see whomever he wanted to see, fuck whomever he wanted to fuck, and she couldn't complain."

She hesitated and looked down at her hands.

"I know there are two sides, and you can ask him when you are up to it. But—" She looked over to me and I think she regretted the look her words generated, especially these last ones.

"But she said that being a 'good wife' meant being available to him sexually. That's all I'll say. You best ask him when, as I say, you think you're up to it."

If my face was panic-looking before, now it was shocked.

I'd never doubted my parents' mutual affection for one another. I knew they had sex, although it wasn't often when I was old enough to understand what they were doing. But there was never a suggestion that it wasn't what they both wanted to do when they did it, though I guess in retrospect I really wouldn't know what the "signs" were.

"Look, sweetie. That's more than enough for now. I want you to think about everything. As to that last thing, I hope you keep it to yourself."

I nodded.

"Not even Kate. Understood?"

I said I did.

As we got up from the bench and walked to my place, she asked what my immediate plans were. Somehow my arm found its way through hers as we walked and in some ways, we got to my building too soon and in some ways not soon enough. I told her that I had some thinking to do but would let her know.

"Nancy," I said, and I think it was the first time I used her name. I was on the steps but turned and stepped to the sidewalk. "Nancy, when I read her things, it seems that something really bothered her about motherhood. Do you know anything about that?"

She waited a second.

"I think you should speak with her parents."

With that, I wished her a good what-was-left-of-the-night and went inside.

14.

I gave a brief report to Kate—excluding the "good wife" reference—when I was in my living room then I put something on Netflix that didn't work so I tried something else and that didn't work, and I put on something that always worked and *that* didn't work. I'd be having a tough time falling asleep and my mind was all over the place. I opened my laptop to Word and began to write. It was crap, about a beautiful fall day in Central Park, but it was cathartic. I didn't bother to save it when I exited the program but at least was able to enjoy the early scenes of *Pride and Prejudice*—the one with Colin Firth—till I was tired enough to go to bed.

I couldn't know whether Nancy was not telling me something she knew or was telling me she didn't know something important. Either way, I'd call my grandma and grandpa. To be clear, they were the Millers, my mom's parents. My dad's parents were always "grandmother" and "grandfather."

The Millers lived in Paterson, in upstate New York. Maybe a hundred miles due north, in Columbia County. It's on our side of the Hudson and south of Albany and not far from the Massachusetts border. Their town had seen better days even when I visited and stayed there while my mom was alive. It had been some type of mill town along a stream. The main factory building was still there, all boarded up and empty. Several large houses for the bosses lined its main street and deeper in were small, ramshackle places, each looking pretty much like all the others.

I spent a part of each summer in Paterson when I was a kid, but there weren't many kids there. Most of the folks were my grandparents' age or even older. The houses were well maintained, and the gardens were a particular point of pride. It was Grandpa Miller who took charge of their garden and even when he worked—he was an executive at a small bank in Hudson, the County seat about five miles to the west and along its namesake river, but retired a couple of years after my mom passed—he spent a goodly portion of the weekend with his flowers and shrubs.

Gardening never took as far as my mom was concerned, and in Bronxville, she left it to our gardeners to keep the yard pristine. Her father would have fallen over laughing if he knew how often—never—she'd fertilized anything and that she probably hadn't planted anything since she left home.

Grandma Miller was a registered nurse. She worked in the county's hospital, which was in Hudson, too, and she also was retired though she volunteered her services once or twice a week at a seen-better-days nursing home just outside of town.

With Mom gone, I didn't go up very often. Every couple of months, I'd take the train to Bronxville and drive one of the cars up. I always asked my dad to come and even Maggie, but he had no interest and because he didn't, neither did she. When all of this began, it was only a few weeks since I'd been up so when I called on Monday night saying I'd like to come up again they were surprised.

I told them I needed to talk about some things concerning my mom, which surprised them.

I said I'd discovered some of her writings at the Bronxville house and was curious about whether there was anything in Paterson. That I remembered she sometimes spent early evenings while she and I were up there—my dad usually came up only on the weekends on Amtrak to Hudson and even then he brought work with him—sitting on their front porch writing in one of his legal pads. I hadn't given it much mind. I was a kid. I never asked what she was writing or why. It was just something she did, and I left her alone to do it while I wandered the neighborhood hoping to find someone to play with.

"Well," my grandpa said, "she left a bunch of those pads here and I think some other things."

"That'd be great, Grandpa," I said, and he said he'd pull them together for me.

We arranged for me to stop by the house late on Saturday morning.

Shortly after I set that up, I called my dad. I was nervous but careful. He asked what the status was regarding the papers I brought down and whether I wanted him to come and collect them. I told him I was slowly working through them, that there were some interesting things, and I'd be keeping them for a bit longer, "If that's alright."

"Keep them as long as you want, honey," he said. "They were just taking up space here."

I didn't say I'd met Nancy. I didn't say I'd arranged to go up to see my grandparents.

It was late but not too late when I was finished with him, so I called Kate. I told her earlier what Nancy said about me calling my grandparents, so I said I'd arranged to go up on Saturday. She, naturally, offered to come with me. She might have met my grandparents a couple of times at some family get-together in Bronxville but neither of us remembered.

"It'll be good putting everything else aside to get out of the city," she said, and we agreed we wouldn't go to either of our folks to get a car but would rent a Zipcar for the trip and share the driving.

15.

Saturday was very warm. It'd be some time before the leaves turned so we didn't encounter leaf-peeper traffic as we headed north and out of Manhattan and through the Bronx into what passes for the country in these parts. Actually, by the time we were about halfway to Paterson, the parkway largely goes between farms as it winds and rises and falls and the expensive cars start zipping past even though we, at 65 or so, were 10 over the limit.

I was up to driving all the way, and Kate let me be quiet.

Paterson itself is maybe a mile from the exit on the Taconic Parkway. As I turned left from the exit and went under the parkway, I was hit by a wave of apprehension. I'd made that turn and gone under that bridge countless times, but this was worlds apart from that.

"You okay?" Kate asked.

"I'm just glad you're here."

"Always."

"I know. But I don't tell you enough."

We stayed quiet as we started down the short hill that leads to town and then took the right on my grandparents' street.

The house itself was a couple of blocks up and one of the last houses before the street went through a small wood and emerged into farmland. I can't say how often I went that way, to where the fields were, when I was a kid. I'd get burned by the sun because there was no shade, just row after row of cornfields and, as the summer aged, corn stalks, and in August the tar used to cover cracks in the road would begin to melt.

But I didn't go past the house this time. I pulled up to the curb. The house itself looked small from the outside. It was in some type of Dutch style with five or six steps from the path to the porch. The front door was white and there was a screen door with an Amish-type carriage on its centerpiece.

The porch was not open but surrounded by a three-foot or so wall that was divided by big round columns that I'm sure have a name, but I don't know what it is. It was where I spent many hours reading, especially when it was raining, and I couldn't lie on a big towel out back trying to get some kind of tan while my grandparents were working and my mom was doing whatever she was doing.

I don't think the car stopped moving before that screen door shot open and Grandma Miller was through it, with Grandpa Miller right behind. It was a bit past eleven and I wondered for how long she'd been staring out waiting for our arrival.

We were there. I'd hurried around the car to stand beside Kate. Grandma Miller hugged me and stepped back so I could introduce her to my friend, "from high school."

"You probably met her in Bronxville," I added, "but it was a while ago." They'd been down to Bronxville only a few times since the funeral.

"And she has grown into quite the young woman," my grandpa said, which got my grandma to roll her eyes in my direction.

"We have some pastries since I'm sure you're hungry," Grandma said, and after the introductions were completed, we followed her into the house, with Grandpa behind.

I didn't bother to tell my grandma not to, well, bother because it wouldn't have done any good. As we were through the door, Grandpa rushed to the kitchen to "put the coffee on" and when we turned into the living room, there on the coffee table was a platter with pastries and bagels and cream cheese.

Grandma pretty much shoved us—politely—to the sofa and handed each of us one of her good plates, which was too hifalutin for us, but we were guests (or at least Kate was) and the niceties were to be observed. Kate was asked to tell something about herself and her parents and siblings and "any children," which got a "none just yet" from her and a guffaw from me.

The chit-chat continued when grandpa brought out a tray on which there were cups and saucers, the coffee pot from the maker, and a creamer and sugar bowl. He put it on the sideboard that was against the wall opposite the sofa, and Kate and I put our plates on the coffee table and got our coffee, ignoring his insistence that he could as easily do it himself.

We settled back deep into the sofa's cushions, and the mood changed. Kate was my dearest friend, I said. She knew my mom and could hear anything they had to tell me. They looked at each other and nodded. Grandpa took the floor.

"You mentioned, honey, about your mom and whether she'd left any writings. I went to the basement, and way in the back by the water heater, I found three boxes. I brought them up—"

"Grandpa, you shouldn't have," I said.

"I'm old, Alex, but not that old." It was true. His hair was not yet white and from his gardening or otherwise he'd always looked to be in shape. Not too tall, but slim with barely a paunch.

Grandma, who was sitting in an armchair by him and whose hair was colored brown but who was also slim and nearly as tall as Grandpa, patted his thigh. She said, "Some of his parts are still in working order," and the pair of them laughed and I said "TMI," which Kate translated as too-much-information. We all relaxed a bit.

The boxes were over to the left, near the window, one on top of the other and very dusty.

Grandma took over. "They haven't been opened in years and we didn't open them when we found them. We thought that would be something you'd want to do. We have no idea what's in them, but we remember her writing when she was here. Your grandpa and I will head into Hudson for a few hours. Give you both some time to open them and take a look. We'll be back at about three and see where everything stands and...talk. Okay? You have our number if you need anything."

They both stood and so did Kate and me. Grandma's handbag was on a table in the front hallway, and she picked it up.

"I got things for sandwiches and sodas. It's all in the fridge so help yourselves." With that, she followed Grandpa out. Kate and I watched them leave from the porch and gave slight waves as they headed to Hudson.

Kate and I stayed on the porch, though only briefly.

"Ready?" she asked.

"Ready," I said, and we were through the screen door and looking across the living room to the boxes.

"Let's open them together," I said, "and then we'll try to figure out what to do."

And what we did was take the two that mostly had documents and put them one atop the other by the coffee table. The third box, though, contained all sorts of things. Photos and cassette tapes. Diaries. Little knick-knacks, some looking to be from when my mom was a kid. I knew my grandparents had plenty of that stuff—the pictures and the knick-knacks—but my mom had put these things aside. Perhaps she had a reason. Perhaps she didn't. Only one way to find out.

"I think I should go through these first," I told Kate when we saw what was in this box.

"You should do it alone. How about in the dining room? I'll start on these others."

It was a good plan. Kate knew what she was about and, more than anyone, what *I* was about.

I carried the box into the dining room. It wasn't heavy. Instead of putting it on the table, I flipped it so its contents spread across the floor. I'd gotten enough practice in doing this whole organizational thing recently, so I leaned down and roughly separated things into categories: pictures, tapes, diaries, documents.

The diaries, of course, were the mother lode (pardon the pun). But the photos drew me in more immediately. I plopped down on the floor, my back to the wall beneath the window, and put them together like a deck of playing cards. Occasionally, I heard Kate mumble something and figured she was making good progress on her documents.

I turned all the pictures to face me and started going through them. Some I recalled from being buried away in one or another drawer or shoebox in Bronxville. Some had dates but most didn't. I had a general sense of time in the undated, though, through my mom's growth.

The photos seemed to begin when she was six or seven. Most were posed. In front of her parents' house, often with one and then the other. Sometimes both. There were shots from Christmas, under the tree and with her stocking. Opening presents. One of the earliest is her first Holy Communion in her little wedding dress next to her classmates. I think she went to the public school, but a goodly number of those in Paterson and neighboring towns were Catholic and so there were enough for the ceremony. One with the priest and who must have been the parish's coordinator for it. Her between her parents, holding a small bouquet of white carnations.

There are some photos of her playing softball. Even some pretending like you see in baseball cards. Grammar school graduation. High school graduation. Just the random sort of photos I think any kid in America would have in those days.

The diaries promised to be more useful. There was a volume for each year beginning in 1976, when she was six. Each was locked, but it was pretty easy to open them with a pair of tweezers. They were filled with her idiosyncratic handwriting, which I got accustomed to in the stories on the legal pads. The entries were so banal I know she'd be embarrassed that anyone read them. But there they were, in her hand in her box in the basement.

There was too much to get through, so after reading the first pages of 1976 and 1977, I merely flipped through the others. I figured I'd read them later, but they suddenly stopped. In 1980, when she would have been ten, there are references to the family getting a dog from the shelter. Entries about Ronnie, the dog, until suddenly he's gone.

And that was the last entry in any of the diaries.

I brought it to Kate, who was mired in the more formal stuff, and asked her about it.

"Remember the date," she said. "It may be significant. It might not be. But if we're being good detectives, we'll check it out. How are you doing?"

I told her I'd gone through the photos and the diaries.

"Do your grandparents have a tape player?" she asked.

Like most people, I'm sure they once did, but whether there was still one in the house that worked had to wait till they were back. That left what I thought of as the more formal things. I asked Kate if she found anything, and she said she was just finishing putting them in some sort of order.

"From what I could tell, it looks like there were some variants on what we saw in the things from Bronxville. I haven't gotten into any of it or any of the new things, though."

She said she was just about finished with her organization, and there were a few piles like the ones we created in my apartment.

"Lunch?" I asked.

"Sounds good to me," and we headed to the kitchen. Grandma, of course, had gone overboard. Way too far. We made ham and Swiss sandwiches on rolls with lettuce and tomatoes and mustard and plenty of cole slaw and potato salad, which we put on the everyday plates, though the good stuff sat on the counter by the microwave.

There were cans of sodas, and we both took Diet Cokes and carried it all on a tray to the porch.

It was deep but a bit dark. It looked to the west, but the trees created plenty of cover, as did the roof that spread across it. On one side of the front door were three wicker chairs and between two of them was a matching wicker table. It was round, and we sat on either side of it with our food and drinks on the table's glass covering.

We thought we were too far from the front and from the street for anyone to notice us, but a couple who looked to be my grandparents' age called "hello" to us and the wife asked if one of us was "Alex" and I said I was, and Kate and I stood to the front of the porch.

"She doesn't stop talking about you, you know," the wife said.

"You make her very proud. I hope you know that," her husband added, and I said that I greatly appreciated it however misplaced it was.

"You? The woman in the city? Oh, don't undersell yourself, Alex," the wife said.

I said, "This is my childhood friend Kate," and Kate and they exchanged awkward how-are-yous before they apologized for disturbing our lunch and started up again with a "Tell her the Taylors said hello," and then with slight waves they headed toward town.

We were just about finished our lunches so back in we went and put our plates and the soda cans in the kitchen, rinsing off the former for the dishwasher and putting the latter on the counter. I put on fresh coffee, and we returned to the living room and my mom's boxes.

16.

Many of the stories in the Paterson boxes were versions of what we already saw. Others either predated her marriage and move to the city and way before moving to Bronxville or were written during extended stays in Paterson. Some seemed to be from her days in college. Mom went to the local high school and her grades and college boards were good enough for Cornell. The Millers' finances were such that she got a fair amount of financial aid, though she still worked several days a week in one of the university's dining halls.

This was all part of the Locus family lore. It was in the dining hall that my parents met. He the rich kid from an upscale Philadelphia suburb and she the decidedly not-rich kid from a mill town in the Hudson Valley who needed a job to pay for her books. My dad would laugh when he told people at a party about it. She hated it when he did. The whole Mr.-Rochester-as-savior bit.

He noticed her working when he was with his buddies. He was too nervous to approach her so one of his pals took it upon himself to do it for him. This guy walked up to her and said he—my future father—wanted to say something to her. She was at work clearing tables, but she followed him to the table in her apron over her jeans and wearing her little name tag on her university-issued, Cornell red polo shirt. The buddy formally introduced them to each other and, that done, she left to finish clearing tables and he wanted to kick the shit out of his friend.

But when she next worked while he was in the dining hall, he said hello and she said hello and finally he got the courage to ask her for a date. It was all very strange since my dad is the last person you'd think would hesitate about preening before a woman he was attracted to, but there was something, he said, that was different, special—so he said again and again—about her.

They dated. He was a junior and she a sophomore. For summer, he worked at a Philadelphia firm and stayed at his house on the Main Line. She got a job in a department store in Hudson and lived at home in Paterson. He drove up to see her a few times, but it was clear that his parents did not approve. They had aspirations for their son and marrying a girl from a down-in-the-dumps town in upstate New York was not among them.

Back in Ithaca—he for his senior year and she for her junior—they became an item. He was her first boyfriend and though he'd had plenty of short relationships with girls, she was his first real girlfriend.

He got into Columbia Law School in Manhattan and shared one of those big Morningside Heights apartments with three other classmates, one he knew from Cornell, for first year. He proposed to her over Christmas at the Millers' house in Paterson, and she said yes. Although it was against tradition, the wedding was held at his parents' Catholic Church outside Philadelphia and, legend had it, a goodly number of the groom's friends from Cornell sat on the bride's side to balance out the proceedings.

No honeymoon beyond a weekend at the Hollister Hotel in Philadelphia. He had a lucrative summer associate job at a New York firm and on August 1 before my dad was to begin his second year at Columbia and not long after my mom graduated from Cornell, my parents moved into a one-bedroom apartment on West 90th Street, though not in a brownstone. A new apartment building on the corner of Columbus Avenue. Yeah, all of a quarter mile from my current place on 85th.

Since I'm filling you in on the details, my mom got a job at a midsized bank with its headquarters in midtown (as it happens, one of the banks later taken over to create my megabank), and that's how the Locuses of New York City began their marriage, first in the city, although they moved to a two-bedroom in that brownstone Nancy walked her to the day they met, and a few years after I came along up to Bronxville since my dad decided to stay in the city and, much to his parents' disappointment, not practice in Philadelphia.

Which is where this all started. Me being a girl in a wealthy suburb whose mother died suddenly when she—that'd be me—was fourteen.

I gave this quick bio to Kate as we drove up. It'd help as she went through things to know that bit of Locus family history.

We sat looking over the mess we created in the Millers' living room. At least Kate had gotten hers into some semblance of order. She looked through the photos.

"Do you notice something missing?" she asked when she was done.

I'd been watching as she flipped through, and she handed them to me for another look.

She answered her own question. "Friends."

"What do you mean?"

"Friends. There aren't any friends."

It was so obvious now that Kate pointed it out. The only photos in which there were other kids were in the group ones at school or on a field. Even those of her at the nearby lake were just of her. I said her diary entries spoke in only general terms about playing with or outings with anyone. If she went to a party, all she said about it was that she went to the party and then went home.

She looked at me. I leaned my head onto her right shoulder.

"Did you find anything?"

"She writes...wrote well. I think she could have been a writer. Some of these were from when she was in high school. They're rough around the edges but she told a good story."

"Any insights into her?"

"I've just gone through first drafts of short pieces, plus what we read before we got here. But more than anything, her heroines were always either fighting for something or looking for something. It's funny. I know she was still young, but they don't seem to be searching *for someone*. They're not romances. If anything, they're adventure stories. Almost old-school fairytales."

She reached and lifted a pad and then another till she found what she wanted. About halfway through, she flipped the pages over the top and handed it to me.

"This one stood out, but it's not much different from a lot of others."

I looked at what was in this case a calm, neat hand and left-slanting lines I long knew. It moved across the page in dark blue ink. It was a fountain pen, and I imagined her fingertips becoming stained.

She usually dated her stories in the upper right-hand corner. The one Kate wanted me to read was dated August 5, 2006. It's entitled *Streaming*.

> *Sometimes the rain frightens me. Not the thunder or lightning. I am used to those. I know they're far away and can't hurt me. But the rain sometimes frightens me. I don't know why. I've never been caught in a flood or a mudslide. The river near where I live, along which I stroll, rarely overflows and when it does it never floods any houses past Mr. and Mrs. Ogden's and there were four houses between theirs and ours.*
>
> *No. I'm afraid because of a story I once heard when I was in camp when I was a little girl. Sleepaway camp. One of the girls, who I didn't know before, told the story of Sasquatch. She swore it was true. I don't think the other girls believed it was true. But I did.*

According to the story, the little girl, now grown-up, feared that if she were caught in the rain without an umbrella, her mask would be washed away, and she would be exposed. In some respects, the story was a variant of Wilde's *Picture of Dorian Gray*.

"She's always hiding," Kate said when I finished. "Afraid she'll be exposed. How could she have something so bad that she was obsessed with people not discovering it?"

I had no idea. Again and again, we saw inside her head. We understood the trees. We needed to see the forest. And at this stage, we hoped we could get at least something from my grandparents. Continuing to pore over the stories wouldn't be enough. We put the piles back in the order that Kate managed to get them in, and I again stacked the diaries by date. It was all we could do till they got back.

17.

As Kate and I were trying to process whatever it was we thought we'd discovered, my grandparents pulled into the driveway, and we went to the porch to meet them.

"Do you want us to drive around a bit more?" Grandma asked as Grandpa took a couple of bags from the backseat of their Subaru.

Kate looked at me and I at her before I said we had some questions.

It came out more ominously than I meant it to, and I wasn't sure that Grandpa heard it, but Grandma sure did, and she turned to look at him and I couldn't say what she was signaling but it was definitely something. As they reached the porch, Kate and I went in and they followed. Grandpa took the bags into the kitchen while Grandma surveyed the stuff spread all over her pristine living room floor. She stood there until Grandpa returned. Kate looked from one to the other of them and then at me.

"I need to use the ladies'," she said and headed down the hall to the small bathroom near the kitchen.

Grandma pulled me aside and said, quietly, that there was something they needed to tell me and asked if Kate should hear it. Not knowing what "it" was, I couldn't say. But I'd come so far with my friend. I saw no reason to exclude her, so I said it was fine. She nodded, and said, "Good. Let's sit in the living room."

I went down the hall and waited for Kate to finish but when she didn't, I knocked lightly on the door.

"You can come out now," I said.

When she did, I whispered, "You were right. They want to tell me something, but I said you can hear it too. I think I might need your support. You okay with that?"

She took a breath.

"That's what I'm here for, isn't it?"

I nodded, and she asked, "Ready?" If I were standing at the door of a plane with a parachute on my back I might not have been, but seeing as I was already in the sky, plummeting to Earth—again—I didn't have much of a choice.

I held her hand as we walked into the living room. Grandma was sitting in one of the chairs across the coffee table from the sofa, and Grandpa was over by the window, looking out. He turned when he heard us come in and moved to the chair next to Grandma's. Kate and I sat on the sofa.

"Since you haven't mentioned it, are we right to think your mother never told you she was adopted?"

Had I not been hammered by the things I'd found out about my family over the last few weeks, I would have been bowled over by this. Now it seemed to be simply another trial-of-Job thing.

Adopted? No, somehow no one bothered to tell me. I felt Kate's hand tighten on mine.

"I can see by your reaction that no one did," Grandpa said. "We didn't think it was our place and we always thought she should tell you and after she passed that your dad would and I think we assumed one or the other had. But apparently not."

"What do you mean, 'adopted'?" I asked. "She wasn't your little girl?"

"She was our little girl," Grandma said, and I felt like a shit.

Grandpa interrupted, calmer than Grandma and I were.

"Actually, we only got her when she was just under five."

"I'm sorry. Where was she before you adopted her?"

"With her mother, her birth mother I guess they call it nowadays."

Grandma said nothing. Just rocking rhythmically back and forth in her chair.

I don't know what Kate was doing beyond holding my hand ever tighter, and I was going back and forth between my, well, between the two I always thought were my grandparents until I reached my free hand to put it on Kate's and thank God she was there.

"We didn't know much about her before we adopted her," Grandpa continued. "Her name was Emily Spencer, and her mother was Dorothy. We only found that out because she was her age when we got her. She was in foster care in Albany for about a year. Her mother was into drugs and...prostitution and they had to take Emily from her. I don't know what happened to her mother."

As Grandpa spoke, Grandma got up. On a wall opposite the sofa and to the right of the entry was a low chest of drawers. It was where things were placed over time so if you were looking for something like a screwdriver or a map, it was where you'd start your search.

She opened the bottom drawer and took out a small manilla envelope. It had some sort of handwriting on its front, but I couldn't make out what it said. She opened it and pulled out a photo. Just a normal snapshot size. There were plenty of photos of my mom at different ages throughout the house at home as well as in that package I just looked through. I'd never seen this one. I realized that for all those pictures of her, there were no baby ones. It was another of those things that were strikingly obvious but that I missed.

"This was the only photo they gave us from before she was taken...removed from her mother."

It showed a sweet but serious-looking girl. What I could see of the dress, a red pattern trimmed in pink with a pink bow in the center, was that it was a little frayed, but clean, as was the face. She was smiling, missing a few upper teeth on her right side. She had a round face, and her hair was reddish and long. Not at all untidy. She stood in some type of park or garden. I guessed she was about four—not much older than TimTim—and Grandma said as she regained her composure that she thought that was about right. I could keep the photo, she said, though I promised to make a copy for them, and I took a photo of it with my phone just in case.

The air was suddenly heavy until Kate somehow cleared it away by asking what they knew about my mom's mother.

They said—they were taking turns filling in what slim details they had—she was unmarried and grew up somewhere in the county. She ran away when she was in high school and got into trouble when she was in New York or Philadelphia. She returned and had the baby—"who became your mother, of course"—and her parents took care of her and the baby. The parents died in a car accident, and she was alone with my mom and things just got worse and worse. She moved to Albany and the authorities had to step in when my mom was about four. That was pretty much all they were told. They asked but no one knew who the father was, and Dorothy wouldn't say. The father was living with her until she got pregnant, she did tell them, and then he disappeared out west, to parts unknown.

My grandparents always wanted kids but couldn't have them. They didn't volunteer why.

"She'd been in foster care for about a year," Grandma said. "They said she hadn't caused trouble but cried herself to sleep most nights. We met with her at the Social Services office in Albany and then were interviewed with social workers there. We saw her a few more times, and they inspected our house and ran criminal checks on us. We must have passed because on April 18, 1975—a Friday, we'll always remember that date—we got a call that we were approved and would get possession of Emily in anticipation of our formally adopting her.

"It was one of the happiest days of our lives, that day. Gradually she came to feel safe with us and she didn't cry so much at night. It was better when she went to school, of course, but she didn't mingle much with the other kids. She didn't have friends she played with after school. Stuff like that. She was invited to birthday parties but would only go if we made her."

Grandpa interrupted. "And she always called us early to pick her up or she'd show up at the door having walked home about an hour before the party ended. The other kids called her 'Ginger' and she hated it and, of course, they all knew she was adopted since she just appeared one day out of the blue."

"We spoke to the other parents about it." Grandma was picking up where she'd left off. "Some didn't think much of her, but they did what they could to make her comfortable. And it went like this for a few years. She was in fourth or fifth grade, though, and she came out of her shell. She didn't mention her mother anymore. She was playing softball"—I doubt she was very good at sports given what I saw of her at the field club—"and spent weekdays over the summer with friends. We thought she had turned the corner. For the first time, she seemed happy."

Grandpa got up and took our glasses for a refill. He came back, and Kate and I took sips and he resumed.

"Emily was suddenly just a normal ten-year-old, although she still didn't have a lot of friends." She turned to Grandpa.

"Do you recall anyone?"

He shook his head. "None she ever brought home." Grandma turned back to us. "She kept hounding us for a dog, and we finally got a shepherd mix at the shelter. Ronnie. She promised to take care of him, and she did. She loved that dog."

Grandma stopped.

"I think that's enough for now." Grandpa got up and went behind her so he could rub her shoulders.

"I think we all need a little break. What were you doing for dinner?"

We planned to head home by four, and it was already three-thirty but leaving now would be a shitty thing so I said we wanted to take them out and asked whether we could stay the night. Again, this wasn't planned and neither of us brought stuff, but I figured we could rough it. Kate and I could walk into town and pick up some toothbrushes and such.

"You can stay in your old room, Alex, but I don't know if there's enough room for your friend"—"Kate," I said—"For

Kate to be with you. She can sleep in the third bedroom if that's okay."

I wasn't sure what they thought my relationship with Kate was, but I admit I was surprised that their attitude might be more open than I gave them credit for in those days. The third bedroom would be fine, Kate said.

Grandma stood. "I'll have to get it ready, then," and she and Grandpa were gone.

"I just love them," Kate said.

"You notice the thing about us sleeping together?"

"I did. But you're the type who probably snores like a freight train so I'm glad I'll have a room to myself."

"Bitch," I called her as I shoved her, and she laughed and said, "And you're not my type."

After our little hysterical fit and again alone, I told Kate I was stunned. "But it does put some of the things she wrote into perspective."

"That it does. It's just so…so unexpected."

She suggested we walk into town to get some air and those toothbrushes and after we called to them that we were taking a walk we were off to Paterson's drugstore.

18.

It turned into a great very early fall afternoon. What clouds had been overhead as we drove up were long gone and the sky was a sparkling blue. Clear skies. No humidity. But still warm, even this far north. The sidewalk was shaded by the pear trees planted decades before with mathematical precision.

Kate had her arm through mine, and we said hello to the three or four people we passed, with me telling them that I was the Millers' granddaughter (several recognized me) and that Kate was my friend. It's strange coming from the city to a country town and wondering how calling another woman my "friend" with my arm through hers would be interpreted but those who came over from their gardens or porches to say hello were sweet as could be and saying how I needed to come up more often to see how my grandparents were taking such great care of the house. "And your grandfather and that garden of his."

I'm embarrassed to say I was embarrassed about Kate seeing the town. Some of the storefronts had been empty for years and though there was something of a sprucing up along Main Street in the spring, there's only so much lipstick you can put on a pig. Kate, whose parents both came from Bronxville and whose family went back at least to the days after World War II in town, was fine, truly fine, with it as I pointed out places I hung out with during those long August days when my mom and I were exiled.

It turned out we were both more tired from all we'd done than we realized, and we felt it on the walk back and were glad we weren't driving home. The boxes and strewn papers and stuff were still in the living room. Everyone understood, though, that we'd done enough for at least the day so we delicately placed it all back in the boxes—we hoped with some semblance of order—and collapsed on the sofa.

Grandma insisted she could make dinner well enough, but we insisted she not. Since the only eatery in town (other than the take-out pizzeria with two or three orange plastic tables and chairs) was Carol's Place, it's where we went. It'd been there forever and had all the comforts of a diner with a few stand-alone tables in addition to the booths and counter, with their benches and stools covered in the traditional reddish vinyl. Carol, who always sat behind the cash register, probably knew and remembered more about everyone in the town than anyone, though she was the daughter of the original Carol, who still lived above the restaurant and had her particular table where she held court and had dinner every afternoon at five-thirty.

On Friday and Saturday nights, Carol's got a bit fancy, with linens on the tables, including those in the booths, and subtle lighting throughout. And so it was when the four of us went in. I introduced Kate to Carol (senior), and one of the kids from town working as a waitress led us to a table near the corner. While she went to get us bread and water, Carol (junior) came by, and I repeated the introduction of my friend.

Grandma ate like a bird, but Grandpa and I had the full meatloaf package and Kate was pleased with the fish filet and salad she ordered. It was an amazingly relaxed evening, with people who I hadn't seen in years stopping by till I was pretty sure the whole town went through the place.

We all passed on coffee though Kate and I shared an apple pie slice with two scoops of vanilla ice cream on top, and it was dark by the time we left and walked back to the house. My grandparents were not so talkative as they'd been at Carol's, and when we were through the door, Grandma pulled me aside and said, quietly, that there was one more thing they needed to tell me and asked if Kate should hear it.

Again, not knowing what "it" was, I couldn't say.

"It's, well, it's another secret about your mother that I don't think *anyone* else knows except…, well, let's sit."

Kate looked at me and I gave a shrug and said, "We'd better sit down again."

19.

Kate and I were back on the sofa with my grandparents across, I noticed a photo in Grandma's lap and an envelope in Grandpa's. She reached over and handed me the photo.

"This is your sister."

"Half-sister," Grandpa quickly added.

I was stunned. Kate's hand hit mine as she looked to see the image. A baby in a pink blanket with a pink hat, her arms flailing about and big eyes looking confused and curious.

"She was born on July 15, 1987." Grandma sat back but had stopped rocking. "It was a party down by a small clearing along the stream. By then she was going out more and there was drinking and smoking pot, and your mother had sex and got pregnant. Simple as that. The father didn't want to have anything to do with her or their baby. She was seventeen. They both were. Before she showed, we found a Catholic charity to take care of her and she gave up the baby right after she—it was a 'she'—was born. All we had, for the longest time, was this little picture."

I asked, "'For the longest time'?"

Grandpa lifted the envelope and handed it across to me, and I gave the photo to Kate. Its postmark was five years old. It was addressed, in hand, to "Emily Miller" at my grandparents' house.

"We'll let you read it," Grandpa said, and the two of them left. I grabbed Kate's thigh to keep her next to me.

Dear Ms. Miller,

My name is Jessica Alpert. I was able to identify you as my birthmother through the New York State adoption registry. I don't mean to upset you. But if you are interested in meeting me, I would like that. I don't need anything from you financially. I am doing well professionally, and my adoptive parents are still alive and have encouraged me to reach out to you. All I would like is the opportunity to meet you. It would mean the world to me.

Jessica Alpert

It wasn't long, and there I was shaking with all I discovered since arriving that morning and handed it, open-faced, to Kate to read.

"Shit," she said quietly when she was done and handed it back to me. "What are you going to do?"

"Do I have a choice?" I asked.

The small paper shook. It had an address in Brooklyn. My grandma coughed and returned and sat back down. Kate was not moving from beside me, and our thighs touched.

"We didn't know what to do. Your mother was dead. And we weren't even her birth parents. I wanted to write to her, but we decided there wouldn't be a point. So, we didn't. I don't know if that was the right thing but that's what we did."

"But what about me? Why didn't you tell *me* I had a sister?"

I didn't mean my voice to rise. It hurt her, and Kate's hand was yet again on my thigh. I reached over and apologized.

"You were going through so much we didn't want to throw this in. And then the letter sat in a drawer, gathering dust. When you called about coming up, your grandpa and I knew we had to tell you. I'm sorry we waited so long." He'd entered the room and was standing next to my grandma, his arm dangling so she could clasp his hand.

I had half a mind to get in the car and get out of there, back to my bed. And maybe I would have, but my grandparents left without a word, and I stayed on the sofa with Kate.

"This is too fucking much," I mumbled. I didn't cry and to this day I don't know why I did not.

*   *   *   *

THERE WAS BARELY A moon but plenty of stars as Kate and I walked away from Main Street after I went to their room and said we were getting some air. We were where the street opened into farmland and the sound of a country fall night, of frogs and crickets and owls and the occasional moo, flowed across the fields.

She and I just walked and walked, not saying much. A few cars and pickups passed before we got back, neither of us saying much of anything on that leg either. At the house, the porch light was on, my grandparents sitting there the way I remembered them sitting in those long-ago summers when I was a girl. It was getting chilly, and they both wore sweaters. Kate and I were warm enough from our walk.

We labored up the steps, and they kept to their Adirondack chairs. They had a portable radio from when I was a girl and the sound of classical music from the Albany NPR station floated barely above the night's sounds, much as I remembered it. Grandpa looked at us when we turned to them.

"You girls alright?" he asked.

"It's just a lot to take in," I said.

"We just hope it wasn't too much. I know we should have told you years ago and after we got that letter. But—"

"But we didn't," Grandma interrupted.

"Now I know," I told them. "Let's talk in the morning."

Before we went in, though, Kate remembered and asked about a tape player. Grandpa got up and went into a little room that he used as his office. It was just off the kitchen and darkly paneled and unchanged since I was last in it years before.

He had a nice but small wooden desk with a maroon leather blotter ingrained on its top, and he walked around it. From a bottom drawer, he out a small SONY tape recorder with a cord wrapped around it.

"I haven't used this in I don't know how long," he said as he handed it to me, and we left together. Kate was waiting in the hall. He went back out and just as he was leaving, I told him I understood why they did what they did. I didn't know if it was enough, but at that moment it was all I could say. He stopped and approached me with his arms spread and I got a hug and he whispered, "We always try to do what's best for you" and I told him I knew that. He stepped away and headed back outside. I heard him say something to my grandma but I'm not sure what it was.

The screen door slammed, and Kate and I went to the living room where I found a socket and she gathered the tapes. The tapes themselves were plain with nothing but a year on them. Whatever mystery we hoped to unlock, though, vanished as we heard that they were simply recordings from the radio of songs that were popular when she was a kid. Madonna. Lionel Richie. U2. "I could so see her in the *Walk Like An Egyptian* video," Kate laughed as she started with her arms and her hands and her head and her shoulders. I reminded her that we were on a quest and after one last hand-fling, she stopped, although it was kind of hilarious.

So, we hit play then fast-forward then play to confirm that that's all there was.

"It was worth a try," Kate said, and I said we had plenty already. I had a strange disappointment that the tapes didn't have my mom's young voice on them. Kate nodded, and we put the tape recorder with the tapes off to the side. By then it was nearing eleven. My grandparents came in not long after we settled down with the tapes. We offered to go into the kitchen to listen, but they insisted we stay where we were. My grandma tidied a bit in the kitchen and brought us milk and a plate of Oreos. They said goodnight and went to their room.

With Kate in her room (the one that was *not* also mine), I knocked lightly on their door. My grandma opened it. She was wearing a nightgown but threw a robe on. My grandpa was already snoring.

"Grandma. What about the father?"

Her head dropped, and she stepped into the hall and closed the bedroom door behind her. "She told us but made us swear not to tell anyone. We don't know if he ever did know about the baby. His family moved away years ago, and we don't know what happened to them. Or to him. I'm sorry."

"Thanks," I said. She was about to open her door and I was about to go to my room when I said, "Grandma. What about Ronnie?"

"Ronnie?"

I nodded, and she said he'd run away—"it was his nature"—and they never could find him. "It took her awhile to get over losing him. She blamed herself, of course. She never asked us to get another."

I told her that her last diary entry was of him leaving. She thought a moment, as the two of us stood in the hallway, lit only by the light from my room.

"I didn't know that. She'd been regular with the diaries, though she always hid them away and locked them. If I found one, I left it be. So, I don't know what she wrote. But as to stopping when Ronnie left, I just can't say why. I'm sorry."

I leaned to her and kissed her on the cheek.

"Goodnight, Grandma," I said. She smiled and told me she'd see me and Kate in the morning and she went into her bedroom and I went to mine. At that point, I didn't know if that mystery about the father was any of my business.

And in the morning, I could barely get my eyes open, having taken what seemed like hours to fall into a deep sleep that led to amazing dreams I couldn't quite grasp when I was up. But I was beginning to grasp that there could be an explanation for some of the things my mom kept saying in her stories.

Kate knocked on my door. She said she'd been up for a while, but was afraid to go down without me, and a quick trip to the bathroom and a change into yesterday's clothing and we went down. Grandma put bacon on when she heard us up, so that sweet aroma filled the place.

"Morning, ladies," Grandpa said. "There's coffee and Grandma is making breakfast. It's nice out. We have *The Sunday Times* so why don't you two sit on the porch after you get some coffee?"

He'd gone into town for the paper, and we greeted Grandma in the smoky kitchen. She rejected our offers to help, and all we could do was get our coffees—milk and sugar already on the table—before she shooed us out.

It was a very nice Sunday morning, and it was damn comfortable on that porch. We left the paper untouched as we looked out onto the street and up at the trees. No one passed by before Grandpa brought out a tray with our plates of scrambled eggs, toast, bacon, and home fries, and he spread the contents on the round wicker table that was on the other side of the porch, the one opposite the Adirondacks. He went back in, and when we were settled, he returned with the coffee pot and the milk and sugar on his tray, and he took care of topping off our coffees before leaving us alone.

Kate got up and came out again with them right behind her. They sat in the two other chairs for the set and just like that we all relaxed and spoke about the weather and my grandparents answered Kate's questions about life in Columbia County.

* * * *

KATE AND I LEFT SOON after we finished breakfast. Grandma asked if we wanted to go to mass, and though she was disappointed, I think she understood that I just needed to get home to process everything, and I promised I'd go with them when I was next in Paterson on a Sunday.

With that, Grandpa helped me load the boxes into the car and we were heading home. We didn't, Kate and I, speak much on the way south about anything of substance, with her driving the top stretch and me taking over about half an hour north of the city.

My mind stayed fixed on the two things I'd learned. The two adoptions. What each must have meant for my mom. For her to be ripped from her mother. A mother she knew and loved. Who got her a nice dress and took care of her but who couldn't cope. What must she, my as yet unknown grandmother, have gone through?

And then my mom. Jessica at least avoided the trauma of knowing her mother before she was placed with another family. My mom did. I don't know who she told, if anyone, but every day she must have wondered what happened to her little girl, if she even knew it was a girl. Looking at me. A daily reminder of another child, who she'd never see again. That it was for the best. But never knowing what became of her.

Kate asked if I wanted to take a detour to Bronxville, but I didn't think that was such a great idea, so we went straight to the Upper West Side, where she dropped me off with the new boxes in front of my place before taking the car back.

I told her I appreciated all she'd done, but that I really needed some alone time to process, though I told her as we stood on the sidewalk that I was going to see if I could locate this Jessica Alpert and that otherwise I did not know what I was going to do about what we discussed and learned upstate.

20.

It was only around one. I settled in and grabbed a pre-made salad that was beginning to go bad and was again searching on my laptop.

It didn't take long to find her. Or at least to find who I was pretty sure was her. I'd done the calculation of how old she'd be: Thirty. The lone "Jessica Alpert" I found in New York City was an associate at a big law firm. Her photo in her firm biography could mean she was my half-sister. Maybe a similar nose and mouth. Maybe her (reddish) hair was a bit curly. Who knew how tall she was?

Several "Jessica Alpert"s were on Facebook and a couple on Twitter and with what I found at the law firm site, I figured I had her. She didn't seem active on either site, but I got a fair number of photos. As far as I could tell, no evidence of having a kid. Most were with her family and with her rather handsome husband and his family (I assumed) and a bunch of friends and one that looked like a firm softball game on the Great Lawn.

There was nothing to be done about it that Sunday afternoon, so I revisited some of the things from my dad's in light of what Kate and I uncovered in Paterson.

I gave him a quick call after dinner, not mentioning my trip upstate let alone what I'd found there. Just telling him I was busy and still working my way through my mom's things, the ones from Bronxville. I'd let him know if I found anything.

A little after I hung up and was streaming a Scandinavian crime show—the boxes from Paterson stacked next to the two from Bronxville but similarly being ignored—Grandma called. Neither of us said much beyond her wanting to be sure I was okay, which I said I was, my voice sounding artificially calm and chipper, and how nice it was to see Kate. After promising to bring her up again, and visiting more often myself, we hung up, and I floated my way through two or three episodes of the show before turning in, though I tossed and turned for quite a while before I found sleep.

On Monday, I was at my desk and figured Nancy was up. I called her. I said I needed—that's the word I used—to see her that night. I went to my grandparents over the weekend, I said. I discovered some things. Not for a simple phone call but in person.

She said she'd "somewhat gotten over" some of the internal difficulties she had when she dredged up the details of some of her memories with me at her place and suggested I come by there after work. I didn't want to go to her apartment, though, so I asked her to come to mine. She'd never been there, and it was small and not nearly as fancy as what she was used to, and it was the only way to do it.

I left work a little early to pick up things for dinner. Nothing fancy beyond an expensive Pinot Noir. The food was microwavable, and I did what I could about tidying the living room, with the stacks of my mom's boxes arranged neatly along the wall opposite the sofa.

The buzzer went. I looked one last time and everything was as good as it was going to be. With a deep breath, I buzzed her up and held the door open for her. Her steps got louder as she climbed, and when she was just about to my floor landing, she waved, with a wine store's paper bag cradled in her arm.

She came in and we hugged lightly as she passed. When she was in and the door was closed, she presented me with her own expensive bottle of wine. I'd changed from work into one of my better pairs of khaki pants with a purple polo, but she'd outdone my suburban chic in flat white trousers over dark blue flats and a black button-down blouse with the pearl necklace she'd worn at Barnes & Noble, which somehow fit perfectly and I was clueless as to how she again pulled it off.

We went into the kitchen, where I handed her a corkscrew. She stood right beside me—quite naturally I realized—as she opened her wine while I tossed the salad. I told her I put a pair of glasses on my little table in the living room, and she left me to fill them and told me to join her, handing me my glass as I did.

We clinked the glasses and drank.

"Sweetie, let's talk about what you found out."

It was very good wine. "French," she said and went to my sofa. I took another, deeper breath and a longer sip and sat in an armchair across from her while she waited.

"Did you know my mom was adopted?"

"Of course. You didn't?"

"No one told me."

She shook her head. "I can't believe she never told you. Or that your father didn't."

"He knew then."

"She said she told him that before they were married. She didn't want to surprise him. As to her, it was such a big part of who she was that I was sure she would have told you."

"Well, she didn't. I only found out when my grandparents, or the couple who I thought were my grandparents, did. They showed me a picture from before they got her."

That surprised her.

"Do you have it?"

It was inside, as it happened, my copy of *Scream* for safekeeping. I got her book and my mother's photo from my bookcase.

"Did you read it?"

"I did. And I'm beginning to understand it."

With that, I opened it to where the photo was and pulled it out and handed it to her. She stared at it. I don't know for how long, but time stood still. She swallowed and closed her eyes and took a hard breath.

"I've never seen any of her young pictures. But she was…so young here."

"They said it was the only one they had from before they adopted her."

"She told me. I think when I asked about one of her stories."

"She wrote a lot about abandonment."

"That was it," Nancy said as she continued to stare at the little image, fighting her tears.

"I wasn't very nice about it. 'What's with all the mother issues?' I asked or something like that. I don't know that she wanted to tell me, but she said, very matter of factly, that she was adopted and so it was important to her. But you say she wasn't adopted as an infant. I always assumed that she was." She looked at me, holding the photo in her lap.

I explained what my grandparents said about it and asked if she thought I should see try to find her mother. She responded by wondering whether my mom ever did, though we'd have no way of knowing.

"I don't have kids," she said. "But I think I'd want to know. Even if it was that she was dead. Wouldn't you?"

I hadn't viewed it like that, but I was pretty sure I'd want to know how my baby turned out, especially if she'd been taken from me like my mom was.

"Well, think about it," she said when I hesitated, and I nodded. She handed the photo back after giving it one more look.

"There's something else."

"Something else?"

I wasn't sure whether to say anything, but it felt dishonest not to since I was confiding in Nancy as much as I was and perhaps relying on her more than I could have expected.

"She had a baby. When she was in high school."

She looked like she didn't understand.

"You obviously didn't know."

"Of course I didn't know." She abruptly stood, balancing her glass in her right hand. "But why didn't I know? Why didn't she tell me? I...I—"

It's a small apartment, as I said, so she couldn't pace very far and all I could do was watch her. She finally stood looking out the window and drank some of her wine. Neither of us said anything till she was back on the sofa with a bit of a thud.

"Tell me."

My sense was that only four people ever knew, and my mom, one of the four, was dead. And Kate and I were the fifth and sixth and Nancy Penchant became number seven.

I said what my grandparents told me and then I went to my room and brought the baby photo and Jessica Alpert's letter. She read it and then read it again.

"Why did the letter go to her parents?" she asked.

I hadn't thought of that. When she put her name in the registry, why didn't she say something about having become "Emily Locus" and living in "Bronxville"?

"She didn't want your father to know," Nancy said.

I knew she was right, and I told her that.

She asked, "What are you going to do? Are you going to contact her?"

Since we'd already agreed that I was going to try to get in touch with my mom's birthmother who had no idea of her existence, it wasn't much of a leap to agree that I'd reach out to Jessica Alpert, who tried to get in touch with her.

I got my laptop and showed Nancy what I'd been able to unearth about the woman who I was guessing was the Jessica Alpert who was my half-sister. She looked at it without saying anything, and she spent a good deal of time gazing at the photos of her.

Finally, she said, "I just can't say whether she looks like your mother." She smiled at me. "Of course, I could say the same about you." She took a last look at this other photo of the little Jessica Alpert and returned it to me.

She smiled. "It's been a long day." She got up. "Are you going to try to contact her?"

I told her I was, and she asked me to keep her posted. She bent down to finish off what remained in her glass, and I got up and walked her to the door. She opened it and turned. She ran a hand across my cheek and smiled.

That was it. She smiled as she pulled her hand away and left me to it. Only then did I realize I hadn't finished making the salad let alone starting dinner so I ate by myself with the plate on my lap on the sofa as my brain ran through scenarios of how I would meet Jessica Alpert and what I would say when I did. That done and the plate in my sink, I poured another glass of Nancy's fine Bordeaux and pondered the question as I swirled and drank the elixir with my legs loosely on the top of my coffee table and a Bach cello suite Bluetoothed through the speakers next to my TV.

21.

Tuesday, the morning after meeting with Nancy and three days after I learned that the two people I thought were my grandparents weren't—I should say birth grandparents, of course—I stood on the southeast corner of Third Avenue and 53rd Street at about noon. It was a bleak, overcast day with a bit of a chill but there were hints of the sun and the threat of rain had passed.

Perhaps it was a sign, the weather turning to match what I felt. *A sister.* I'd seen her baby photo and the far more recent ones. What about her, though? *Would she be bitter and would that bitterness be aimed at me when I told her, as I would have to almost immediately, that my...that our mother was dead?*

I stood and was nervous. What happened soon would affect me forever, for good or ill, and as I stood watching each woman come out, I prayed—I'm not a religious person—it would be for the good and Jessica Alpert would like me and in time maybe even love me.

I stood hoping she'd emerge from that door soon so I could get it over with. 875 Third Avenue is one of those big, black office towers with a public atrium included as a trade for adding a few stories at the top. Strangely, it had two main entrances, one on the southeast and the other on the northeast corner. Since each wasn't squared to the corner but cut across it to create a triangle at the property line, the doors were at an angle.

Given the two entrances, I had to pick the one I would watch and chose the southern one. I told my boss I had something personal to take care of, so I was there right at noon, with no idea if and when she'd be going to lunch and which exit she'd use and whether she'd be alone if she did. Plus a zillion other things. And not counting whatever might happen if I guessed right and she appeared.

I tried to be inconspicuous near the curb. At about twenty past noon, I saw the first who might be her. The hair was a clue. She was alone. She came through the revolving door quickly and wore a nice, dark suit and low heels that branded her a professional. She was staring at her phone as I crossed towards her and as I got close, I was pretty sure it was her.

"Jessica Alpert?"

She stopped and gave me a WTF look as she lowered her phone. I was trying to be as non-threatening as possible, like just another woman working in a Manhattan office. I'd worn my best office suit.

She paused, and I had her attention. "Yes. Do I know you?"

It was my turn to pause.

"I think I'm your sister."

She gazed at me like I had two or maybe three heads.

"Sorry?"

I directed her toward the curb, next to and upwind from a falafel vendor's cart, to keep the entrance clear. From my handbag, I pulled her letter out. I handed it to her, and she looked at it and back at me.

"Where'd you get this?"

"The Millers are my grandparents and...and your mom was my mom."

Her eyes narrowed. "Was?"

"She died in 2008."

She was processing it like a just-the-facts-ma'am lawyer, which somewhat amazed me.

"So I'm clear. If what you say is true, and I've no reason to doubt it, you're my...half-sister? Full sister maybe?"

You could almost see the gears working and I swear a wave seemed to rise within her, and she rocked side-to-side and her eyes seemed to lose focus. I was ready to grab her, but she stabilized. A guy walked up to her. Probably another lawyer from her firm.

"Jessie. You okay?"

The interruption brought her back to Planet Earth. She nodded at him. "Thanks. I'm good. I just was...surprised by this long-lost friend. I'm good."

He looked at me and I smiled and nodded and with a "just checking" he headed wherever he was going for his lunch.

"Half-sister," I said.

"Look, I know it's a shock. You should have seen me when my grandparents gave me the letter—"

"When was that?"

"Over the weekend. Can we go somewhere? Grab something. Maybe sit in the atrium here and talk?"

Without a word, she turned, and I followed her back into the building and down an escalator to a food court. We each got salads and bottles of Poland Spring water and found a small, round table in a nook off to one side.

I don't usually get on well with strangers, but I felt at ease as I gave her my background. She knew vaguely about Bronxville, and she knew my father's firm. She lived in Brooklyn. Happily married to Peter O'Toole. ("Yes. That really is his name. Blame his parents.")

"I can't believe she'd dead."

"She had a stroke. We were with her when they disconnected her life support—and sometimes I can't believe she's gone either."

She took a breath and seemed to compose herself. "Just so you know, my parents adopted me when I was an infant, from the organization that handled my birth and the adoption. They told me when I was a kid, old enough to understand, and they always said it was up to me to decide whether I'd ever seek out my birthmother.

"After college, I decided to see. I was living with Peter. He and my parents supported the decision. There's a state registry that tries to connect birthmothers with the child they gave up, and it only works if both register and she must have. This was about five years ago. With her name—it was 'Miller' of course—I got more information, and it didn't take me long to get that letter out to the Millers, who I figured would forward it to my...our mother."

"She was gone when you did."

"Which I didn't know, and it makes me sad that I might have met her if I tried a bit earlier."

"But that means that she thought or maybe hoped you would try to contact her. Why else would she register?"

She took some of her water. "I know. It makes it even sadder, don't you think?"

It so did. I nodded.

We had gradually worked through our salads and waters as she spoke.

"Do you know anything about my father? There was no information about him."

"My...our grandparents said they know who he is—though they didn't tell me, and I didn't press it. I'm sure they'll tell you. They said he and his family moved away and he might not even have known about you."

"Well, first things first. Look. I don't have anything pressing this afternoon. I need to speak to Peter and my folks, but I'd like to learn more from you. Do you live in the city?"

"West 85th."

"Closer than Cobble Hill. Can we cab it? If you can get the rest of the day off."

That latter was no problem since I didn't have anything scheduled either so after we both called our offices, we were in a cab heading to the Upper West Side.

22.

My apartment was its typical mess, though lessened by my having tidied it for Nancy's recent visit. I went to the bedroom. Jessie stayed in the living room as we made our calls.

For me, it was first to Nancy and then to Kate. For both, I kept it short: I met Jessica. She's with me. Things seem to be going smoothly.

I then called my grandparents. Grandma answered, and while I was a little bit longer with her, and I heard her report to Grandpa about what I was reporting to her, with them, too, I promised to call that night.

"You okay?" I called to Jessica when I cleared the bedroom.

"I'm good. Spoke to everyone and they're good and pretty excited. As am I. So, where are *we*?"

I wasn't sure where we were. The sun had won out over the morning's clouds and things had warmed up. I suggested walking and talking and so that's what we did. Three laps around the Great Lawn (where one of her Facebook photos was taken)—a half-mile loop around a bunch of softball fields with the Shakespearean Festival theatre on its southwest corner.

We walked as if we'd known each other for years, her arm through mine as we took deliberate steps, neither of us quite sure of what to say next.

Most of the fields were busy with softball games and constant shouting that reminded me of what my mom wrote about what she heard from the tennis courts on that afternoon she met Nancy. The loop itself was not crowded, and I bet those who paid us any attention thought Jessie and I were the longest of friends. Or maybe sisters.

And I gave her my life story and what I knew about and recently learned about our mother. It was at first awkward to refer to her that way, as "our mother," but I got used to it.

"What did you call her?" she asked.

"'Mommy' usually, but 'Mother' when I was pissed at her."

She laughed. "I always call mine 'momma.'"

Finally, she asked how it happened.

"She wasn't old. What? Thirty-eight, thirty-nine?"

"She was thirty-eight." I thought it best that we sit for this, so we found an empty bench on the eastern side of the oval.

"There's no easy way to put it, and it was less than a mile from here. She had a stroke when she was in bed with a woman with whom she had a long-term relationship."

"An affair?"

"An affair."

She looked ahead of herself. "Shit."

"I only just found out. And, well, it started this whole adventure that led me to discover about you."

"What about searching for me?" she asked.

"I only found out on Saturday." I told her how my grandma said. How I got the photo and the letter.

"As soon as I knew you existed, I had to find you. I didn't mean to ambush you. But I stared at your photo on your firm's website for a while. I thought we might have the same nose. I don't know. But I couldn't wait. If you hadn't come out, I probably would have gone to the Brooklyn address."

"That wouldn't work. We moved out of there about three years ago."

"Good thing I found you, then."

She nodded and looked at the lawn, some sort of excited play happening in the field in front of us.

"I remember putting it in the mailbox. I carried it with me for a while before I just did it. You know? Just put it in and see what happens. I was excited for a while about getting a reply but then nothing came. I searched online now and then, and I think it said they still lived there but I never found anything about her. Our mother."

I paused.

"There was more isn't there?"

"There was more...She was adopted too."

Her eyes again got large. I told her the story, or what I knew of it.

"Poor thing. We have to find her parents. Our grandparents."

"And your father."

"Eventually," she said. "For now, let's deal with this part. I don't know if I can handle anything more. Agreed?"

I agreed.

23.

J essie and I began doing research, searching for Dorothy Spenser. Since my grandparents knew the name, we didn't have to search for adoption records and get a court order to have them opened. We were in constant email and phone contact but didn't find much. Until Jessie uncovered a "Dorothy Spenser" with a police record in Hudson, New York, not far from Paterson. She paid to get more information and found records of someone with that name who once lived in Hudson.

That breakthrough came on Wednesday. On Thursday night I found a single further record of "Dorothy Spenser": a small, long ago wedding announcement in the local paper. She'd married Edgar Davis in a ceremony at a local church. It said she was the daughter of the late Eric and Susan Spenser—my great-grandparents—and he of the late Edgar (Sr.) and Barbara Davis. There was one Edgar Davis in Columbia County, and he lived just north of Hudson.

I reported this late on Thursday. Jessie said she and Peter had to fly to Chicago the next afternoon for a wedding and wouldn't be back till Monday night.

"Look," she said. "It's probably a good thing. We don't want to overwhelm her, say her daughter also had an illegitimate daughter." She insisted, though, that I go up myself, with Kate if possible, to meet her. She knew about Kate as Kate knew about her, but they hadn't met. We agreed not to mention Jessie's existence to our grandmother just yet.

Only a week after she schlepped with me to Paterson, Kate ("I don't have a life") Winslow agreed to repeat the journey, this time to Hudson. We were both more relaxed this time. I told her all I could about Jessie, and she'd done her own internet sleuthing.

Kate and I'd learned so much about my mom since we last picked up a Zipcar and while new mysteries were popping up seemingly everywhere we looked and under every stone we turned over, we were making progress. Neither of us knew where it would take us and whether we wanted to go there, but we were caught up in the thrill of the chase and again heading a couple of hours north of Manhattan to meet another relative I had no idea existed a week before.

24.

The Davis house was very much like the Millers' in Paterson. It was few miles north of Hudson and on a small lot with houses close to it on both sides. It, like the Millers', had a wide, covered porch. There was a blue Subaru wagon, five or six years old, in the driveway. The sidewalk and the path leading to the front door could've used some repairs, but they were passable. It looked like the house was painted a few years before Kate and I showed up, and firewood was neatly stacked on the porch not far from the door.

I rang the doorbell, and Kate and I stepped back. We didn't wait long before the door opened. The woman was old but not elderly or frail. She asked what we wanted in the homey accent I was used to hearing when I was at my grandparents'. She wore the type of sundress I also saw all the time on retired women in Paterson.

"Are you Dorothy Davis?" I asked and after she said she was, but "it's 'Dot,'" she wondered what she could do for us.

"May we come in? There was something important we need to speak to you about."

She hesitated. A man called out, "Who is it and what do they want?"

She looked at us, one after the other, and shook her head. "Pay him no mind. He thinks you're trying to sell us something. Are you?"

"No, Mrs. Davis," I assured her, and she seemed to believe me. She opened the door wide and invited us in.

The inside of the house was like the Millers' too. A long-in-the-tooth sofa and two newer armchairs. The coffee table had books scattered unorderly on it. The rug was an oriental, also showing its age, and there was a large TV on a table. The mantel was lined with photos. To me, though, one stood out.

Before I could do anything, Dot Davis asked if she could get us tea. Kate and I thanked her and said that would be very nice of her.

"Please. Sit down. I'll be right out."

As we waited on the sofa, the man, well-built with short, neatly trimmed gray hair in jeans and a flannel shirt, who we rightly thought was Edgar Davis, entered. He introduced himself.

"So, what do you pretty women want with my wife?"

I said, "There were some things we would like to speak to her about." I hoped he didn't notice my shaking. Kate did, though, and her hand moved to my wrist.

Edgar was suspicious. Here were two women obviously from New York City wanting to speak to his wife alone. He sat in one of the armchairs, plainly weighing what to do. His wife returned with a tray. She poured three teas and there was a creamer and a cracked sugar bowl with a teaspoon in it as well as a small stack of cookies leaning against one another.

"They say they want to speak to you. I get the sense that it's about you and not us." He turned to us, "Is that right?"

I nodded. He got up and said, "We don't have no secrets, but if you want to speak to her first and she don't mind, that's okay by me. Dot?"

"Go on. Let 'em talk to me. No harm there. Go out back. I'll call you when it's time to come in."

He got up and nodded, "I'll be right out back if you—"

"I think I'm safe. They've told me they're not trying to sell me anything."

He laughed. "That's what all good salesmen...and saleswomen, say. Just don't sign nothing."

He shook his head and nodded as he went into the kitchen and then the back door slammed, and it was only the three of us in the house.

"Well?"

I'd rehearsed what I would say to Dorothy Davis dozens of times and tried variation after variation on Kate as we drove up. "Just do what comes naturally," she said again and again, but *nothing* felt natural. Whatever I was saying. But it all vanished when we were sitting in the Davises' living room. I got up. I stepped to the mantel and took down the photo that got my attention when I entered the room.

I brought it to her.

"This is my mom."

I was looking straight at Dot Davis. My grandmother. I don't think anyone is prepared for such news delivered in such a manner. She last set eyes on my mom over forty years earlier. Except for this photo. She saw it every day.

She was very confused. She put the frame in her lap, and her hands gripped her chair as she began to rock forwards and backwards. She kept turning from me to Kate, from me to Kate.

"Should I get your husband?" Kate asked, starting to get up.

"No, dearie. Just give me a moment."

I waited until she nodded, and Kate sat back in her chair but kept her eyes locked on Dorothy.

"You are my grandmother."

"I can't be. No. I can't be." She was leaning at the front of her chair, still going back and forth between us and shaking her head. "No. I can't be."

She reached up and ran the top of her right hand across the bottom of her nose. Keeping physical distance was not an option, and I squatted down in front of her and placed my hands around each of her wrists.

"I promise you, you are. The Millers, who adopted her and who I thought were my grandparents, showed me this photo when I went to see them just last weekend. She died eight years ago."

Her head shot up, and I regretted what I said. None of this was going to plan.

"Dead?"

"I'm so, so sorry. She was only thirty-eight. She had a stroke, and we couldn't save her."

Her hands were back on the chair's arms, pulled away from mine. I lifted the frame with the photo.

"Every day I think she'll come through my door. Every day. Always have. No matter where I was."

Seeing Dot spiral, Kate jumped up and headed to the back, and the screen door to the yard slammed.

I said, "I think that every day since she died."

She was shaking but had regained some control over herself. Edgar hurried to her and took the space in front of her where I had been.

"She told me what they said. Ya think it's true? Dot. Tell me."

She looked up at him.

"She says she's got the same photo of Emily. It must be true, don't you think?"

I backed away and Kate stood beside me as we watched the pair. Dot began to speak, in an even, controlled tone, and Edgar slipped into the chair beside hers, never taking his eyes off her. Kate and I moved together to the sofa and sat.

"I was at rock bottom. My parents were killed in a car crash when my Emily was three. My dad was drunk and it was icy and they just ran off the road. The car turned over. No seatbelts. I had no one. No one could take care of her. I was in such a bad place. Everyone in town hated me as the runaway who'd gotten pregnant by some stranger, a stranger who ran off at the first sign of trouble.

"When my parents were alive, they gave me some protection, but once they were gone, I got no support. People wouldn't even come up to me at the funeral. I stood there with my Emily by my side and people ignored us both. I asked people to come to the house afterward, but no one came."

She was sniffling and chortling as she fought to speak, with Edgar holding and rocking her hands, his eyes fixed on hers, which were staring into her abyss.

"I had nothing. I had no one. I started going places I shouldn't have gone. Carrying Emily with me. I was snorting coke when I could find it. I couldn't get a job and got welfare. I headed up to Albany, figuring I might get something there where no one knew me. But I didn't. I would pick up spare change by...by doing things to men and letting them...do things to me. I'd leave Emily home and pray she'd be safe when I got back after I scored.

"Then one day in February 1974, I didn't come back. I was lying in a freezing stairwell, my puke all over me and they brought me to the hospital, and I asked 'em where my Emily was, and they asked who Emily was and they saved her and took her from me. She was four. They let me see her a few more times before I was sent to the County Jail for ninety days. I never saw her again."

She had fallen completely inside her memory. The torture of that last day she would ever see her daughter mixed with the realization that her dream of somehow, someday setting eyes on her again was crushed when I told her that her daughter—my mom—was gone.

I couldn't imagine what it'd be like to see another human being collapse and lose all hope in ten minutes and I will never forget it. She heaved in agony, prevented only by Edgar's arms from throwing her face back into her palms.

He whispered, "You now have her," loud enough for Kate and me to hear it, and he looked up after he said it and I nodded. "You'll always have me."

She looked up too, with the slightest smile. It drew me back to her. I handed the picture to Kate and squatted on the carpet again in front of the old chair, and I held my hand up to her and she grasped it and it was an incredibly intimate touch. She said, "I know, dearie, I know."

There was a silence, more a calming than anything, in the room as we all processed what just happened.

Edgar tapped my shoulder and said quietly so I don't know if Dorothy heard it clearly, "She's been living in the hope that

Emily would be back. She sometimes just sits and stares at the front door. Been doing that since I knew her."

He began to rise, and I pulled my hand from hers and moved away as he put his arm delicately around his wife's shoulder and helped her stand.

"I think you should lie down for a little bit while I speak to them, okay?"

She nodded and let him guide her from the chair and then up the stairs. We heard her begin to lose it again as they slowly started up, her sobbing seeming to roll down towards us like a wave.

"We shouldn't have come," I told Kate. "We shouldn't have told her. Not the way I did."

Kate leaned over. She pulled my head down so she could give its top a kiss.

"Thank God for Mr. Davis. Let's talk to him about it."

He was coming down, and we stood, but he waved us back down to the sofa.

"She's gone through so much. She's come very far. But we're both going to need you."

"Should we have come?"

"Of course you should have come. She's been waiting, waiting, waiting. The fact is that Emily is gone. That Emily's never coming back. And we now have you. Do you know why she never tried to find Dot?"

I hadn't thought about that. I told him I'd only found out a week earlier, from the couple in Paterson I thought were my grandparents.

"They're still your grandparents," he interrupted. "Never forget that or what they did for your mom. Paterson you say?"

"Yeah. My grandpa was a banker, and my grandma was a nurse at the hospital, both here in Hudson. They both retired not long ago. We—my mom and me—used to come up all the time. But I never knew about Dot, and I just don't know whether my mom ever tried to look her up. Maybe she tried and failed. She never even told me she was adopted."

Edgar looked a bit uneasy. He was quite a handsome man, and I could already see that his face tended to reflect his thoughts. "Maybe she didn't want to remember. I hear that Dot made things pretty tough for a little girl." He smiled and hit the arms of the chair as he stood. "Let me get you girls some more tea," and before we could say anything he'd grabbed our hardly touched cups and put them on the tray and was heading into the kitchen.

25.

Kate and I didn't know what to do while Edgar was gone. I took the photo and restored it to the mantel and sat back down. We were both afraid to speak after he got back with our teas so we listened to him tell their story. They met about twenty years earlier. Dot had moved back to Hudson and almost had a standing reservation in the Columbia County Jail. Mostly drugs. Sometimes prostitution. He was a cook at a diner on Route 9.

"Dot'd come by the back now and then, trying to scrounge something. She knew I was a soft touch. Not just with her. The owner didn't like it, but it wasn't like I was making anything special for her, or the others. Just stuff that we'd throw out anyway. 'Yeah, but they'll be like raccoons if you keep doing it,' and he threatened to fire me. I wasn't worried. Who else could he get to do the job?

"And I got to speaking to her when she came by, and she got to waiting for me when I got off at three in the afternoon. She didn't have a job. Tried, but couldn't hold one down. She'd come back to her home, but everyone hated her, especially when they saw the baby was gone. Some thought the baby was dead, that she killed her, until word got around that the state took her away. It was horrible for her. But it was the only home she had.

"She was on welfare, but that was harder than it had been. Food stamps. At least she had a place to stay. Her clothes were old, but she kept them tidy and clean.

"Dot'd walk the mile or so from town, and I started looking forward to her coming. And we'd walk down Route 9 together. Finally, I took her to a real dinner at the diner in town. Our first quote-unquote date."

Edgar told of how he started to like her and how she was starting to like him.

"Then she didn't show up for a few days. I called someone I knew at Hudson PD, and he told me she was nabbed for shoplifting. It was ladies' underwear mostly but also a man's belt. I went to the DA's office and spoke to some young lawyer. He knew her pretty well, having prosecuted her a couple of times, and was no happier about sending her away for six months than I was. For some underwear and a man's belt.

"The belt was for me, of course. He told me that if I got the store to drop the charges and promised a thousand ways to Sunday that I'd take care of Dot, she'd get one chance. He said he'd hold the paperwork for a few days, while she was sitting in the county jail to see if I could pull it off.

"I mean, the store didn't want to press charges much, either. It knew she was screwy but saw no reason to help her out since she'd just come back and shoplift something else. Now, I didn't go see her. I didn't want her to know I knew or to say anything about helping her out unless it worked."

In the end, he said, he got the store to drop the charges and made my grandmother promise to stay with him until they could work something out. His place wasn't very big and he said he'd sleep on the couch.

"She insisted that it was my place so *she'd* sleep on the couch and I told her the couch wasn't big enough for two and there was no way I was sleeping in a bed and making a lady sleep on the couch so she gave in and I got the couch." He smiled and said, "though the truth is that that didn't last too long," and he gave me a wink.

"I got her a job washing dishes in my diner—my boss took a shine to her—so I could keep my six-to-three hours. She's been straight ever since, swear to God."

He asked her to marry him a month or so later. She sat him down and told him about her Emily and what she went through. Her family dying and losing her girl. He didn't care. They got married and have been together ever since. That was fifteen years ago.

Life settled down for them. They still worked at the diner, but just weekdays. And she was now a waitress. They were able to save and get their little house. They were regular churchgoers.

The Davises had an equilibrium that held them together. Did I ruin it for them? By showing up?

He asked how I found her, and I explain our little detective work. I lowered my voice and said that while I was the only child in my family, my mom had another child, a girl, when she was in high school.

"I just met her. But we didn't want to pop it on...Dot off the bat. Now that we're talking, you can help me in figuring out the best way to do it."

He took what I said in stride.

"In high school? In Paterson?"

"Yeah. She went away and had the baby who was put up for adoption. She's now a lawyer in the city and is anxious to connect with my mom's side of the family, especially with Dot, but as I say we didn't want to pop it on her. I only met Jessie—that's her name—earlier this week."

"You have been going through a lot lately, haven't you?"

Kate chimed in. "You don't know the half of it. She knew none of this a couple of weeks ago."

He looked at me, and I told him in very broad strokes about the Barnes & Noble reading, being very careful to keep Nancy's relationship with my mom out of it.

We returned to the Jessie Question. "Let me speak to her about it first," he said. "I'll tell her, I promise you. But let's see how she handles this horrible news about Emily first. And then maybe you and this—"

"Jessie."

"Maybe you and Jessie can come up to meet her. And you, of course," this last bit directed at Kate.

"Listen," he said, "let me check on her," and he was heading back up the stairs. Kate and I got up and went to the front porch. It was set up much like the Millers' with several chairs amid a small, round table to the left of the front door. Kate sat in one, and I leaned with my ass against the railing. We were just off the main road and could hear its traffic but only vaguely in the distance.

"What do you think?" she asked.

"You know, you can't anticipate what'll happen and we'll just have to see how she gets through it."

"I'm glad she has Edgar."

"Could you imagine if she didn't?"

We heard the screen door.

"Speak of the devil," Kate said.

"I thought you might come out here."

Kate stood beside me, our backs to the railing.

"I think we need to give her some space. Is that alright? You came all the way up here."

26.

While Dot was napping and the three of us again sat in the living room, Kate and I got the story, or at least the story Edgar pieced together of her life before she met me. My mom's birth name was Emily Spencer, which we knew.

"Most of this, at least till I met her," he said, "comes from Dot. Over the years she'd tell me things." He asked if we wanted anything to drink, but we said we were fine.

"Dot wasn't married. She worked as a waitress until she had to stop when she went into labor. She was all of eighteen. She came from a good part of Hudson. She ran away when she was sixteen and her parents didn't hear from her for nearly two years.

"She lived on the streets of New York City for about a year before following someone to Philadelphia. Someone she met in New York. She was just seventeen. She and this guy found a cheap apartment. Lousy part of town. She got pregnant shortly after they moved in together. By the guy she followed. He was a little older than her and had a respectable job at a bank.

"Dot said that when she told him she was pregnant, he told her to get an abortion. He asked around and said he found someone who'd 'take care of it.' He gave her money, and she went. It was a dirty ratty place, she said, and whether because of that or because she couldn't do it, she never went in."

He paused and looked at each of us.

"She knew it might mean sacrificing her life with her boyfriend, who made it clear he wanted nothing to do with it. She wanted a baby. Her baby. She got back to the apartment and he came in after work and she told him. She was keeping the baby. He flew into a rage. She said he didn't hit her or nothing. Still, he left her the next morning and she never saw him again. She thinks he went out west."

He again looked at me. "He is your grandfather."

Having started, he was in a hurry to finish the story, Dot's story.

"Dot had no money beyond the little she made as a waitress in a local diner, and she couldn't afford the rent on her own. When she squirreled away enough, she took a bus to New York and then the train to Hudson. She called her parents. She heard her father and mother shouting at each other, but her mother came to get her.

"At the house, though, it was clear that her situation was supposed to be temporary. Even after she said she was five or six months pregnant. Her father wanted to throw her out. He wanted to do that simply because she ran away. Now it was made worse by the fact that she got herself knocked up by some guy who then left her.

"Dot said her father kept asking, 'Do you love him?' and she kept saying she did, and her father said that it was clear he didn't love her since he left her to go someplace far away from her.

"Her mom protected her. She heard her parents fighting all the time about whether she should have an abortion. She was just over eighteen, and it was still illegal back then. Her mother insisted that it was her decision and ultimately her decision ruled. But her father kept his dealings with Dot to a minimum. She said he barely said hello to her.

"She had a job in a local Kmart until she left about a week before Emily was born. She and Emily stayed with her parents for another two years. Dot tried to work odd jobs when her mother could watch the baby. She got her own place, a dive in downtown Hudson, when Emily was just over two. She got a job as a check-out woman at the local grocery store with regular hours and a friend who watched over the baby while she worked.

"Then her folks died in that crash and, well, she told you the rest."

We, the three of us, were silent until I broke it.

"Do you want us to stay around? Maybe come by later this afternoon?" I asked.

"No, girls. I think just leave her to me for the next days. Give me your number—Alex, is it?—" I nodded. "Give me your number, Alex. Head back to the city. I'll give you a call late this afternoon or tonight, and I'll let you know how it stands."

He gave each of us a hug, and we pulled away in the car and I gave Kate a tour of Hudson. Hudson was a major whaling town in the mid-nineteenth century, along the river. Like much of the region, though, it's had some rough years and the city itself has been only partially rescued by becoming another of those Brooklyn Norths that *The Times* writes about like clockwork.

Being the home of restaurants and boutiques and various other businesses that cater to the city folk intermingled with the more old-school places the locals frequent, Kate and I wandered aimlessly, as they say, for a bit. We stopped in places and browsed before she suggested that we go to my grandparents, the Millers. The 800-pound gorilla in the room.

"Would I be a horrible person if I said I just wanted to go home?"

We were on the sidewalk outside a place with large, overpriced furniture that I could not imagine anyone buying.

"Honey," Kate said, turning to look straight at me. "I don't know how you've gotten this far. Let's head home and you can call them when you get to your place."

With that, we got the car. I was too drained, so she drove all the way down. We dropped it off together and she walked me to my stoop.

"Call me, okay?"

I nodded and hugged her before turning and heading upstairs. It was three, or half-past, and I plopped down on my sofa when I was through the door and fell into a deep sleep until the need to pee overcame the need to sleep. I splashed some water on my face in the bathroom and looked in its mirror. Not great. But not like shit either.

It was still light out and tired as I was from the drive I changed into some running things and made it to the park, where I did three easy laps of the Reservoir. A bit under five miles. It wasn't that crowded at that time on a Saturday and with each step, I felt more alive. I was glad not to be wearing my headphones for a change and sprinted the last hundred yards or so to the path's southwest corner, just a stone's throw from my apartment.

A new person after the effort, I showered and decided that after I made simple spaghetti with bottled marinara sauce and a glass (or two) of my normal cheap Pinot Noir I'd go to the Barnes & Noble and just wander around.

Before I left, Edgar called. He said Dot was doing much better and how I had brightened her up by simply...being. He said he'd come up with a plan to let her know about Jessie, and I promised to speak to him later in the week.

I called Jessie in Chicago and with a wedding band playing in her background, I reported on the meeting with Dot and Edgar and the call I'd just had from him. She agreed to defer to his suggestions about actually heading up with me to see her. Meet her.

"She took it remarkably well," I told Jessie, referring to Dot, "considering the news about Mom. My guess is that we'll be able to go up on Saturday if you can."

"I will make sure I can. But report back on what Edgar says, okay? I'm home on Monday night and we can talk then."

I promised to and headed out to the bookstore. It's quieter on Saturday nights than it is, say, on Thursdays since anyone who has somewhere to be is at that somewhere—though one does sometimes see people on a date wandering around—

and your classic lonely, single Upper West Sider is what you're most likely to encounter.

I walked past where they do the readings, though there was none that night. I looked at where Karen Adams did hers and how Nancy Penchant spoke of the Emily Locus Award and how she hoped it would help someone do something my mom never did. All these books in the store and all these authors who did take the next step and did seek out a publisher and did find someone interested enough in the story on the page to ship it to the Barnes & Noble on Broadway and 82nd Street.

I wandered over to Classics. It's always been a bit of a refuge for me. All the familiar names and the collections I've aspired to read but rarely had. I suffered through a couple of classes in English Lit at Villanova—it didn't take—and my knowledge of the canon was essentially the BBC and Netflix adaptations that I binged on now and then when there was nothing else worth watching.

I'd not thought much of the writer's craft. A talented person sat down and, *voilà*, out came a wonderful story and hundreds, thousand, millions of times they populated bookstores and some were good enough or insightful enough to merit inclusion in anthologies and English Lit courses (or, you know, Russian or French Lit courses for the linguistically adept).

Now, though, I'd seen the scrawls—the "sausage-making" as someone famous said about laws—in my mom's drafts and redrafts. Her dead ends. Her wordsmithing. So, it was different this time. I ran my fingers along the spines of the books on some shelves. Which one, which one?

I liked the *Jane Eyre* cover. It was an old painting with a window to the left and a pair of women's shoes on the floor. A broad table with an ornate edge was in the foreground and a woman sat by the door at the end of the room. A man appeared in another, far-off room, behind a half-open door to the rear.

I'd probably seen at least one version of it and remembered reading it in college. So, ambition being the order of the day, I bought it.

Like my simple laps of the Reservoir, the quiet evening with a book did a world of good for me. It was raining on Sunday morning with quite a chill, so I wore tights and a long-sleeve shirt to do a five-mile loop of the Park Drive, which I got in before a half-marathon took over the place. I may have stayed under my shower stream longer than I ever had before. It was a cleansing.

Kate called in the late morning, asking if I wanted to do something with her but I said I was just hanging out alone for a change. Nancy called in the early afternoon, and I told her what I told Kate and I told Jessica the same thing when she called about an hour after Nancy did, though since, you know, she was in Chicago she didn't suggest us getting together.

Scrambled eggs and toast for lunch with more cups of coffee than I should have and sitting in my favorite chair pulled near the window so I could read Charlotte Brontë, and I watched the water drops slide down my window until I again dozed off. The next thing I knew the book was splayed across the floor. The rain had stopped, and the sun had broken through and when I looked out its beams were reflected off the puddles that dotted West 85th Street.

"Alexandra Locus," I asked aloud, "what is to become of you?" I had less of an answer to that question than anyone else in all the world.

27.

"What are you doing for dinner?"

Seeing as it was not yet noon on Tuesday, I hadn't given much thought to Jessie's question. She'd gotten back to town late the prior night.

"Nothing, right? I want you to meet Peter. There's a place on East 47th Street west of Madison. Irishy place. I made a reservation for six-thirty. You can bring Kate."

As I said, I'd told her quite a bit about Kate (and *vice versa*), but they'd not met. I decided, though, that we were Musketeers, all-for-one/one-for-all, "in this together," so after Kate said she was in, I texted the fact to Jessie.

I knew the restaurant. The lunch crowd was pretty much banker- and lawyer-like given its location and the dinner crowd looked to be the same. There was a bar on the ground floor, though most of the restaurant tables were upstairs.

I went in. A tall woman with long dark hair and fair skin approached. I told her I was meeting a Ms. Alpert. She checked her computer monitor. "Table for four, six-thirty?"

"That's it," I said.

"She's not here yet. You're the first. You're welcome to sit at the bar while you wait."

I was not in a sit-at-the-bar mood. I declined and said I'd stay near the door.

Peter was the next to arrive, and he went through the routine I did with the hostess, except that when I heard him mention "Ms. Alpert," I tapped him on the shoulder. He must have seen pictures of me and didn't seem surprised when he turned. Jessie's Facebook photos did not do him justice. Peter was tall, maybe 6' 2", and solid. Perhaps a swimmer or a rugby player and *very* handsome. His hair was dark brown and a little on the long side, with hints of curls trying to rebel against his combing. He had a nice, round face, and its features blended well with each other, especially his, what?, rustic hazel eyes.

I've mentioned that I'm not good with strangers. Peter was more than a stranger. He shook my hand, and I was glad he didn't try to kiss me since that would have been Very Awkward. Instead, he simply said he'd been looking forward to meeting me after I suddenly parachuted into his wife's life. "Instant family," he said, his arms exploding out. He had an easy laugh that helped loosen me up.

The wait wasn't long. Jessie came through the front door.

"I see you two have met," she said. They exchanged a sweet kiss. "He's taken, so you know," she informed me when she turned in my direction. "What about Kate?"

Before I could answer, the woman herself appeared. She locked onto me before I introduced her to the others. Seeing the four of us, the hostess grabbed some menus and led us up the stairs. The floor was perhaps half full. Its walls were a tasteful forest green on which large, old-fashioned hunting prints were hung. It was not loud beyond the murmurings of and occasional laugh from the diners and the clanking of silverware on plates. We took a booth on the righthand side. Trendy this place wasn't.

Our waitress showed up as we sat and when she asked what we wanted to drink, Peter interrupted.

"Is it alright if I get a bottle of champagne? It just seems like an occasion."

Kate and I exchanged glances and then nodded and so that's what was ordered and that's what came shortly after we began.

Things turned serious quickly. I don't think any of us plotted along those lines. It happened during a lull in the conversation and after our champagne toast. Peter started the ball rolling when he asked me how I was holding up.

"I'll say Jessie has been, well, confused about all of this. Discovering what she has about you and about her...your mother and her grandparents and everything."

"The thing is," she interrupted, "for all the disruption and confusion, I'm glad I'm finding out this stuff. It's hard, especially about her having passed, and it's not as though I felt a big hole in my life I needed to get filled. It's just that I feel more complete in ways I didn't imagine. Maybe I couldn't have imagined."

After that, we tried to just, well, get to know one another. We were all just mid-twenties/early-thirties frazzled New Yorkers who were happy to be sitting with other, pleasant people with whom we felt a new but somehow deep connection.

Peter was nice and dinner was nice and we spent the evening generally avoiding the topics that were foremost in our minds but the very act of doing—or not doing—that was a relief to me. By nine, Kate and I, both a little buzzed from the champagne, were sharing a cab to our part of town and after I was deposited in front of and walked through the door to my place, I once again drifted off to sleep still dressed in what I'd worn to the restaurant, though at some point in the night I was down to my panties and burrowed into my blanket, and I discovered my regulation dark blue skirt and cream blouse and utilitarian white bra thrown across the top of my dresser.

Jessie deferred to me regarding what we covered at dinner, and I think she was disappointed that we hadn't gotten to any detail about the meeting with Dot and Edgar. The thing was, though, that I felt so comfortable being with them, which meant more than any details. Meeting my sister, albeit half-sister, and her husband and being in some crazy whirlwind of conjoined existences.

So, yeah, there were things we didn't talk about. Those things we pretty much took care of at lunch on Wednesday, and I told her what I could, emphasizing that Dot was particularly upset—"I can understand that," Jessie said, and I could tell that *she* was upset about it—and that I was waiting to hear from Edgar to get the all-clear to go up with her.

And Edgar did give the all-clear that night, and he got me to promise to visit again on Saturday and to bring Jessie.

I called Paterson and had a long chat with my grandma. It was mostly telling her what happened when I went to Hudson with Kate and how I felt about it. I avoided the details about Dot's life except in the broadest strokes. They were not my details to give.

I'm afraid she was a little hurt that I'd been in Hudson and not stopped by, but I told her that while I thought of it, the strain of the meeting with Dot was too much, and I just couldn't. I don't know that she was happy, but I think she did understand.

28.

I left it up to Kate to decide whether to come with Jessie and me. She was relaxed with Jessie when they met at dinner, but she said it probably was best that it be a "sisters thing." I had to agree.

A little before nine on a clear but chilly Saturday morning, then, I sat on my stoop dressed as if I were posing for a cover shot of a Talbot's fall catalog for our trip to the country after Jessie called to say she was starting across the park. She pulled up in her light blue Volvo wagon, and from what I could tell she had the same fashion mojo that I did. We were soon fighting traffic up the West Side Highway and into Westchester and on and on through thinning traffic until we got off at the City of Hudson exit.

"It was a bit of a splurge, and it doesn't make a lot of sense," she said about the car, "but it's nice to have it when we go to the Hamptons or upstate."

She confessed that she and Peter rarely headed upstate. I let her do the driving and control Sirius, but things quieted between us as we got close to Hudson itself. The confidence I'd grown used to in her was ebbing away and she found it difficult to complete thoughts in the few times she tried to speak in those final miles. I cannot say how many times I assured her that Dot and Edgar would love her. "If they like me, they'll definitely love you."

I don't know if it had that much effect, although it did get a smile out of her, and I was in no position to judge her since I'd been similarly anxious just a week earlier when I was driving these same streets.

Unlike that earlier visit, this was announced and a fair amount of work was done to the house since. And that was just the outside, where the lawn was cut and paint applied to the railings and the columns of the porch plus the front door itself. What had been untidy shrubs were trimmed.

I called when we got off the parkway, and when we pulled up, Dot and Edgar were waiting on the porch, and I was afraid they'd hurt themselves as they hurried down the steps to greet us.

I was not, however, prepared to see how Jessie reacted as this sophisticated New York lawyer seemed their equal in enthusiasm as she ran to them, and I was left to stand to the side and gawk until Edgar turned to me and gave me my own hug as I watched Dot and Jessie holding each other tightly. Only when Edgar intervened did they stop as he said there was freshly brewed coffee inside. He had us sit on the porch while he got the tray. I left the other two alone, though, and followed him in to help.

If the outside of the house was tidied up, the inside was transformed. No paint, this time, but everything was shined or polished within an inch of its life, including, I made a point of checking, the frame of that one photo they had of Emily. The cups and saucers in the kitchen were new and fancy. As he poured the coffees and I got the plates for the pastries that were on the counter, Edgar said, "It was a little rough at first. About your sister. But once it set in, she couldn't wait to meet her. I mean, she'd met you already. But she hadn't met Jessica. She was up at six and still polishing. She's told half the neighborhood so don't be surprised if some old bat 'happens to stop by.' In fairness, though, we couldn't have gotten things in decent shape without their help."

He lowered his voice. "She's a different woman, is Dot. She'll never get over what happened to Emily. Not in a million years. I don't know what shape she'd be in if she didn't have you two girls. I'm glad we don't have to find out."

By this point, the tray was ready. We could hear the animated conversation of Jessie talking about her own family and how they were from the Island—"Long Island, so you know"—so didn't come upstate much and how, yes, they hoped to have kids but how busy she was at work and all and how busy her husband—"Yes, that's Peter"—was at work and...

They both looked embarrassed about our overhearing them but nothing that a bite or two of a strawberry Danish couldn't take care of. Edgar had pulled the round table away from the wall and the porch was wide enough so that we could have four chairs surround it, and that's where we sat, with Dot between her granddaughters.

I doubted what Edgar said in the kitchen, but on its face at least Dot did seem like a different person. She'd gained ten years when I told her about my mom but seemed to have lost that and another ten in anticipation of our visit and were I not of a generous disposition I would have been jealous that she was more excited about meeting Jessie than in seeing me again.

Edgar was right. A few neighbors did amble by, claiming "just being on a little stroll" as they stopped to get a glimpse of the sudden additions to Dot's family. Each time she made us stand on the porch and introduce ourselves and several, referring to Jessie, said, "Oh, you're the lawyer," once or twice followed by "And what do you do, dear?" to me.

It was all done with such magic that I couldn't and didn't take offense about the plainness of my own position in a bank.

The time went very quickly and perhaps too quickly for Dot. So, after we had sandwiches and coffee with her and Edgar on their porch, we decided to leave so Dot could have the chance to process all that'd happened to her in just the one week.

Hugs and kisses on the sidewalk, and Jessie and I started heading home. We were not far when I asked whether she wanted to go to the Millers.

"I'm a little scared, to be honest," she said.

"Look. I came up last week but decided it was too much to see them. So, I understand. But if you can, I think it'd be good to stop by and for you to meet them."

She took a deep breath and gripped the steering wheel tightly and said, "Okay. Let's do it."

I pulled out my phone and called them. I hadn't told them I was coming up with Jessie. If I did and we didn't stop by, they'd be more than a little upset given that I hadn't stopped by the Saturday before.

It was a short call. I said Jessie and I had met with Dot and that we'd like to stop by in Paterson if we could and of course my grandpa said we could and before we knew it, we were in front of their house and they were running to meet their daughter's other child and it was only with some effort that we all climbed to *their* porch and somehow there was a platter with cookies ready for us when we got there.

This time there was no agenda. No "I want to look at my mom's stuff." It was the type of meeting we had not three hours before at the Davises', filled with tears and emotion and memories of Emily Miller.

Grandpa suggested that we best leave before it got dark, so we were soon heading south to the city and Jessie was able to drive, though at times she fought the tears that she tried to laugh off by saying how "unbecoming" they were for a New York lawyer and more than once I reached over and rubbed her upper arm to assure her that I understood.

* * * *

WHAT I UNCOVERED UPSTATE went a long way to explain why my mom wrote again and again about abandonment and about her questioning her worthiness as a mother. I was largely exhibit 1 in this, and I didn't think I turned out so badly. I realized, though, that she must always have wondered what she did wrong and whether I became who I was becoming despite not because of her.

With this new family, I thought of bits and pieces of the stories I read and tracked them down to reread and I felt the agony that sometimes flowed from her onto the paper. I spoke regularly with Nancy about this on one level and with

Kate on another. As for Jessie, we were not far from square 1 and just learning about each other, never mind our mother. And I found I liked her and that I liked Peter and suddenly a new vista opened before me.

The reunions or whatever they were with my grandparents and bringing Jessie into the fold were not the only thing going on, of course. As I was trying to get my footing, I kept my dad at something of a distance. My excuse to him was that I was "still working through Mom's stuff," supplemented after my first trip to Paterson with "and I got some things from Grandma and Grandpa." He said he figured there might be other things with them since she often was writing when she was there.

I spoke to all these folks about my dad and particularly how I was going to broach the subject of their existence to him. I knew he knew my mom was adopted but if the Millers didn't know who her birthmother was, I doubted he did. Or, of course, that she herself did before she died.

The existence of Jessie was far more delicate. My dad was open-minded but also conscious of his social standing. His marrying my mom was perhaps the most unusual part of his life, what with growing up on the Main Line and all. The moment to tell him would come. It just wasn't there yet.

I'd go up to Bronxville to speak to him about most of this—still not sure what to say about Jessie but confident as to Dot—and called on Tuesday to see if I could come up on Saturday, and he seemed pleased that I was finally telling him what was going on.

29.

I don't know how I made it to Saturday. Everyone knew the signs:

Leave

Alex

Alone

Other than super-quick how's-everythings? with Jessie, Kate, and Nancy, I had to figure out what to say to my dad on Saturday. I wanted to speak to them, to tell them what was going through my head, and to know they'd give me the advice I had to get from them.

I *needed* alone time to consider and contemplate what this all meant to me. I knew quite a lot from my "detective work." Shifting through the clues. But, I said aloud on Thursday night—something that was becoming a strangely comforting habit—sitting on my sofa and looking at the boxes, "Alexandra Locus. What will you do now? What will you do with all of this new information? These people? What will you *do* with it all?"

I didn't know the answers beyond knowing I had to head up to Bronxville, and I slept poorly that night and on Friday.

I got up early on October 14. It was foggy, and the brownstones across 85th Street were blurred. I puttered around for a bit until I was ready to repeat my trek of four weeks earlier, when I went for the boxes. By the time I left my place, the fog had burned off. I spoke to my dad on Friday and asked that we speak alone so Maggie and TimTim were at the field club when I got there. We had the place to ourselves. The living room was the neutralist spot and though it was big, it's where I asked him to go.

"Why all the cloak and dagger?" he asked after we sat. By the window looking to the winding street and not far from the Steinway were a pair of comfortable armchairs in a cream pattern. I sometimes sat in one and put my feet on the other to read when I was a kid. It was a particularly great place to be when a spring rain came through and the new leaves on the elm out front glistened.

Those leaves were beginning to turn, though, and there was no sun to brighten them. They fit my mood. We each had coffee in our laps, in blue mugs with the first two people in his firm's name wrapped around in a fancy white print.

I answered his cheerful question with the feigned cheerful, "I wanted to tell you what I've found out." I took a sip of the coffee. "It's a lot."

He took a drink from his mug and placed it on a coaster on the table that was between the chairs. He leaned back and crossed his legs and waited.

"First, why didn't you tell me she was adopted?"

I don't think he expected this, though it wasn't hard to realize I'd find out from the Millers.

Still, he looked surprised.

"I knew. Your mom told me before we got married. But for some reason, I didn't want anyone to know. Her folks—the Millers—did know, of course. But I had enough issues with my parents and why did it matter? We rarely spoke about it. I think the only time we did was when we talked about telling you. 'Is she old enough?' 'How will she react?' That sort of thing.

"In the end, we never found the right time, but it didn't seem to be an issue for her."

It was all so matter of fact.

"She was obsessed by it."

No question he was surprised by this.

"How do you mean? How do you know?"

"It's from the stories. She was obsessed with abandonment and whether she could be a good or even a not-bad mother."

"But she never said anything to me. How'd you find out?"

"The Millers, of course."

"Look, honey. I didn't know."

I put that aside. I would just keep checking off the mental boxes of what I found, there being no point in doing anything else.

"I met her birthmother."

"You what?"

His left leg was no longer across his right thigh. It was firmly planted on the floor, and his back was no longer against the chair's.

"She lives in Hudson. Not far from the Millers. She's married to a wonderful man who, as far as I can tell, rescued her from where she was. I broke her heart when I told her that her little girl was dead. But I didn't know what else I could have done. I went to see her with Kate—"

"Kate Winslow?"

"Yes. She's been my rock through this."

"She's a good kid. I'm glad she's been with you."

No time like the present, I thought.

"I went to see Dot—she's Mom's birthmother—again a week ago with Jessica."

"Jessica? Who's Jessica?"

"Mom's other daughter."

He was shocked by this. No doubt about it.

"She's not younger than you?"

"No, Dad. From Mom's high school days. She's thirty. A lawyer in the city. Married. Lives in Brooklyn."

He was doing the math in his head.

"Did your mother ever meet her?"

"No. Jessie was given up just after she was born but tried to get in touch about five years ago, after Mom was dead. Which she didn't know. The Millers gave me the letter she wrote when I went up there a few weeks ago. They didn't know what to do with it and it just sat in a drawer all these years. Kate and I tracked her down and we met her and have met her husband and she and I went up to Hudson to meet with our grandmother, as I say, just a week ago."

"Well, you've been up to a lot of secret sleuthing," he said with the hint of sarcasm that sometimes slipped out, often with my mom.

He got up and began to pace.

"I swear, Alex. She never told me anything about that. Her parents, I mean the Millers, never said anything about that. So, you've met her?"

"She's very nice and very smart. She was shaken up about Mom being dead, but I think she was happy to meet me."

"What about her parents? This sister?"

"They're fine with it. Always told her she was adopted. She grew up on the Island. They encouraged her when she was old enough to try to contact Mom. It's just sad that she waited too long."

He reached for his mug on the table and asked if I wanted a refill. I nodded, and while he was in the kitchen, I went to the window. Things had gone pretty well, so far. I'd dropped a lot on him, but he took it, even the stuff he clearly knew nothing about, as well as could be expected.

He was near me when he called to me and reached out with my mug.

"I hope I got the milk and sugar right," and I told him it looked perfect.

We sat.

"Then there's Nancy Penchant."

He leaned back in his chair, cradling his coffee, and nodded with a creepy kind of smile I'd never seen on him before.

"Ah. Nancy Penchant. The writer who started this whole quest. I take it you've been back in touch with her and I take it she didn't have very nice things to say about me."

I took a sip of the coffee. It was a little heavy on the sugar, but drinking it was something to do.

"I need to know your side of the story. I'm not saying anything about what she said. Just tell me, Dad, what you know about her and Mom. All I'll say is that she told me you found out through a private detective and that you, well, you entered some type of arrangement with Mom that allowed her to continue to see Nancy once a week. That's all I'll say." I put the mug on the table and leaned forward, my elbows on my thighs and my fingers interlaced. It was the height of feigned calmness.

"So. Tell me."

"Jeez, Alex. You sound like Lennie Briscoe and a perp on *Law & Order*."

"Dad. Just tell me."

He put his mug next to mine on the table and sat back. I leaned back too.

"Okay. You'll never get me to admit marrying your mom was a mistake, but a lot of people think it was. Especially your grandparents. There was something about her, though, that I couldn't put my finger on. I was so used to the types of girls who grew up in my neighborhood and who were that type at Cornell. Like the girls you grew up with here in town.

"And she was...different. I ran into her type, the 'other-side-of-the-tracks' kind, when I was a kid and maybe I was a fool, but I liked it. And I'm afraid I liked pissing my parents off, if I'm honest."

"Is that one reason you didn't practice in Philadelphia?"

He laughed and clapped and broke into a legitimate smile.

"If I'd gone to Penn I might have. But it was so different at Columbia. I knew I wouldn't be happy in Philly. And your mom was important to that, given her in-laws, and I didn't blame them."

Things had lightened dramatically. He never spoke of either of these things to me before and he was relaxed in a way I rarely saw.

It couldn't last.

"And Nancy?"

"Ah." He'd moved forward in the chair in his animation but slumped back again. "Nancy. Do you know how they met?"

I said I understood it in broad strokes, not admitting the existence of *The Love of My Life*.

"She was lonely. I can't say I blame her. It was mostly my fault, but I was trying to make a good life for both of us. And for you when you came along. It's what lawyers, ambitious lawyers, did. Still do. Work like dogs and work even harder when they get signals that they might, just might, make partner.

"And, you know, New York suburbs are so much more expensive than those on the Main Line outside of Philadelphia and the salaries and rewards so much greater. It's the brass ring they hold out."

He was again relaxing. "I worked my ass off. We all did. So, she was alone and she was going for walks as she got bigger and bigger and...and this woman picked her up. I never blamed your mom. It was Nancy whatever-the-fuck-her-name-is."

You'd think she was Voldemort he fought so hard not to say her name. I was on this roller-coaster ride and thought it best to sit back and try not to puke—figuratively—till it was over.

He got up and turned to look down on me.

"Again, I never blamed your mom. She had...needs and this woman made her think she could fill them. It grew from that. So, yeah, I had her followed and found out. I was straight— ha, ha—ultimately with both. I left it up to your mom, and she accepted what you are calling our 'arrangement.' It was only fair. She could do what she wanted and I could do what I did.

"As to intimacy, I don't think she was gay or anything, but this woman filled a need. I admit I didn't give her the attention she deserved in some ways, but that was for her. She came from nothing, and I was giving her the world.

"Look around this house. I've been to the shack where she grew up. Nothing compared to what I gave her here. And friends. She had no friends up there."

"Did she really have friends here?" I asked.

"Of course she had friends. Tons of them. At school. At the field club. We were always meeting people. Going to people's houses."

"But what did she think of that?"

"Your mom? She was fine with it."

I had my doubts, but I let him go on. He started to get animated but slipped back into his more usual controlled lawyer mode and sat back down.

"Sometimes she didn't appreciate it. I worked hard, but for her and for you. I thought she was happy, or at least happy enough. She went into the city regularly, and I figured she wanted to go to the Met or places like that. I didn't think she had any friends there. She didn't meet any as far as I knew while we were there.

"Then I noticed she wasn't as...available on those days. I noticed hickeys sometimes, and I'm not as big a fool as she apparently thought I was so I got a private detective to follow her. She was oblivious, he said. It only took two trips and I had her. And this other one.

"So, I confronted her. The lover." He made air quotes for that last word. "It was clear that's what they were, though your mom was never like that. I told her to back off, and she agreed."

"Because of me."

"What?"

"She only agreed because she knew you'd take me away from her."

"Is that what that woman told you?"

"It was kind of important. That's why I said I wanted your side."

"Well, no. It was simply that if your mom...It was essentially to have what I guess they call an 'open marriage.' That was it. Nothing about me leveraging you. Nothing of the sort. That's bullshit."

He was up and after grabbing his mug he was heading into the kitchen, and I heard cupboard doors slam.

"You want anything?" he called out, and I shouted that I was fine. I wasn't, of course, but I got up and when I reached the kitchen, he was there, bent over the counter, his hands holding its edge.

"She didn't understand. We were so good. And then everything fell apart."

He might have been crying if he were the crying type, but he decidedly wasn't. Crying or the type. I put a hand on his shoulder and said how sad I was that she was gone.

And then *I* was gone. I still can't explain it, but something made me want to leave that house as quickly as I could, and he was there, still standing at the counter when I grabbed my bag—which I'd left on the kitchen table when I went in—and headed into town.

30.

Fortunately I didn't have to wait long for the train, and as I rode back to the city, I replayed what happened. Of course he resented her, Nancy Penchant. She'd taken advantage of a horribly vulnerable woman and created the unhappiness reflected in my mom's stories and, I guessed, in her life. I still didn't know the "why" of what she'd done, not as I would have liked to. But I didn't know what more I could do.

By the time we got to the Harlem/125th Street Station, it was nice and not late, so I walked the three miles or so to my apartment. On the way, I stopped and sat on a bench overlooking a small lake at the northeast corner of the park and called my dad. He apologized for getting "so damn emotional" and said he was fine about how I walked out, that he understood. Just that I'd brought back happy memories that were gone.

That done, I gave progress reports to Kate, Jessie, and Nancy as I resumed walking south and before I knew it, I was at my apartment, and it wasn't even two. Tired as I was, I changed into my running gear and headed out to do a very easy counter-clockwise five-mile loop of the Park Drive. I felt like shit at first, but as I warmed up the breathing became easy and the slightness of the rolling terrain got me into a rhythm and before I knew it, I was more than halfway done, passing the Met on my right.

There was a fair share of Saturday afternoon clueless walkers but not so many that they blocked the running lane and with a final burst up the final small hill I was done. I felt like a new woman.

During the run, I concluded that I had to sit down with Nancy. While I was really close to her place in my last mile, I went home and showered and called her. And she was in and anxious for me to talk to her at her place.

* * * *

"I'VE TOLD YOU. THIS ALL was very much my fault. If he wants it to *all* be my fault, I can't say I blame him, and if you're alright with that, I'm not going to blame you either. I told you, there are two sides to this."

"That's all you have to say for yourself?"

We were on the couch. She ran her hand across my chin.

"Sweetie, what's happened, happened. It was hard for her, for him, and for me. None of us can dwell. Be glad you've learned as much as you have about your mom and your grandma and your sister and be done with it. I'm here if you need someone like me. But can't we just leave it? I moved on when she died those years ago. You need to do the same."

She went into her bedroom and returned with *The Love of My Life*, what I'd left on that bench.

"I've read it several times. I haven't copied it. That's for you to decide. But I would like to get a copy, if you'll allow me."

I took it and promised I would get her one. As I started to the door, she reached out and asked me to stay just a moment more. She didn't bother to sit or ask me to.

"I can't have you think for a moment, sweetie, that telling you to put this behind you lessens what I felt for her. What I'll always feel for her. And what I want you to feel for her."

My back was towards the door through which my mom went so many times and that one last time she came in and that one last time she went out (on a damn gurney). Nancy often seemed lackadaisical about my mom, but I knew from the many times she wasn't that she thought it best to put on, literally, a brave face. This had turned into not one of them.

Now it was me who ran a hand across her face, with an intimacy I'd known but never felt with her before. Before I could remove it, her hand grabbed my wrist and simply held my fingers against her cheek.

"That's all I want to say."

She released my hand and me, and with an awkward, embarrassed smile she reached behind me to open the door and said "*Ciao.*"

With that, I left and walked home. I knew my mom was better than just being taken in, especially given the words she used in so many of her stories about hope and love, in such contrast with those other ones of self-hatred.

But if Nancy was willing to at least try to move on and accept my dad's spin—or at least pretend she was—so was I. I didn't know whether I'd see her again. I was happy to have seen the woman my mom loved, but I had no other connection to her. At least our passing-in-the-night brought closure to how my mom died and set me off on the adventure in which I learned so much more about my mom and that I had another grandmother (and, with Edgar, a grandfather) and more than anything that I had a sister.

So, for the first time in a month, since that Thursday night trip to Barnes & Noble, my life resumed its boring but satisfying course, and I was on the phone that night planning with Jessie a visit up north to see about getting the Millers and the Davises together.

31.

We picked a neutral forum, a nice but not too nice restaurant on Warren Street in Hudson. I knew no matter what we said, they'd be dressed to the nines, so it would be brunch on Saturday at noon at a reserved table back in the corner that would offer some but not too much privacy.

It went off great. Edgar, Jessie, and I assured Dot I don't know how many times that the Millers would love her. She was still super nervous. Jessie and I picked her and Edgar up and I discovered that when she was nervous, she became a Chatty Cathy, so we got a running commentary as we drove in Jessie's Volvo wagon into Hudson.

The Millers were at the table when we got there a little after noon. The introductions were a little awkward, but I also found that a bit of alcohol calmed Dot down so mimosas all around had the desired effect. Dot spoke so very well about the little girl who grew to be Jessie's and my mom, and Grandma couldn't stop complimenting Dot on how well little Emily grew. In a break, Grandpa reached to the floor and lifted a gift, which he handed to Grandma who passed it over to Dot.

If I didn't think things couldn't get more emotional, I was wrong. "You shouldn't have," Dot said, as she delicately removed the wrapping paper and found a plain box, the type you'd use for a sweater or blouse. She opened it and moved the tissue aside. It was a collection of photos of Emily at all the later stages of her life. After looking at three or four, Dot dropped them in the box and started to chortle and thank God again Edgar was there to put his arm around her and she moved her head to his shoulder for a minute or so while we all let them be, pretending to ignore them.

But after that minute or so, Dot took a deep breath and reached back into the box and Grandma started to tell her what each one was until we were interrupted by our food, and it was agreed to put the box aside until we were done. The plates were cleared and we were on the last of our coffees when Grandma moved to sit next to Dot, and the two of them went through all of the photos, with Grandpa occasionally interrupting with his own memories of some event or another.

When this started, Grandpa told Jessie and me that he discovered an old computer back in Paterson that my mom sometimes used and that I was welcome to take it to see if there was anything of interest on it. It was in the back of his car. I told everyone that I was happy with what I found and that my quest was officially over now that I tracked down so many more members of my family. Jessie said, though, that she'd take it if I didn't. She was still unsettled about her father and our grandfather.

We left the restaurant with Grandma's arm through Dot's and Dot clutching the box of photos. Grandpa led us to his car. He said he'd plugged the computer in and attached the keyboard, mouse, and monitor and it seemed to be in working order. Though the monitor was huge (though its screen seemed tiny), Jessie and I could carry it to Jessie's car, which was not far, and after goodbyes on the sidewalk and a brief walk, the paraphernalia was in the rear of the Volvo, and the Davises were in the back seat. Dot was quiet heading back to her place, saying how nice it was to meet the Millers and what sweet people they were. Her hands caressed the sides of the box the whole way to their house.

"Are you going to see them again?" Jessie asked from the driver's seat.

"I don't know," Edgar said. "They are so different from us and I'm not sure about stirring up things too much. But we'll see."

"We'll see," Dot echoed with a nod as I looked back at her, and she then turned to look out the window. I told her that

I'd put together a set of photos for her too, though I'd have to get most of those from Bronxville.

We dropped them off, and I told Jessie I'd call the Millers and say that the Davises weren't quite ready for a two-on-two with them just yet.

Jessie and I spoke about the computer as we headed south, and she convinced me that we'd gone so far with our mom's stories that we owed it to her to see if there was anything worthwhile so she dropped me off and double-parked to help me carry the pieces up—it was a dinosaur—and I put it on the floor by the boxes. I didn't know how much longer the boxes would remain, but there they were and now even more of my floor was occupied.

32.

It took a while to get the computer set up. I didn't bother moving it beyond putting the monitor on top of one of the boxes, so I sat on the floor and figured out what plug went where till I finally got it right and turned it on.

It took a bit of whirring, but the monitor flashed on, and I had the home screen. The screen saver was a photo of me from one of my field hockey games when I must have been about eleven with a blue jersey that was way too big and the "14" on its back over white shorts. The ball was at my feet, and I was maneuvering it with my stick. Such a dweeb, but there it was on my mom's screen and I began to cry. I hadn't cried much throughout this last month or so, but this hit me very hard. I just stared and stared at it. And cried and cried about it.

Once I'd cried myself out, with a sigh and a final sniffle, I grabbed the mouse and put it on a mouse pad on the box for traction. I found the directory.

Everything seemed pretty vanilla. It must have been one of my dad's old desktops he'd deleted all the work files from. The directory "EMILY" was all that remained outside the system and program files. It had a "Stories" subdirectory. I clicked on that, and it brought up a list of, well, stories. I recognized most based on their file names.

I'd have to figure out how to get them from the computer to my laptop but for now, I simply went through the ones I didn't recognize and took quick looks. It wasn't very comfortable, sitting on the floor and scrolling through the stories like that, but it didn't take long since as soon as I recognized a story, I moved on.

Jessie called when I was nearly done. I told her my issue about getting things off the antique to my laptop and I heard her call to Peter.

"Pete asks if there's a disk drive on your laptop." I checked and there wasn't.

"Okay. He says if you can download the files onto a three-and-a-half-inch floppy disk he can get them onto a flash drive."

There was a disk in the drive that I'd put in my bag when I booted up the computer. I grabbed the bag from the doorknob and put the disk into the old computer and said I was ready.

"Great," she said. "Just copy the files to it and we'll take care of it. Pete says there should be plenty enough room for Word files since they're not so big. You can get it to me on Monday and I can get it back on a flash drive on Tuesday. Make sense?"

I told her it did and thanked her and Peter and set out to make the copies.

Before I began, I saw several files already on the disk. There were five, and four of them opened. They were duplicates of files on the C: drive. The fifth was not. "MyWalls.doc."

I tried to open it, but it was password protected. None of the other files was locked. I called Jessie.

"I don't know, but I may have found something."

I explained about this file and how I couldn't open it. She said she had to speak to Peter and then I was on her speakerphone.

"Do you have any idea what password she'd use?" he asked. I said I didn't. "Try birthdays," he said.

"Four or six digits?" I asked.

"Both. See if any works. We'll wait."

I tried hers, with and without the year. *Nada.*

"Look. It can't be that complicated and there are programs we can use to get it, but let's see. Did you try yours?"

I did and told him it didn't work.

I didn't know what else to try so I put in "100112" *et voilà*, it opened.

"What is that?" Jessie asked.

"My eighteenth birthday. Nancy said it was a special day for our mom."

"Okay. Clever Girl. Let me know if there's anything interesting. *Ciao.*"

"Thanks so much. Both of you," I said and ended the call.

33.

It wasn't ideal. This story, *My Walls*, was on the little monitor, tethered to the computer. I got a wooden chair I used at my table and bent to the screen and set about reading it.

I knew they were coming only because the lights went off. The lights, cheap glaring fluorescents that ran the length and width of the room's long walls—which were not very long—were always on except for this. They'd go off and a moment later the door opened. The door had no knob on my side. There was just a keyhole, which I knew from examining it soon after I arrived. As I'd examined everything in the time I was there. As to that, I did not know how long it was. It just was.

The walls in the room were painted in an institutional blue and for all I knew I was in a wing of a psychiatric hospital somewhere in the northwest, though I couldn't say where even generally it was since I was in a room with no windows. The paint job was recent enough so that there was no peeling. The floor was similarly institutional, a sort of speckled yellow linoleum. It had browned in places and gook built up along the walls but periodically—again I had no sense of what the period was—a woman entered with a mop and pail and other cleaning things, and she mopped the floor and cleaned the bathroom and changed the sheets. I can say nothing more about her since she wore a full covering that left only her eyes exposed—though she never answered my own eyes while she was there—and she said nothing as she went about doing her duties. I learned after numerous unsuccessful attempts that she would not respond to anything I said or to any questions I asked.

Those long walls with the lights were twelve feet or so in length and the short ones were eight. I'd measured them with my bare feet, which I assumed were about nine inches each. The ceiling was high. If I jumped, I could not come close to touching it, so it must have been at least ten feet top to bottom. And the cameras. There was a camera in each corner. Each had a red light, which was always lit.

There was an iron bed with a thin mattress and a pillow. The sheets, as I said, were changed when that woman cleaned the room or when I stained them, while I stood in a corner out of the way. There was a light blanket as well, but somehow the temperature was never too warm or too cold.

There was a hard metal chair with a hard metal seat and a metal dresser, both gray. The dresser was attached to one of the long walls. I had four wide drawers.

The top two drawers had clean clothing—underwear, shirts, shorts—and when I first woke up after arriving there was a note on the top of the dresser that told me to place my used clothing in the bottom drawers. I understood eventually that at some point the rears of the drawers were opened on the other side of the Wall and the dirty clothing was removed from the bottom and fresh things were put in the top drawers. That's all I wore. White cotton panties, a white bra (that fit me perfectly) beneath a plain gray t-shirt and plain gray cotton shorts. Plus black sandals.

There was a table beside the dresser. It had two levels and, like with the dresser, food and drink would be put on the top level and I was told to put my used things in the lower. I never saw food come in or plates go out because of the bathroom.

It was small, maybe twice the size of a toilet on an airplane. It was set up much like such a toilet with everything that horrible metal but there was a drain in the floor and a nozzle in the ceiling. The wall had a button. "On/Off" was stenciled on the wall above it. It controlled the shower. Next to the button were two small nozzles, and "soap" was stenciled above the left one and "shampoo" above the right.

The water was cold but not frigid. I could not bring a towel in because there was no place to put it where it wouldn't get wet. When I showered, I had to leave the stall naked and collect a towel from a (gray metal) table by the door. When I used the toilet, thankfully, I could get tissue from a shelf well above it, which also held feminine products, kept high I imagined so they would not get damp when I showered, and I was able to flush.

Whatever I was doing there, I had to close the door, and when I did the door locked. When I finished using it, I pushed a button, which would release the door, and food came and plates went only when that door was closed. Several times I tried to open the door right after it locked to catch this process, but there must have been a separate lock because each time the lock would not release for many seconds so that by the time I opened the door the exchange at my little table was complete.

I had, as you can imagine, much time to take these measurements. My days—I did not know how many there were since all I had was the rhythms of my body—were saved only because a book appeared with my first meal. It was perhaps ironically meant: Fahrenheit 451. I wondered if my task was to memorize its text as when I finished it another did not take its place, so I read it a second time. Then a kind note appeared with a meal. "If you want another book, you must send the one you have back." It was printed by a printer and not by a person but I cherished it still.

I kept Bradbury's novel for several more days before placing it with my used plates and glasses. When the next meal came, a novel was with it. And I devoured it and placed it with my used plates and glasses and so began my routine. Once the book was in French, a language I did not know. Instead of returning it immediately, I read it aloud and it became my companion, the sing-songy words.

Before I finished it, another novel appeared. It was in English, and I understood I was being allowed to retain the French book as some sort of Crusoe-like companion or the volleyball Wilson in that Tom Hanks movie.

There seemed to be no rhyme or reason to the books. Old. New. Hemingway. Austen. Some I'd read before, others I hadn't. Jane Eyre was one of the former. I'd read it a few times and always loved the ending. As I devoured it in this horrible place, though, I realized that Mr. Rochester was a brute.

Each word I knew and knew again. How his eyes and other parts of him to Jane Eyre "were more than beautiful to me; they were full of an interest, an influence that quite mastered me,—that took my feelings from my own power and fettered them in his."

But, yes, over time, I was not so assured in my opinion of him and of the governess. "You elf," he calls her. "My lamb, my pet lamb," likely as not to forever treat her so. Protected from the wolf, but to what fate?

Instead, I read again and again about Jane Eyre's rescue in the moors. The Rivers. St. John. But mostly the Rivers sisters. How they rescued her and took her under their wings. How I would have taken that money and let St. John go wherever he was doing his missionary work and go with the (newly rich) Rivers girls to some oasis. Perhaps the south of France. It wouldn't matter where we went as long as we went together.

I refused to put Jane Eyre—the book—on the lower level of the table. If I had one book to keep, this would be it. I must have read about the meeting of Jane and the Rivers siblings a half-dozen times and it got to the point where I didn't bother to follow her return to Thornfield

Hall. How pat I found that romance to be with each rereading.

I cannot say for how long this went on, but sometime later a new book appeared though I'd not returned the Eyre. *And the routine continued, excepting I would alternate my reading between* Eyre *and whatever book was also provided. Sometimes I read snippets of the French novel aloud simply to hear the flow of its words.*

Thus was my routine. Day in. Day out.

Except when the lights went off. When it first happened perhaps a week after my arrival, I did not understand. It was suddenly dark for the first time since I was brought there (when the room was pitch black). I heard the door open and felt hard hands on my arms and was forced down to the bed. My ankles were placed in cuffs and the cuffs were attached to the foot of the bed. Cuffs were placed on my wrists, and my arms were clasped to the head of the bed.

I screamed and screamed but was ignored and I felt a needle in my arm and realized that I was not being injected with anything but that my blood was being drawn. I cannot say how much but it was drawn, and I was released with military precision and as soon as the door closed behind however many came to take my blood the lights were on again and I was nearly blinded by their cruel brightness.

So my life became.

The story went back to how the narrator found herself in this dystopian nightmare. Being deceived by someone she trusted and waking up in this hellhole, having no one who would care if she disappeared from the face of the earth, as for all intents and purposes she had.

It ended:

I recalled little more of what happened to me before I awoke in a plush four-poster bed, naked and covered in a comforter. I had to climb down it was so high. There was a light robe across the foot of the bed, and I put it on and tied its belt. The room was painted in a light yellow with white trim, including a strip of wainscoting. The curtains were closed, but it was light enough to see, and when I opened them, I found a pair of French doors.

They opened inward and there was an iron railing that went to my chest and from there I saw what I knew was a Parisian street, une rue Parisienne, *and the traffic—cars and people—was moving as if it were the most normal thing in the world, me looking down at it all.*

A tray was on the dresser, a dresser in what I thought was the Louis XIV style in a cream color with gold trim and an oval mirror attached of the same design and on that tray were a cup and saucer and a silver coffee pot and matching creamer and sugar. A linen napkin with a narrow raspberry border was beneath a knife and spoon, and a fresh baguette lay across the tray, with several pats of butter on a small plate and some type of strawberry confection on a separate one.

I broke off a large piece of the bread and ate it with neither the butter nor the preserves. It tasted fresh from a boulangerie, *and I quickly followed it with dense black coffee I'd poured. I could not help looking into the mirror, and the face that looked back at me was very much the face I saw when I last looked into a mirror, I did not know how long ago, except the eyes were more drawn and the cheeks were shallower.*

Within minutes, I lay in the large tub in the warm water and only lifted myself when the water turned cool. I dried myself off with a large, white towel and wrapped myself in a terry cloth robe that was warm.

I can't say whether that was how the story ended or where she simply stopped writing it. I wouldn't have attributed anything particularly significant to what she wrote if it was not the only one that was password protected.

I tried to dismiss it as just another story, but my mom did not write fantasy. She tackled the range of emotions, but always in a realistic setting. Without anything beyond the words, though, I decided it was a part of her imagination that was experimental. As extreme as the story was, there was no reason to think it anything but a story.

I called Jessie and said there was nothing revelatory in *My Walls* and with it read, we'd exhausted the stories. They proved invaluable in getting me started on what I was doing but in the end nothing more. Still, I said, I'd download it all to the three-and-a-half-inch disk and give it to her the next day so Peter could convert it into something I could put on my computer.

34.

I only spoke to Nancy once or twice after this. I didn't mention *My Walls*. I was on the phone several times a week, though, with Jessie and met her for lunch at least once a week.

Just before Thanksgiving, I met her parents at a Sunday brunch near their Brooklyn apartment. I liked them and think they liked me and, most importantly, they showed no signs of, well, jealousy in what their daughter found after I went up to her some weeks earlier.

On Thanksgiving morning, Kate and I went to Bronxville on the train and to our respective houses, bundled up because it was freezing. In my case, it was just the four of us—my dad, Maggie, TimTim, and me—and was relaxing in the way Thanksgivings are meant to be. Okay, it was very boring. No one wanted to say anything of any significance and TimTim left as soon as he could. I helped clean up before going for a walk on my own, passing couples largely doing the same in the narrow, winding streets in the neighborhood.

Friday wasn't quite as cold. Kate and I met up. We walked through town with some classmates who were there for the holiday, ending up being too loud at the small coffee shop on the main street and going to her house for heated turkey and stuffing for lunch before, for laughs, piling into her parents' black Range Rover and driving to the upscale mall in White Plains where we tried on things we'd never buy and made fun of girls from Bronxville or Scarsdale or Chappaqua who were doing pretty much exactly what we were doing when we were their age.

It was getting dark as we got back to town and after dropping the others off, Kate suggested we spend the night at her place. "Like old times," she put it, and who was I to refuse such an offer?

I think my dad, Maggie, and TimTim were disappointed, but I had dinner with them before schlepping my stuff the few blocks to *Casa Winslow* and we entrenched ourselves in the basement.

We'd raided the kitchen, and everything was set up on the coffee table in front of the couch opposite the huge TV in the furnished basement with sliding doors out to the dark patio and Kate hit play and *Jane Eyre*—the BBC one with Ruth Wilson and wasn't she so great in *The Affair*?—began. The desert as Jane imagined traveling as she paged through the large book. Discovered by the horrible cousin John and being struck in the head by the book and knocking the brat down and being carried by two housemaids to the red room, begging and begging not to be taken to the red room and abandoned to the ghosts she knew haunted it and seeing the ghost...and my stomach churned and my head grew light and I rushed up the stairs into the kitchen, nearly running into Kate's mother.

Kate was on my heels as I fought for breath with my hands spread on the kitchen counter and my head rocking back and forth. Her mother got me water, most of which I downed with barely a break.

"What is it, Alex?" Mrs. Winslow asked as her daughter stood beside me panicking. Kate pulled out a chair, and I collapsed into it as her mother refilled the glass and grabbed her phone, but I told her I was okay.

"I have to go," I said again and again. "I have to go."

Kate's hands were tight at my shoulders, preventing me from getting up.

"Alex. Talk to me."

Her mother was off to the side, staring until I looked at her.

"I'm alright, Mrs. Winslow. Really. Give me a minute with Kate," and when Kate nodded to her, her mom left, though I don't think she went far and she had the phone with her. I finished the water and put the glass on the table delicately.

"I never told you about one of the stories I found."

"What do you mean?"

I caught my breath and said we should go to her room. "It's too much for your mother to know," I whispered. I had no idea the extent to which, if at all, Mrs. Winslow knew what was going on in my exploding life.

We were sitting on her bed with the door closed when I told her the rough outlines of *My Walls* and how *Jane Eyre* fit into it. I made a point of saying it was the one story that was password protected and one of the few that didn't have a paper copy in some form or another.

"Do you think your dad might have taken it out?"

"I can't say, but he said he went through the boxes before I showed up."

"Do you have a copy?"

"I never printed it out, but I got Jessie's Peter to put it on a flash drive. That's at my apartment. It was dystopian, the only one in everything she wrote."

There was nothing to be done about it then, so we both went back down. I told her mother that I was fine and asked her not to mention my little "episode" to anyone, especially my dad. Kate supported me on that, and she and I went back to the basement, and she picked a different, far lighter movie and it was still early when it ended, but we went to sleep together, and I nodded off shortly after she draped her arm around me as we (platonically) spooned, my mind horribly unsettled by the reminder of my mom's story.

Kate and I got up early, and I think we were both a little embarrassed about what happened. We had some cereal and as I went up to get my things Mrs. Winslow pulled me into her bedroom and sat me on the bed. She stood in front of me and bent down.

"You know I'm here for you, Alex," she said, and I nodded. "I don't know what's going on and I won't ask Kate anything and I promise I won't tell anyone what happened last night. You tell me when you're ready, okay?"

"I know, Mrs. Winslow."

She smiled and ran her fingers across my cheek. She'd been as much a substitute mother to me after my mom died as anyone, and this made me feel guilty about allowing her to drift away, especially since I'd moved to the city.

"Good. I told Kate I was going to speak to you, so feel free to report to her about it as you head home." She smiled and I stood.

It was a little awkward, but I reached and put my arms around her and said I was sorry not to have included her in what was going on and she pushed me away and said she understood and that I better hurry or I'd miss the next train.

We didn't miss the next train after saying our goodbyes. We took a cab from the Harlem station and hurried up the flights to my apartment. I booted up my laptop and found the flash drive in a bureau.

I opened the file with the password and showed the story to her. She sat on the sofa, spread across with the laptop on her thighs, and I made some coffee. She said nothing the whole time except "thank you" when I gave her a mug.

I pretended to be busy tidying but always with at least one eye on her. She closed the laptop.

"Shit." I moved near her, and she handed the computer to me.

"Tell me what you think, first," she said.

I put it on the coffee table and sat on the other side of the sofa after she swung her legs to the side.

"I tried to view it as just another story and didn't want to make anything special about it. But something triggered something when I saw the movie."

"So, you think the prisoner is your mom."

"How could it not be?"

She paused. "And the jailer? Could that be your dad?"

I hadn't articulated it but...

"Alex. Could the jailer be your father?"

"That's the problem. No way it's not."

"But I thought you said they'd worked it out?"

That's all I'd told her. That they'd "worked it out." I never said what the terms were, and now that I did, she was shocked. She began to say something, but I put up my hand and she stopped. I said Nancy hadn't disputed that there was an arrangement between my parents from that point on. I told her Nancy and I agreed to move on, that enough had been disturbed about things that happened long, long ago. That if he was allowed to...well, fuck whomever he wanted while she was allowed to fuck Nancy that would be a win-win. Which is what I assumed happened and Nancy told me to leave it there.

"She takes full responsibility for what she did, and nothing will bring my mom back."

"What's the date of the story, *My Walls*?" Kate asked.

I opened the directory. It was last saved on 05/15/08. A few months before she died.

"You have to speak to Nancy again. Has she read it?"

35.

Kate was right, of course, and after I told her Nancy hadn't seen it (nor had anyone else, not even Jessie), she left with a kiss and an "I'll leave you to it."

It was nearing noon on the morning of Thanksgiving Saturday and Nancy answered on the third ring.

"Can we talk?" I asked.

She said, "I need to, um, finish up with something but that won't take long. You want to come here? Or I can come down."

Neither place was quite neutral, but I was not in the mood to see whatever the something Nancy had to finish was so I asked her to come to me when she could.

It turned out to be soon, and my buzzer buzzed about twenty minutes after I called, twenty minutes largely spent pacing back and forth on my little floor. Nancy was in her normal perfect outfit of dark blue pants, cream blouse, black pumps, patterned jacket, and midnight blue Prada scarf, and no jewelry except a small gold heart necklace.

While waiting, I printed the 47 double-spaced pages. They sat on the coffee table when she came in. She took her jacket off and I hung it up for her as she went into the living room.

"I need you to read something she wrote. Just tell me what you think about it."

"I don't understand."

"It's just a story. Not too long." I walked around her and picked it up from the coffee table. I handed it to her.

"I sort of stumbled on this. I just want your opinion about it."

She looked from it to me and back.

"*My Walls*? I never heard of it, and I read most of her things."

"I'm going over to Columbus to pick up a few things. I'll have my phone. Call me when you're done."

With that, I took my keys and phone and left her. I did need things at the local Korean market and picked them up and then returned slowly back to my building, where I sat on the steps scrolling through my phone. I wasn't there long when it rang. Nancy was finished, and I was through the building's front door the moment she ended the call.

My apartment door was open, and I went in.

She was not in the living room, but I looked to my right and she was drinking a glass of water in the kitchen. She finished it and ran the tap for a refill and drank some more before turning to me.

"Tell me what you think," she said.

"I want your view."

She put the glass on the counter harder than I think she meant to and walked toward me. When she reached me her misted eyes locked on mine and her hands lightly touched my upper arms.

"I need to know what *you* think, why you wanted me to read it in the first place. Okay? If you go through this door, sweetie, there's no going back. So, tell me."

I couldn't understand why she was playing a game. For all she knew I just wanted her assessment of the literary value of the piece. I broke from her grip, of her hands and her eyes. The story was back on the coffee table, its left side now creased. I picked it up. I turned.

"Is it true? That's all I want to know. *Is it true?*" I shook the pages in her direction.

She surrendered her stiffness and her shoulders dropped. She stepped to the sofa and told me to sit.

"Perhaps it'd be better if you hadn't seen this."

"You said you didn't know about it."

"I didn't. This comes as a shock to me. But...but I know how hard it must have been for her to write it. Where'd you get it?"

I pointed to the computer from my grandparents' and how it was password protected and how I figured out the password—"It was my eighteenth birthday"—but then putting it out of my mind until the night before, when I was thrown back into it by a movie version of *Jane Eyre*.

"Cat's out of the bag, as they say," she said. "If you want the truth, you'll have to come to my place. There are some other things you need to see. Okay?"

Over the months, I'd become more comfortable in her apartment as I became more comfortable with Nancy herself. I knew she'd taken me as her charge because she felt my mom would've wanted it that way. Maggie was my stepmom and more an older friend like someone I worked with. Mrs. Winslow was Kate's mom.

Nancy was far different.

We were both quiet as we walked the nine or so blocks to 94th Street. It was cold on Thanksgiving but had warmed up. She wore her to-perfection jacket, and I threw a sweater on.

We went into her place. Again, I was sure and not sure about crossing its threshold. Apartment 3F was in its usual immaculate condition. It was too early for wine or harder stuff, so she went into the kitchen to put on water for tea. While we waited for the kettle, she pretended to tidy, and I studied photos arrayed in the hallway to her bedroom. I now knew some of their stories, who they were, where they were taken. She led an enviable life, at least as far as her gallery was proof.

The kettle whistled, and she poured the tea. She handed me two Limoges cups and saucers which I carried to the coffee table, and she was behind me with the teapot and her sterling milk-and-sugar set on a tray, which she put on the table. She poured the tea through a strainer and let me add my milk and sugar, and she did the same with hers. Though it was chilly outside, the radiator heat was intense, so the windows were opened a bit and we heard the street noise that had grown for both of us to be strangely comforting.

She waited a beat or two too long after we sat. I jumped in.

"Why'd you lie to me? About how well everyone got along like some Hallmark movie?"

She took a deliberate sip of her tea. "What would be the point? She was gone. He was here. You found me. You found Jessie and the others. What's the point of ruining that?"

I got up and put my cup and saucer on a table beside her sofa. Yes, we'd agreed to let things be. That was, though, before *My Walls* and *Jane Eyre*. I stopped my bit of pacing and not looking at her said, "I tried, I really tried, to let it go. But her story grew and grew and I can't anymore." I stopped across the coffee table from her and looked her way. "I won't blame you for not telling me before. But now just tell me. Was she a prisoner?"

She got up. She placed her right hand around my waist and pushed a little to get me to return to the sofa, and when I did, she joined me.

"Okay. To be clear. I've been completely honest about your mom and me except for this, all the *details* about what happened when he found out. Some I learned then. Others I discovered later. Yes, there was an 'arrangement.' She hated it. But it was all about you."

"What was it? Tell me."

She reached for her cup of now tepid tea and took a sip and again with deliberation returned it to her saucer.

"It was largely as I said. She could see me every week. He could see—"

"And fuck."

"Yes, and 'fuck' whomever he wanted. She had no problem with that. She didn't want anything physical to do with him at that point anyway. The problem was when he couldn't find anyone."

I stared at her.

"As a rule, she was with me on Friday afternoons. He stayed out late on many Thursday nights. I'm sure he slept with women other times, but he was primed for Thursday nights."

"Mom said he had meetings and other firm stuff and dinners on Thursdays. Sometimes I heard him come in after midnight. I didn't think anything of it."

"Which is what they both wanted. But sometimes he couldn't, well, he couldn't get laid and he'd be home early and wait until you went to bed, and he'd exercise his rights over her to use her body."

I was stunned. I had some vague memories of him coming home early when my mom and I were relaxing together as we usually did on Thursday nights. She even called it our "special time," when it was just the two of us girls and she'd have rented a movie and I'd make popcorn in the microwave and we'd sit on the couch together and how they were among my happiest moments growing up.

Now that Nancy mentioned it, there were times when my dad would surprise us. Sometimes he'd call from the car, but sometimes we'd hear the front door open, and he'd be standing in the hallway looking into the living room where the big TV was in those days—before Maggie remodeled—and my mom would turn white. He'd say the meeting ended early or something and head upstairs after telling us to "carry on." I remember him saying that. "Carry on." Sometimes he'd come in and go to the wet bar and get a Waterford glass and some Scotch and go to the kitchen for ice and carry it upstairs or to his den.

Sex? They were "old" to me and when I eventually learned the bits and pieces of "sex" I don't recall them doing it. I probably would have been shocked had I heard them and had I given not hearing it a moment's thought—which I didn't—I would probably have assumed that they were keeping things quiet so as not to corrupt or contaminate the kid. Plus, the master bedroom was down the hall from mine. My dad began to sleep in a separate bedroom when I was nine or ten. My mom said he snored, and I had no reason to doubt that.

So, other than my dad usually being out very late on Thursday nights and that I remembered hearing things fall upstairs sometimes when he came home early and that my mom sometimes looked particularly worn on some Friday mornings, I hadn't a clue about, well, anything along those lines with my folks.

"Your father can think he and she were Ozzie and Harriet till the cows come home"—she said that referred to the ideal husband and wife—"but she came to me and, more important, she stayed with me because she realized his whole relationship with her was based on some savior complex. That he—what did you say?—saved her from being on the wrong side of the tracks.

"That was the problem. She was always on the wrong side of his tracks. She told me he paraded her around the rich blondes in Bronxville—which is what she called them—like a trophy to his benevolence. She hated every minute of it. It wasn't so bad at first, when you all moved up there. But in time, she came to loathe it. Though I'm sure she did all she could to keep up appearances and especially for you to think everything was as it's supposed to be in an upscale Westchester suburb.

"Only you. You were the only thing that gave her life meaning outside of the few hours she and I got to spend together. Part of the deal was that you would never know about me or about...the affair."

She said she somewhat generally kept tabs on me. She didn't dare go to the funeral mass, but she went to a few of my field hockey games when she knew he was at work. She made sure to stand off to the side of the visitors' families.

"I knew you moved to the Upper West Side from your Facebook posts, but I didn't know more. I wondered whether we ran into each other now and then when you were going to work or shopping or going out to eat. Like we said when we went to the burger joint.

"I thought of contacting you after you turned eighteen—"

"You knew my birthday?"

"Of course, sweetie. October 1, 1994. Your mom always thought of October 1, 2012, as her 'Independence Day,' the day she no longer had to worry about him taking you from her."

"That was the password for the story. You mentioned it once to me."

"I don't remember that little detail."

"I did. But about me. She was worried?"

"Don't you understand? You were the key to everything. She knew your father had proof that she'd had an affair and while that wouldn't be a big deal about getting the divorce, it would be a very big deal about custody. She'd have been ostracized by your quaint little village—though she didn't care about that—but it was you that mattered. In the end, you were all that mattered to her."

"What would have happened if she left him, putting me out of the equation?"

Neither of us moved a muscle this whole time beyond, at some point, her placing her hands over mine.

"I don't know if it was a dream or something we thought might happen. I loved her. You'd turn eighteen, and she and your dad would agree to an uncontested divorce. She didn't care about the money—though I wouldn't have allowed her to walk away for anything less than what was fair—and she'd move in with me."

"You spoke of her moving in with you? It was that...serious."

"Don't you get it? My dream was to be with her, and as gay marriage was percolating, I wanted her to marry me. And she wanted to marry me."

"So, if she didn't die, we'd all be one happy family?"

"That was the plan."

"What about me?"

"Once you turned eighteen, the decision was yours, but she knew that even if you didn't accept her—"

"Of course I would have."

"She didn't know that. People can be...funny about it. But she was confident that you'd still love her."

She paused and a range of expressions crossed her face.

"Stay here," she said, and she got up and disappeared into her bedroom.

36.

Nancy returned from her bedroom with a medium-sized boot box. Ferragamo.

"You wanted it? Here it is. Your parents went through all the motions I was pretty sure because of you. And face it, your mother had plenty to be blamed for."

She looked down at the box. Almost speaking into it, she said, "What were his parents like?"

That came out of the blue, and it took me a moment to go from wondering what was in the Ferragamo box to what she'd asked. I told her they lived in a Philadelphia suburb, on the Main Line. Growing up, I saw them only a few times a year.

"I didn't know them that well," I said. "But I didn't like them. They were my grandparents and they doted on me, being their only grandchild. Unlike my mom's parents, they always gave me expensive gifts for Christmas and my birthday. My mom didn't like them. He was the prince. She called her father-in-law by his first name. But her mother-in-law was always Mrs. Locus. I think my mom believed they thought she was below their son. At least his mother did. His father was kind of distant from us when he visited. He often went out to play golf with my dad, whose game was tennis. Of course, that left me and my mom stuck with his mother. Which was pretty awkward, and his mother pretended to have things in the house that needed taking care of.

"But I did hear the two of them, my grandparents, snipe at each other all the time. She would have been a very difficult woman to live with. I didn't even see them that often after my mom died. I saw her parents more than them."

As a kid, I spent parts of each summer in Paterson with the Millers. But I didn't give a lot of thought to my father's parents. I told Nancy they were always distant. I didn't think that he was thrilled when they came, and he always seemed relieved when they were gone.

Nancy asked if they ever were affectionate.

"Definitely not my father's father. I don't remember him that much."

"Tell me, what did your father call them?"

"It was always 'mother' and 'father.' I guess I kind of erased them from my memory. But it was a pretty fucked up relationship. Doting mother. Distant father."

"And he comes to New York to practice law."

I never gave this much thought either.

Nancy continued, "And they resented him marrying below him."

"Perhaps that's why he married my mom. The poor girl from the upstate mill town. But, you know, she never came across, as best as I can remember, like that. She always fit in with the women who'd been in Bronxville for generations."

"Perhaps he had this whole Professor Henry Higgins thing going on."

I didn't get the reference.

"You know. *My Fair Lady*. Taking the lower-class girl and turning her into a lady."

"Audrey Hepburn?"

"Yes, Audrey Hepburn."

We were quiet briefly, and I was mostly thinking about the boot box on her lap.

"Why did she stay with him?" I asked.

"Don't you understand?"

"Understand what?"

"She couldn't leave him because she couldn't leave you. She knew that if she did anything, she'd lose you. He would say she was in a gay, adulterous relationship. That she was an unfit mother. With his money and resources, she knew she'd lose custody. She'd be lucky to see you on your birthday. You were everything to her. Everything."

"What about you?"

"Okay. I became important to her. But nothing compared to you."

"What if she promised to leave you? Would she then be able to keep me if they split up?"

"No. It didn't matter."

Nancy stood and began. "You don't understand. He was glad she was sleeping with me. It was his leverage."

She sat back down and turned to me, her hands reaching for mine and her voice losing some of its edge.

"He used it to get what he wanted. You and your mother gave him respectability. I don't know when, but he probably agreed at some point with his parents that he married down. But she could pass and so with his colleagues and people in town he could pretend to be the sweet professional he portrayed himself as.

"But it also meant that he could sleep with whomever he wanted to. She knew about it. Sometimes we'd laugh. She was happy he didn't make 'demands' on her more often than he did."

"What do you mean, 'demands'?"

She paused.

"As I said, he forced himself on her sometimes, though he wouldn't see it that way. She knew there was nothing she could do and she let him. Sometimes, she told me, he was gentle with her. Usually when he was drunk. We laughed, as far as you can laugh about such things, that those times he usually fell asleep as soon as he started so he'd be snoring with his, um, 'equipment' dangling harmlessly against his fat stomach.

"But often it was a rage, um, fuck. If he struck out with another woman. She hated the nights when he got home early. Because she knew what was likely to happen. He had expectations of sex and they hadn't been realized. So, he took it from her. He was always careful not to leave any marks.

"She always called me when it was over. She knew I didn't care what time it was. Usually, she sounded like she was in a bathroom; I could hear an echo. I was here for her. That's what mattered more than anything. She wouldn't say much. Just that he did it again and then I let her cry and I told her I loved her and she told me she loved me and she hung up. I wouldn't bother trying to go back to sleep. I did some of my best writing on those nights, recovering from her calls at one or two in the morning.

"I'd put some coffee on and sit at my desk and," she nodded at what was in her lap, "write."

She held up the box and passed it to me.

"I put them on a shelf in my closet. I look at this almost every day. Some of the things I wrote on those dark mornings I used. Put some of them in stories I published. Built stories around others. And some were too personal to share."

She looked down.

"Until now. I haven't read these often since she died. They're something tangible that I still have from her. Horrible as they are. She was so vulnerable, and I was so helpless to do anything about it."

I didn't know what to say. I'd read all of Nancy's works I could find, and I thought I saw (or perhaps imagined seeing) traces of my mom in lots of it, and her presence haunted every page of *Scream*. There was nothing obvious, but after a while and knowing of their relationship I picked up the threads. This stack, though—these stories were *all* about my mom.

As I shifted through them, reading words here and there as I tried to get a sense of what was there, she went back into her bedroom and after a little time, she was again beside me.

"And then there are these. The last, most treasured *tangible* things I have from her."

They were in various colors of stationery and tied in a red ribbon like in some Regency novel and she handled my mom's letters as if they were made of the finest crystal. She passed them to me with the caveat that there were no copies, and I told her I would make some and "treat them with the care they deserve."

"She swore to me that she burnt mine and since they haven't appeared I believe she did. I, of course, kept all of hers."

With that, she rose. She offered to walk me home, but I told her the alone time would do me good. I put the Ferragamo box and the letters into a purplish Bergdorf's bag she retrieved from under her sink and walked through the still air home.

With nowhere else to put them, I plopped the boot box on the top box from Paterson and the letters, being too precious, I put in the bottom drawer of the dresser in my bedroom but not until I gave them a good sniffing and ran my fingers along their edges. My head wasn't in a place that allowed me to delve into this latest group, so I left them there. I called Kate to report that I'd met and spoken to Nancy but wasn't ready to talk about it.

"That bad?"

"Kate. I just can't say anything about it, okay?"

"Love you," she said. "I'll have my phone with me. Okay?"

I thanked her and hung up and spent the rest of the day wasting my time online and was too knackered to even try to go for a run. I found something in my freezer to microwave and ate that with some water and watched a mindless RomCom before turning in.

I didn't sleep well. I stared at the ceiling for a while and debated simply getting up, but I didn't know what I would do if I did so I just lay there staring at the ceiling and listening to the buses going up and down Central Park West.

It was everything. I sometimes regretted going to that reading at Barnes & Noble. This was one of them. I was happy. Blissfully ignorant of...everything. Now nothing was simple. I put off going through these landmines.

I told Nancy I "needed" to know, and in the end, I still thought I did. But I was no longer so sure.

37.

I kept putting off reading the papers and the letters, but I couldn't do that forever.

I started with the Ferragamo box. The papers were folded so they'd fit. Some were hand-written in Nancy's neat penmanship with compact letters but end-of-word flourishes on quality stationery with a tint of purple. Especially her "g"s and "y"s, which displayed big loops. The words ran into one another and "t"s were sometimes left uncrossed and "i"s sometimes sat undotted. The occasional "l" got crossed. She used a pen on lined paper, much like my mom's legal pads, and most of the pages had edits in the narrow margins. She hand-printed her corrections. Tiny corrections wherever they fit with lines and arrows pointing to where they went. They all had dates.

Nancy, of course, was a polished, professional author. Her skill with a pen was evident from the first words. The thoughts flowed freely. I plopped on the floor and read bits and pieces almost randomly. I knew these snapshots would require closer examination, but I couldn't resist the pull of my mom's letters.

Those I then took to a chair by the window, which I'd again turned to look out as I had with the Brontë a lifetime ago. I put them on the table beside it and read the passion my mother exposed to her lover. I wanted to feel, touch, and even smell the originals. And within two or three of them, there was no doubt that Nancy was the love of her life.

If I thought my mom's stories were a look into her, nothing prepared me for her letters to Nancy. I understood why Nancy hesitated in showing them to me. They were in chronological order, and that was how I read them.

My mom sometimes wrote little ditties, doggerel really.

When the sun dances in each of your eyes
And in them, you answer all of my whys
And in them, I hear each of your sighs
When you've allowed me between the flesh of your
    thighs.

She often wrote of how she hated herself, but the source of that hatred varied. At times, it was because she could not keep away from Nancy. At others, that she wanted Nancy to keep away from her. This passion and even obsession dripped from each page and in the sometimes-splattered ink—at times, my mom used a fountain pen, perhaps for its dramatic effect.

They alternated between the happy and the miserable and, as with her stories, there were stretches dominated by the rawness of one or the other of those emotions.

After a time, though, they melded together. The one-sided expressions of love. Desires and lust. Hopes and fears. And always the dreaded reality of the cruelty of each too brief rendezvous.

It was one thread that I was obsessed with, but I only realized it after my read-through. I did that in a bit over two hours, and by the time I was done I was well into a second glass of Pinot Noir.

It was me. The thing next to love was her daughter. I was stunned by the frequency of the references. More than—far more than—the implications in the stories were the reality of what she said about the first true and sustained love of her life.

Nancy had told me about this, but it wasn't quite real until I saw it in my mom's hand. And I saw her, Nancy, in a strange light. She was the complete friend to my mom. The woman who received her love and lust, of course, but also her thoughts and dreams and because those dreams were limited by the real world—and how things would be different today!—they were her thoughts and dreams about me. Unfiltered. Unbound.

She used a variety of names to describe me. "My Baby." "My Sweetie." "My Alex." Nearly always "my" (never "our") and more and more the last of those as I grew. Nancy told me of going to some of my games after my mom was gone, but it was clear that when she was alive my mom was reporting on every aspect of my life almost in real-time.

It was embarrassing to think of her going on about me while they laid naked under the sheets of Nancy's bed after a session in the time before she had to get up and get dressed and get a cab to the station to stand—all of the seats would have been taken at Grand Central—on a crowded Friday train that took her home to her...prison. Her "walls."

I cannot say when she wrote her letters. Perhaps after dinner was made and she was waiting for my father to get home from work while I was at practice or up in my room. Never did I see a reference to his knowing about her letters. That was perhaps part of the bargain about her continuing a relationship with Nancy. Perhaps it would have been a comfort to him that the relationship was more than physical. Probably not. I don't know what she could have had left after what she wrote to Nancy. If he did know about these letters, it would have driven the wedge between them even deeper.

I won't get into the particulars of those love letters. Some were almost juvenile. Most unveiled a deep, emotional attachment between the women. At times, my mom bristled at the reality that Nancy could not limit herself to just three or four hours of passion a week, and much as my mom said she understood Nancy being with other women, she feared taking a back seat. Always, always my mom feared that Nancy would tire of her, would tire of the transient nature of what they did and had. I could only assume that Nancy frequently promised my mom that she would never leave, as there were the frequent apologies from my mom for being both so possessive and so apologetic for having doubted her place with Nancy.

My God, Nancy loved her. The sentiments she expressed to me that first day I was in her apartment when she spoke of being with my mom in the hospital was proven by these letters. How she tolerated what my mom did or could not do. It broke my heart. Two people deeply in love yet separated.

I was such a fool. It took the proof of these letters to impress upon me that suffering. How Nancy felt on that August afternoon when suddenly my mom shook and perhaps gasped and collapsed on top of her, never to be alive again. Nancy's world vaporized in that one, sweaty moment.

* * * *

IT WAS LATE. NEARLY ELEVEN. But I couldn't wait and walked to Nancy's. I paced back-and-forth in front of her building I can't say how many times before pulling out my phone and calling her. She answered on the fourth ring, asking if everything was alright. Of course, it wasn't, I told her. "I'm downstairs. Let me up."

In the apartment, I didn't know what to say or what to do. I asked, "Why did you put up with so much for so little?" I gently passed the letters to her, wrapped in their ribbon.

We were standing, but she had me sit on the sofa. She'd thrown a robe over her nightgown.

"I told myself to end it countless times. I'd be in some bar on Saturday night, thinking about her in her fancy house with that...husband of hers. Allowing her a few hours a week to do something that she needed to do. I know it was complicated, but at times I thought it the simplest thing in the world. Let me go. Keep you in her life. But she wouldn't do it, and I'd be in a bar the next day, sometimes even hours after she left, and I needed to get laid, and I'd find someone. Never someone who could remind me of your mom. Just a woman who I could take care of and who could take care of me. At her place. Sometimes in the bathroom for a quickie.

"The point was the emptiness of it. I needed to feel someone in me, and I hated myself for it and I sometimes hated your mother because she was not the one in me except for those hours on Fridays.

"She was always telling me how sorry she was for what she was doing to me, but it was me doing it to myself. I could not *not* be with her. I could not *not* love her."

I conjured up an image of the two of them, my mom and Nancy, on this sofa talking yet again of the mess they found themselves in. My horribly damaged mother being loved and believing herself greedy for taking it from a wonderful woman who loved her.

"She told me again and again—and you saw it in the letters"—to which I nodded—"that I needed to leave her. I needed my own life. But. I. Couldn't."

Nancy couldn't continue. She was heaving and leaned in so I could hold her. For a moment I felt she might mistake me for my dead mother, but the thought must have occurred to her because she pushed herself away and apologized, wiping her nose with the back of her hand.

"I'm sorry, sweetie," she said. "I'm still feeling the effects of seeing and holding her letters again."

38.

It was well past midnight when I staggered home. Nancy'd thrown something on and half carried me down Central Park West to the steps to my building and I declined her offer to see that I got inside safely. I did, on my own, and again had my clothes on when I fell asleep. It was late on Sunday morning when my phone rang. Jessie, checking in. I last spoke to her on Wednesday night.

"Hey, sis." I didn't feel like being flippant, but it's what I always said when she called.

"Are you okay? You owe me a call."

"Sorry. A lot of shit came down—"

"About Mom?"

"About Mom. And my dad."

I looked at my watch. It was after one.

"Look. Can we do it face-to-face? It's really...bad. About my father. So not directly to do with you. I could use talking to you about it though. Are you home?"

"Yeah. Pete's out playing basketball and won't be back for hours. Do you want me to come over? I can just get an Uber."

"I've been inside...I'll tell you when I see you. But I have to get out. Can we meet in front of the Met at twoish?"

"I'll see you on the middle steps then."

"Okay."

"Alex?"

"Yes."

"You know I'm always there for you, don't you?"

"I do. I don't know what I would do without you."

"See you at two."

We didn't go in the museum. Instead, we strolled down Madison. As we maneuvered through the late-autumn strollers—it was another beautiful day—I brought Jessie up to date on these latest developments. I told her about *My Walls* and the "arrangement" and that maybe what my dad did wasn't so bad since they had a deal and my mom got what she wanted out of it.

"That's bullshit." I don't know that I'd ever seen her so angry so quickly. "About her agreeing. He held a gun to her head. He was holding her hostage. Of course, she'd 'agree' to whatever he wanted. That did not make it a deal. It did not make it consensual. It was like a guy who pulled a woman into an alley, pulled a gun out, and said he wouldn't shoot her if she let him fuck her. And doing it again and again. Now, how is that not rape?"

That word struck as no word struck me in my life.

She calmed and ran her fingers down my cheek. "I didn't mean to be so...brutal, Alex, but that how I see it." She smiled.

"I know. It's just spinning so out of control."

We'd taken only a few steps when she said, "You know, it used to be that a husband couldn't 'rape' his wife as far as the law was concerned."

I stopped and glared at her.

"Really. Not so long ago. Thank God that's changed," she said as she started up again and I followed, saying, "Thank God."

I think we both regretted what should have been a nice chat and walk took this dark if inevitable turn, and before I knew it, she hailed a cab and brought me to my place. She asked whether she should come up. While I gave it a moment's thought, this was not her battle, so I thanked her, as I'd thanked Nancy for her similar offer very early that morning, and she waited till I was through the door before the taxi headed west to take her back to Brooklyn.

39.

I entered a going-through-the-motions phase. There was the period after that mid-September Thursday reading with Karen Adams that ended when I had my long chat with my dad and followed it with Nancy acknowledging her responsibility and advising me that it was time for everyone to move on. I accepted the reality of what my mom did. I didn't fully understand it, but I accepted it.

Then came *My Walls* and the tsunami-like impact of watching *Jane Eyre* with Kate right after Thanksgiving and then Nancy warning me about crossing this Rubicon and at my insistence showing me what she showed me, and I was even deeper into the quicksand that my family's history had become (or perhaps always was).

Into this insanity came a call from Maggie. It was Monday afternoon. My dad, she said, was heading out to Chicago for a case and wasn't coming back until Thursday. Might I want to come up for dinner, say, Wednesday night? Some TimTim time. I could sleep in my old room.

I was in no mood to go anywhere near that house and that town, but if he wasn't there perhaps it made sense to take advantage of her reaching out to me. So, I made it a date and got back to work.

As I walked home, a name I hadn't thought of in dog's years popped into my brain. Agnes Hall. She was my dad's secretary and had been forever. I assumed she still was, though she must be getting on in years. She always had a lollipop for me on the visits my mom and I made to him every once in a while. After my mom passed, I don't think I went to the office more than once or twice, but even then, she reached into a drawer and pulled out a lollipop. Always red or orange. Never yellow or green. Even when I was way too old and rolled my eyes when she did.

Most of the lawyers did their own typing by that time but she stayed on as something of a mother hen for the associates and was the go-to person for using Word.

Agnes Hall would be more likely than anyone to know the truth about my dad, so at lunch on Tuesday, I went to his office. They let me in through security, and Agnes was waiting in the firm's ornate, well-furnished reception area off the elevators.

"I'm sorry you came, dear. He's not here."

She reached and hugged me, and when she pulled away there was an orange lollipop in her fingers for me to take. Which, of course, I did.

I pretended I didn't know about my dad and said how nice it was to see her anyway.

"It's lunchtime, Agnes," I said. "Can I take you?"

It was a first, but she smiled and said she just needed to get her bag and, in a moment, we were taking the elevator down. There was a small restaurant mid-block between Fifth and Madison a few blocks south of my dad's office. It had been there for decades probably, and he took my mom and me there sometimes. It was truly old school, and I imagined the average age of its patrons was "deceased." Down three or four steps to a black door festooned with a window and Zagat's decals. The restaurant itself was on the old-school dark side with a few large tables but mostly small, rectangular ones along the wall to the left, lined up against a long maroon leather bench that stretched the length of the wall itself. Beyond that, the décor consisted of two rows of what looked to be paintings of the French countryside and a couple of Paris.

I regretted picking it when we stepped in since it was such a fossil, but there we were, led by a maître d' in a tuxedo with a pair of large, leatherbound menus under his arm to one of those tables. I don't know whether it was too early or that this was the normal lunch crowd but fewer than half the tables were occupied so Agnes and I were seated with no one on either side of us.

A busboy brought us bread and water as we looked at the menus before we were interrupted by a waiter, also in a tux. We declined wine, and he left us and, in the end, we each ordered a simple chicken with peas and potatoes dish.

Alone again, I took some of the bread—I can still almost taste the baguette's freshness—and Agnes asked how I was. We'd not spoken a serious word until that moment. Not in the elevator. Not on the short walk to the bistro. Not after we'd decided on our lunch.

I hadn't seen her in, oh, seven or eight years. I felt like something of a schmuck.

"I confess that I know he's in Chicago. Maggie told me. It's you I wanted to see."

She grabbed the baguette and ripped off her own bit just as our salads arrived. We ignored them and we each pushed our plate a bit to the side.

"You've known my dad as long as just about anyone. I've been looking into some things my mom wrote."

"He mentioned something like that."

I looked up. "What did he say?"

"It was just in passing. Only that you took a sudden interest in your mother when you found out she'd written things. Are you thinking of becoming a writer?"

"Far from it. I wanted to see if I could learn something about her."

She reached over with her fork and began on her salad, so I did the same. The chomping and the taste and the simple act of doing something lightened the mood.

"And have you?"

I chewed a bit more and took some water and dabbed my lips with my napkin.

"I learned that she was a lot more complicated than I always thought."

"When you become an adult, you find that out about your parents. It can be quite a shock. Especially about how complicated it is."

"Which is why I wanted to kind of ambush you. About her. And about my father."

She concentrated on her salad, as did I, and our plates were quickly clean and our chickens with peas and potatoes were quickly in their place but ignored.

"He's been very good to me. And I guess things that go on in the office are best kept secret."

"Agnes. I am not asking you to betray him. I just need to know. From what my mom wrote, issues have come up about their relationship."

The restaurant was, I realized, perfectly apt for this John le Carréish conversation.

"There's not a lot to say," was how she began. "Other lawyers bitched about their wives or husbands now and then. They'd slam the phone down and say—not thinking anyone would hear—'stupid bitch' or even...," she leaned forward and I did too, "'fucking asshole.' Things like that. They'd take a minute to recover from whatever happened in the call and be back to business." She sat back.

"Your father was never like that. I never heard him say a bad word about your mother. Or you for that matter."

Her attention turned to her chicken with peas and potatoes, so I did the same. It was a relief, what she said. He wasn't like other lawyers in the office. He was kind to her.

"Did things change in how he treated her?" I asked.

"Like when?"

I sucked in. "From my mom's stories, it seemed that something might have happened between them. I don't think I was even ten."

"It's not for me to say, Alex, but there did come a time when she wasn't calling as often as she had before. I didn't notice anything when they talked, not that I often heard what they said to each other. But, no, I don't think other than that that there was a difference."

Somehow our plates were nearly cleared except for remaining bones and some skin, and the waiter swooped them away. He was back as the busboy cleaned the table—using whatever they call the blade that clears the crumbs from the tablecloth—handing us the dessert menus. Agnes and I, though, said just coffee.

The place was no more crowded than when we arrived, and we still had no close neighbors at the tables along our wall. Our conversation fell into simpler things, and I asked about her and her background, none of which I'd bothered to ask before, though in fairness to me I don't know that I'd seen her more than a few times even since I was a teenager. She'd been at the wake and funeral mass for my mom, but my dad never asked me to come see him in his office anymore. She was a widow. Her husband was a pharmacist who worked in Queens, not far from where she still lived. He'd died quite suddenly and, she said, my dad was very supportive.

"But it was a long time ago, and I've settled into the life of a relatively content, childless widow living in Forest Hills." She smiled and I did believe she was content.

We finished our coffees, and I paid the bill—over her objection—and we thanked the maître d' and busboy as we left and went up the steps to 52nd Street. As we approached her office, she turned to thank me for lunch, making me promise not to be so scarce in the future. I asked that she not mention our little rendezvous to him, and she smiled and nodded.

As she was about to turn through the revolving doors, she stopped and moved off to the side, out of the flow of pedestrian traffic.

"Brenda Jackson. That's all I can tell you. She may talk to you." She paused and put her hand on my upper arm. "Tell her that I suggested you call. I can't say she'll talk to you, but that's all I can do.

"Alex. He's a good man. He went through some tough times with your mother. Please don't blame him."

She went, carrying with her something about my mom she would not reveal.

40.

The trip to Bronxville the next night, strangely, helped clear my head. My dad wouldn't be there, so it was like a return to an earlier age. As the crowded commuter train headed from Grand Central, I was glad not to have to do *that* twice a day. There were pockets of conversation here and there, but for the most part, people were sitting and standing in their own little worlds, silent and reading the *Times* or the *Journal* or the *Post* (or in the case of one man *The Good Earth*) or reading nothing, interrupted only when the conductor came through and they flashed the monthly passes on their phones (or in the case of us non-regulars, handed her our tickets) and the train was an express until Fleetwood, the stop before Bronxville, so I was in town in about twenty-five minutes.

I didn't recognize anyone and was glad of that as I walked up the hill and into the kitchen where Maggie stood at a board chopping onions for a pasta sauce on the counter.

She sent me to TimTim's room, where he was playing a computer game with headphones on. He took them off when he saw me and ordered me to sit beside him as he resumed, his headphones back in place, his game of who-knows-what and spouting colors until he reached a resolution or destination or something, at which point he removed his headphones, told me he won again, and said I had to help his mommy make dinner.

The sauce was already simmering when I returned to the kitchen and the kitchen smelled great. She'd opened a (very good) bottle of Merlot and already had her glass and filled mine when I came in. We simply sat on either side of the kitchen's island as we drank, and she opened the fridge—did I mention it was Sub-Zero?—for some cheese and olives as we waited for the water to boil.

The night went much like this. The conversation was at times slow with bits of local gossip (that I cared little about) and background (I found some things she told me about herself interesting) and generic things women talk about. She put some of the linguini aside and put butter on it for TimTim while I put the rest in the pot with the sauce.

It was so comfortable that we didn't bother to go to the formal dining table but ate at the island, with TimTim beside me and the wine between Maggie and me. TimTim asked to be excused, and she gave him permission and promised that I'd tuck him in when it was time.

With him gone and us having tidied the kitchen, I told Maggie I wanted to collect some old photos of my mom without explaining why, which she said was fine, and I found them in the cabinet below one of the bookcases in my father's den. They were haphazardly thrown in a shoebox, as were those ones in Paterson, and I selected an assortment of my mom at various times and with varying folks so I could send them to Dot (which I did at lunch the next day).

That done, and my collection in my bag, I joined Maggie in the living room where she'd brought our glasses, and we sat on either end of the couch, the one by the coffee table that I first saw the boxes on. Though she tried to probe me, I avoided it and since I was keeping better track of my alcohol intake than she was of hers, I did get her to admit that things were a little more flirty between them when she was an associate at his firm than anyone had let on—"though no more than that"—though otherwise we only talked more about the generic.

She suggested we watch a movie together. So, after I came down from fulfilling my pleasant commitment to put TimTim to bed, with a story, I went to the snug at the end of the hall where the large TV was and it brought back memories of my Thursday nights with my mom and we sat beside each other on the loveseat with our legs on the ottoman watching *Notting Hill* and having a great time.

As the credits began, I went to my room and she went to theirs and after a quick just-saying-goodnight/having-a-good-time call to Kate and a trip to the bathroom, I fell quickly asleep in my old bed.

And the last thing I remember was wondering who was Brenda Jackson? And how I was supposed to find out?

41.

It didn't take long for me to track Brenda Jackson down. She was a senior vice president in the legal department at a midtown bank (not mine). Her photo was right there on the bank's website. Attractive, particularly with how her reddish hair framed her round face. Some more searching and I discovered she was married and living in Manhattan with two kids. A boy and a girl.

That was the easy part. Do I ambush her the way I did with Jessie? She didn't work far from me, but it was best to ask to meet her.

Late Thursday morning, I called the bank's legal department and was sent to voicemail. I didn't leave a message. I mulled it over that night and decided to try again on Friday. I was again sent to voicemail. This time I left a message.

"Hello. Ms. Jackson. My name was Alexandra Locus. I believe you know, or knew, my father, Steven Locus. I, um, I would like to meet with you if possible. I work in midtown."

I left my number and hung up. I had no idea if she'd return the call and I jumped each time my phone rang, but it was never her.

For the rest of Friday and into Saturday morning, I puttered around my apartment. The phone rang but it was only Nancy, touching base. I said nothing about my meeting or conversation with Agnes Hall or my efforts to contact Brenda Jackson. Not yet. I simply said I was working through things—that was my go-to phrase in this period, "working through things"—and that maybe we could go for a walk on Sunday. I hadn't told anyone else either.

About half an hour later, the phone rang again.

"Hello?"

"This is Brenda Jackson. What can I do for you?"

A voice to the picture.

"I am—"

"Yes, you said. What do you want?"

It was a cold, cold voice. Before I could respond, she said, "It was long ago when I knew your father. I really don't have anything to say about it. It was a long time ago."

She paused. Before I could tell her what I wanted, she continued, "Why do you care?"

"My mom died some years ago."

"Yes, I heard. I am sorry."

"And I'm trying to understand her. I've learned a huge number of things about her recently, and I was trying to get a complete picture."

"What does that have to do with your father? And me?"

I wait a moment.

"Ms. Jackson. It's so much more complicated than I thought. Can I just meet you? I am across the park if you're still on the East Side."

I waited, hoping she'd agree to it.

"Does he know? How did you get my name?"

I explained about Agnes. I ignored her first question.

"Well, if Agnes trusted you, I guess I should too."

So, we arranged to meet. It was a nice day. We picked a spot on a wall behind the Met. I'd be wearing a Mets cap.

I was there early. The runners and cyclists on the Park Drive were behind me and the back of the museum with its big, glassy Egyptian wing in front. I studied each person who approached but there wasn't a lone woman for a while. Till there was. I recognized her from the picture. Not quite as made up as in the bank's portrait, but still attractive even from a distance. And the rusty hair.

I stood and tried to smile, but her expression was frozen.

We sat on the concrete top of the stone wall lining the path.

"Ask away."

No formalities after the simplest of greetings. I called her "Ms. Jackson," and she never asked me to do otherwise.

42.

"**I** don't know."

I didn't know if I'd see Brenda Jackson again so that's what I told Nancy when I plopped on her sofa while she opened a bottle of Merlot—yeah, this adventure was wreaking havoc on my liver and I wondered if I were becoming a cliché—and when she sat with me and I'd taken a long sip—it was again early but this time I more than earned it—I gave my report.

I went to 94th Street directly from my walk and was relieved that Nancy was home. I gave her the quick version about how I came to learn of Brenda Jackson and to meet her.

Ms. Jackson and I got up and walked shortly after we sat, ignoring what was going on around us. She told me of being attracted to my father from almost the first moment they met at the firm. They'd flirt a little, then they flirted a little more when they met in the elevator—they were associates in different departments on different floors—but things changed when they happened to see each other at the same lunch spot.

It was crowded. They were next to one another on line at the soup place, so they sat next to one another. She knew his name. He didn't know hers.

"She said they started to have lunch there together occasionally. They felt comfortable with each other, as I suppose associates at the same level of dog-eat-dog big law firms often do. She wasn't married but knew that he was. He said he was having issues with his wife. Post-partum issues, so it'd have been shortly after I was born. She'd just broken up with a fiancé she knew from college and was glad my dad was there to give her a shoulder to cry on.

"She said it all began innocently enough. She swore she didn't know quite how it happened, but they were checking into a midtown hotel using cash he got from an ATM and calling the office—separately—to say something personal had come up they had to see to and he was calling my mom to say something'd come up at the office and he'd be working late at a client's.

"She said she didn't have anyone to call. She realized it was a mistake on the elevator going to the room that first time and she told herself it had to stop but it continued every few weeks for a couple of months before she ended it. By then, she was falling apart and hiding it at the firm and began trying to find a bank job somewhere and she took the first one she could and was gone and, she said, she never saw him again.

"She said, 'I won't say a word against him. It was as much my fault as his. Maybe more. I was in a bad place and those afternoons were maybe the only good thing I had.'"

Nancy was quiet and attentive through all this, occasionally sipping her wine while I kept mine firmly in my lap, now and then running my fingers along its bulb.

"She said she'd found herself when she left the firm, which she called a 'toxic environment.' She liked her new job and her bank and worked her way up, found the right man for herself, and now has two kids and she's quite happy.

"'I hope I have been of help. You seem nice enough,' she said when she got up to leave. 'I am sorry if I hurt your mother. And you. And I'm sorry she's gone with you so young.' She smiled. With that, she turned and headed out of the park and I came straight here.

"So, he cheated on her too."

Now I took a big slug of the wine, and she waited.

"Yes," I said as I twirled the glass's stem lazily back and forth.

She continued. "In some ways, does it matter? I don't think she knew. I'm pretty sure she didn't. Her being with me was on her. And on me. That he cheated, too, doesn't change that. Which is what I told you those months ago."

"You're right. Except for the hypocrisy and what he did to her after he found out about the two of you."

"Which, sweetie, changes everything, doesn't it?"

Yes, it did.

43.

One of the last people I expected called about an hour after I was home from Nancy's. Agnes Hall.

"I just got a call from Brenda. She wasn't happy I gave you her name but, in the end, she said she hoped it would give you some closure."

"It was a bit of a shock. Her story about my father."

"I know it's late," Agnes said. It was a little after four and starting to get dark. "But can we meet? I think that there's more you should hear now that, well, now that you know about Brenda."

It had turned rainy, so I grabbed a cab to Queens and when I got to the Forest Hills coffee shop she suggested—it looked like the one in *Seinfeld*—she was sitting alone in a booth with half a cup of coffee and lipstick on the cup. I asked for the same when the waitress came over and I'd hung my raincoat on a hook by the door.

"You said you wanted the truth, so I have to tell you."

She paused as the waitress put my cup and saucer down and poured the coffee and dropped a handful of portable creamers on the Formica table.

"You have a brother."

I stared across at her.

"No one is supposed to know. But I handled the payments. It happened some years after Brenda Jackson was gone so it isn't hers."

She stood and put a ten on the table before putting her raincoat on. She sighed and reached into her pocket, removing a slip of paper and handing it to me. As I looked at the handwriting, she was already through the door.

"Andrew Grayson. 53 Jackson Avenue, Newton, Mass."

I stared at it. A name and an address.

I pulled out my phone and searched as my coffee sat untouched. Born in August 1997. Three years younger than me. Probably still in college. If he was in Newton, it was probably BC. I couldn't get much info on my phone, so I dropped a five on the table and rushed out to get a cab home. Less than an hour after Agnes handed me the name, I knew a fair amount about Andrew Grayson. Most particularly that he was, yes, three years younger than me. And at Boston College.

On Facebook, he was handsome with short hair. He gave Philadelphia as his hometown, and some sleuthing led me to Diane Grayson. She gave *her* hometown as a town on the Main Line, which I checked and saw was next to where my father grew up. Exactly my father's age. Curiouser and curiouser.

It didn't take a Sherlock to figure out. And Nancy, who I went straight to when I recovered, agreed. This time, I wanted to go through the next step with her, unlike with Brenda Jackson. We agreed to wait before I did anything.

Even though I wasn't going to contact her right away, I continued searching. It wasn't hard to locate Diane Grayson online, particularly for someone of my suddenly vast investigating experience! There were seven or eight, but my screening found the one who had to be her. My father's age. Living in Philadelphia. A search for photos revealed someone pushing middle age with a round face and a nice nose and somewhat dreamy eyes and the hint of a smile. Wrinkles likely from too much sitting in the sun. Auburn hair, but definitely and very professionally treated.

I wasn't ready to do anything with this information, but I stored it. My intent was not to confront my father with his past. It was simply to get whatever information I could to know my father, warts and all. Like I did with my mom.

Another reason to wait was that my dad's folks were visiting New York for a few days and while it was a long shot, I might get some useful information about this Diane Grayson from them if, as I suspected, my dad knew her when they were both in high school.

44.

"I never knew why he did it."

"Nonsense, Lydie. You know exactly why."

Grandmother Locus looked at her husband and sighed.

"Alright, then. I knew why. I just never understood it."

It was quite unusual, but when my dad during one of our brief I'm-doing-fine/still-looking conversations mentioned that his folks were coming to New York, I called Grandmother Locus and asked if they could stop by to see me on the way to Bronxville. They left home early and reached the city before eleven on Saturday and found a parking space not far from my apartment.

I tidied as well as I could for this unprecedented get-together. The boxes were still along the living room wall, but the old computer sat on the floor of my living room closet. The Ferragamo box was under my bed and my copies of the letters to Nancy—I'd delicately scanned and printed them and sent them to the cloud—were safely covered in the bottom drawer of my dresser.

My grandmother was more bundled up than was my grandfather and though it was not cold they were happy with the fresh coffee I made. I got bagels and lox and cream cheese from the Korean market on Columbus.

We had the mugs (none of which matched) and plates (which did) balanced on our respective laps on the sofa (them) and an armchair (me) in my living room. I told them in the broadest strokes that I was exploring my mom's background. I pointed to the boxes as I explained about the discovery of her stories and that I'd sat with the Millers—I told them no more than that about what I learned in Paterson—and thought it would be a good idea to sit down with them and find out more about my parents, something I'd never really spoken to them about. I'd asked how my parents got together, beyond the family lore aspect I'd so often heard.

"I have to go back," Grandmother Locus began. My grandfather nodded, and slipped back deeper into the sofa, balancing his plate on his lap with his mug on the side table. I sat with my coffee mug wrapped in my hands.

"Your father was not the easiest of children. You know how you turned after your mother died"—apparently news of my breakdown reached Philadelphia—"well, your father was like that in high school. He was a good athlete," and my grandfather chimed in, "that's for sure," and my grandmother ignored him. "Very good-looking, smart, charismatic. He never, all through high school, never had trouble getting a date. He had a few steady girlfriends in high school, but nothing came of any of them."

I couldn't gauge the extent to which my grandmother disapproved (or my grandfather approved) of this.

"We thought he'd go to Penn or Princeton, but he didn't want to be too close and picked Cornell. A bit of a rebellion, maybe, heading to the hinterlands of Ithaca, New York, but it was what he wanted to do so we gave him our blessing."

My grandfather spoke up.

"I give him all the credit in the world. He knew he lacked discipline and decided to head away to see if he could straighten out. It wasn't that he did anything bad, as far as we knew. It was just that he wanted a new experience. Of course, he met your mother there."

"I don't think, God bless her, either of us was happy about that."

"Oh, Lydie, that's not true. I was fine with her."

"You were not." She pivoted to him and then back to me. "And then when he went to law school in New York and decided to practice here and not down near us, you weren't happy."

"That's natural. Philadelphia was the perfect spot for him. For them."

"And Emily?" my Grandmother asked.

He turned to me. "Maybe I wasn't fair about your mother. Since we're being honest here, we didn't think she had the right class. I hate to say that, but it made us uncomfortable."

"Even with a Cornell degree?" I asked.

"I'm not proud about it, but you wanted us to be honest and that's how we felt."

My grandmother nodded, and he continued. "We've never been up to where she grew up, you know. We might have been asked, but we never accepted. We've only met her parents a few times, and that includes the wedding."

"And the funeral," Grandmother added.

"Yes. And the funeral.

"We never knew much about her before they married. And your father didn't speak about her much until one day, out of the blue, he announced that they were engaged. I wondered if she was pregnant," he added, somewhat under his breath.

"We both did," she said, making clear she wanted me to hear. "But he swore she wasn't. And we believed, and still believe, that."

Our conversation went like this for a while. It was clear that this simple we-don't-know-why-he-married-her story was short of the truth. I knew my father was much closer to his mother than to his father. She was the one he talked to the most. I didn't push it. The history drifted down Memory Lane with them, back to Year One and as I didn't want them to be too late getting to Bronxville, I walked them to their car at about one.

I called my father to tell him they were on their way. I'd said I'd asked them to stop by and gave him the same pitch that since I was looking into my mom, I wanted some information about him.

"Did they embarrass me?" he asked.

"No more than usual, Dad. Pretty much as I expected, about you and Mom. But it was nice to feel like an adult with them."

He said he was glad, and I was off and decided to see if Kate was around and since she was, we hopped a cab and wandered for a few hours around the West Village from overpriced boutique to overpriced boutique, trying on and rejecting outfits neither of us could afford—though one or two did make us look "fetching" (as Nora Ephron might put it)—and taking a coffee/bathroom break at a small place on Spring Street until it was suddenly chilly and dark, and we leaned against each other and I (at least) smiled as we took the C local back to 86th Street, with me using the opportunity to fill her in on Brenda Jackson and (what I knew of) Andrew Grayson and what my grandparents told me.

45.

Grandmother Locus called early Sunday. She wanted to meet. Discreetly. I'd planned on going to brunch with Jessie in Brooklyn but canceled, and my grandmother arranged for a car to take me to Tuckahoe, the town north of Bronxville. She'd ask where we could meet, and I knew of a tavern there she could walk to but that was unlikely to have anyone from town.

I got there at about eleven-thirty. She was there, sitting at a round table in the front overlooking the street and the plaza where the train station was with coffee and what looked to be a mimosa, so I got the same.

We engaged in somewhat uncomfortable chatter until I had my drink and then ordered brunch. We clinked our mimosa glasses and took sips, and she placed her glass lightly on the table as a busgirl brought over some bread. As I felt for the first time the day before, I was a grown-up with her. She told me my grandfather didn't know what she was about to tell me but that I was old enough that I had the right to know.

"I'm not a fool, and I know how badly your father sometimes treated your mother. Be honest with me, Alexandra. I won't tell a soul. But what have you learned about your mother?"

Again, she and I were never close. Even when I went to Villanova not ten miles from their house, I rarely saw them. I don't know whose fault that was, but that's how it was. She may have resented that. I don't know. But I was always closer to the Millers.

I took a sip of my mimosa and put the flute back on the table with its stem between two of my fingers and my thumb as I moved it around the table. And for the next half hour, I somehow told her everything. Nancy. Dot. Brenda Jackson. Jessie.

She'd let me drone on till, at that last one she asked, "Did your father know?" and I told her he didn't but that he now did.

She just listened as I rambled on about all these discoveries and during it all, we had our eggs benedict (her) and cheese-and-mushroom quiche (me) and coffee refills. The place grew crowded, and it was nearly one before I knew it. Somehow, I shed no tears. I was a train hurtling down the tracks, and I was barely staying on them until out of sheer exhaustion I stopped. I just stopped.

"I knew about her affair with that writer. It was a very bad business," she said. "I only found out some years after it apparently began, but before she passed."

I looked across at her.

"Your father called one day. He said he confronted her with proof of her affair—he never said what that proof was—"

"He hired a private detective to follow her," I said.

She looked at me. "I should have guessed. In any case, he said she confessed to it. You must have been nine or ten. She swore to him, he said, that you knew nothing about it, and I guess you didn't."

"No. I had no idea until recently."

Her voice low, she explained that he thought of leaving my mom, taking everything, especially me, and never looking back.

"'She can go back to that hellhole I found her in,' I remember him saying. Your grandfather was right. We were never sure why he married her. She wasn't right for him."

She asked about Nancy.

"She's nice," I said. "A well-regarded writer. She lives a few blocks to the north."

"Where they found your mother?"

"Yes. The bedroom there is almost a shrine. I think she was deeply in love with her and still is. I think Mom stayed with Dad because of me."

With this last piece of business over, I said, "Please don't tell anyone. Especially my dad."

She was quiet. She placed her credit card in the leather check holder, and it was swooped away by our waitress.

"I won't tell anyone until you tell me I can." The waitress returned, and my grandmother signed the receipt and before I knew it, we'd both used the ladies' and were in the chill Westchester air.

It couldn't hurt to ask, so I did.

"Do you know a Diane Grayson?"

Her head shot up and for a fraction of a second, she might have glared at me. She buttoned her coat.

"Is there someplace where we can walk?" she asked. I took this as a yes and nodded. She asked me to wait as she pulled out her phone and called, I assume, my grandfather and told him that she was being delayed, though I had no idea what story she'd told him, and my father, about what she was up to in the first place.

I was not quite familiar with Tuckahoe, not being quite up to Bronxville standards, but I knew there was a paved path along the small Bronx River, which led back home, so that's where we went.

"As I told you I wouldn't repeat what you said to me, the same holds for this. Agreed?"

"Agreed."

She put her arm through mine as we walked the few blocks to the path. Her shoes didn't look particularly comfortable, but she didn't object and we took our time.

"Why do you ask about Diane Grayson?"

I was committed to being open, so I told her about Agnes and the piece of paper.

"Andrew Grayson? Fuck."

She stopped and I stepped in front of her and looked at her. In a million years I couldn't imagine my grandmother saying "fuck" but there it was.

"I don't know anything about any Andrew. Only Diane."

"I think she's Andrew's mother."

She resumed the walk, but her voice was low until I reminded her that there was no one to hear us. She smiled and continued.

"As a senior in high school," she said, "your father did something very stupid. I knew he was sexually active from about when he was sixteen. Not with the girls at his school's Catholic sister school but with girls at the local public school.

"Over the summer before his senior year, he got involved with a particular girl there. Yes. Diane Grayson. He brought her to the house a few times. Nice girl. Early in senior year, though, a condom broke, and she got pregnant."

I stopped but she kept going, forcing me to follow.

"How do I know this? He told me. He was in a panic. What to do? What to do? I wasn't allowing his life to be ruined. Or hers. She was a nice girl. She was afraid to tell her folks, of course. They thought she was a virgin. I sat the two of them down in our kitchen when your grandfather was out, and we discussed their options. Your grandfather knew none of this. Still doesn't. Only the three of us.

"In the end, it was a pretty easy choice. I gave them money, and the two went to an abortion clinic and she had the procedure and that was that."

"But you're Catholic."

She might have laughed at that. "I'm a woman and a Catholic but I'm not a fool. Was it wrong? Was it wrong to avoid saddling her with a baby in her senior year of high school? Would your father have remained? I like to think he would, but I was glad, frankly, not to have to find out. I think she already decided anyway. It's funny. I became some type of mentor to her, I guess. I didn't know her that well, but she looked up to me and was looking for an adult to say it was okay to get an abortion. Whatever my religious feelings about it, I didn't, and don't, feel strongly that it's wrong.

"Surprised?"

I said I was. I agreed with her, but she was...she was Grandmother Locus, a pillar of the parish.

"If it was a test, I failed it."

"I didn't mean it that way," I say. "I'm just surprised."

"At that I helped with the abortion or that your father was put in the position where he got a girl pregnant?"

"Well, the religious thing I don't have a problem with. But the other."

She put her arm around my waist and pulled me close.

"What about her?" I asked.

"The pregnancy and the abortion pretty well ended it. It was too bad. It was high school, of course, and nothing would probably have come of it. But I liked her. In fact, you remind me of her in some ways, though I didn't know her that well."

"And?"

"Well, I didn't know her family. I'm afraid I didn't keep track of her. I think I've seen her now and then in town. She must be visiting her parents. If it's her, she had a boy who, I guess, would be a few years younger than you so probably all grown up."

We were quiet as we kept to the side of the path, as the runners and walkers and dogs went the other way.

"You know," she suddenly said, "your father may have married your mother because she reminded him of Diane. I don't know. But I do know they were about the same size, your mother and Diane."

"And the hair?"

"Now that you mention it, yes."

As we reached town, my grandmother wanted to get a car to bring me back, but we were by the station and a quick check said a train would be coming in shortly, so I got a ticket from a kiosk and stood on the platform waiting.

"There's one thing I need to do," I told her.

"About Diane?"

"I need to call her. I was going to before we spoke."

She was looking straight down at the tracks.

"I can't object to that, Alexandra," she said, looking in front of herself across towards the movie theater. I reached for her arm, and she turned to face me, her hands in her pockets.

"Thank you, Grandmother. I'm sorry I've been so difficult over the years."

Her hands came from her pockets and she smiled, her hands reaching to mine.

"What's done is done. I've always loved you."

She hugged me as we waited on the platform.

"What did she think of me?" I wasn't sure that this was directed at me and not across to the other platform.

"I think you intimidated her and that she always, well, always thought you believed she was beneath my dad."

Finally, she said, "Do you think she hated me? I know you were too young. But given what you've learned about her. Do you think she hated me?"

I looked up, and she turned to look at me.

"She had so much heartbreak. She hid it so well. Did she hate you? I think the only person she hated at times was herself. I think she felt your disapproval of her. Her background. Her parents. Even without knowing the true story there. But I don't think she was capable of really hating someone."

"I just didn't know how to connect with her." She turned to me. "I'm sorry for that."

My train appeared up the tracks.

She gave me a hug and kissed my cheek before pushing back. "Always know I love you."

"I do. I love you too," and we separated and stepped back just as the train came in and before I knew it, I was aboard, and she was heading back to the house and I realized neither of us mentioned Andrew.

Back at my apartment, I went to the boxes. There was a story that I think answered my grandmother's final question.

A Misty Morn is about a woman staying in a small house that has a lawn that runs down to a small lake. A pond, really.

There were a few houses sprinkled around the lakeside with docks reaching into the water but for the most part, it's all woods and vegetation. It's a summer retreat, and her husband was in the city during the week, coming up on Friday night and leaving on Sunday night. In some ways, it was like Karen Adams's *Lonesome*, which seemed apt given that story's importance to everything.

Wednesday, of course, is the worst of my days. I am tired of him being gone and anxious for his return, but his return is forty-eight hours off and my loneliness is crushing. I wish he'd allow me to stay at our apartment as he allows the rest of the year. But he insists that I need the clean air of the mountains.

He means for it to take my mind off it, and he will not listen when I tell him the loneliness only makes things worse.

On this particular Wednesday night, in early August, I see activity across the lake. I am, as usual, on the screened-in porch. The mosquitoes are frightful this year—though he scarcely notices when he's here, they're upon me within seconds of my exposing my skin—and I have just a small candle on the table by the lounger on which I lie. Being lonely.

There's movement across the lake, as I say. This is unusual since few people come up during the week. A light suddenly flickers. Not electric. A candle, much like mine. I can't make out anything visually, but I hear the strumming of a guitar. It's not great strumming. Perhaps the player knows only three chords, and those imperfectly.

But if her playing is not pleasing, her voice is. She begins to sing a sweet melody. I cannot quite make out what it is, but I'm certain it's not a standard song. Not Dylan or Baez or even The Beatles. The words are beautiful but can't be made out.

She sounds older. Far older than me. I don't think of my mom. She would never sing so plaintively. Somehow my thoughts run to his mother. The one who disapproves of me. Who is sure he could have done better. I shouldn't be thinking of her, though. The song has feelings, and she has none. Yet, she is the one I think of.

Her playing melds in with her singing, and the weakness in her guitar complements the strength of her imperfect voice. She surely does not realize that her music is reflected off the surface of the lake as if I were standing directly in front of her. And I wish I were standing directly in front of her.

She does not play or sing for long. Perhaps four minutes. No more. When she is done, I can see in the low light her returning to the cottage. Her candle is extinguished, but then the cottage's lights go on. It's too far away from me to see anything clearly, and I don't have time to get the binoculars that are somewhere in a drawer in the den. That would break whatever remains of the connection I have with her.

When my own candle flickers out as its flame reaches the end of the wick, I head inside my own cottage. It's almost nine. My husband calls at nine to check in. See how I'm doing.

When he does, nearly on the dot, we have the conversation we have each Wednesday.

"Miss you."

"Miss you."

"Wish you were here?"

"I'll be up on Friday night."

"I can't wait. I'll have something made for you."

"Good. I won't eat until I get there. Sleep well."

"You too."

All this occurs in the dark. I'm afraid to turn on my lights in case she would discover someone is across the pond and perhaps listening to the intimate minutes when she played and sang that song.

I must, though, acknowledge reality, and I turn on the lights, though stealing a glance across at her house before doing so. I continue with my Wednesday till it's time to turn in. The bedroom overlooks the lake. I turn off the light and stand by the window, looking out at the neighbor. Her lights are still on. I wonder which is her driveway on the other side of the lake. Should I go to see her? I hadn't noticed any sign of life at that house. Even on the weekend. I think I should very much like to meet this woman.

I turn and get into my bed, under a sheet because it gets cold during the night although it's August, and I fall asleep.

It was another story that registered with me when I read it but didn't resonate, if you know what I mean, till I had more context.

I put it down. I didn't know whether I could, would, or should show it to her mother-in-law.

46.

I was adept now at cold calling people.

"Is this Diane Grayson?"

"Who's calling?"

Show time.

"Ms. Grayson, my name is Alexandra Locus." I stopped. It'd either sink in or strike a nerve. Or she'd hang up.

The pause was brief, and without a change in her flat voice, she said, "Yes?"

"I believe you know my father, Steven Locus."

"I did."

Now she was waiting. Letting me fill in the gap.

"Ms. Grayson, I was trying to learn some things about...my parents."

"Your mother is dead, yes?"

"Yes. She died some years ago."

"Look. I haven't seen or heard from your father since before your mother died. I have no interest in having anything further to do with him or with you or anyone else."

Before she could hang up, I asked, "What about Andrew?"

She didn't hang up. It seemed forever but probably was very brief and her voice lost its coldness and if anything hardened.

"What do you know about Andrew?"

I didn't know much beyond what I found online and the not insignificant tidbit from Agnes Hall that he was my half-brother. Before the call, I didn't know what I would say. I didn't know how the conversation would go. It wasn't going well, though in all honesty it was going about as well as could be expected.

"I know he's my brother."

I decided to throw it out there. It was a mistake, though. She hung up.

Before I came up with an appropriate interval before I tried a second, and likely last, time Diane called me back.

"Who knows?"

"Agnes Hall told me."

"Good old nosy Agnes Hall."

"Look. There was a reason she told me."

"Yes, your exploration of who your father is. I will speak to you on one condition. You will not try to contact Andrew unless I specifically okay it. Is that understood?"

I wouldn't have done it otherwise.

"Of course. I promise."

She asked if I was comfortable, that she had a story to tell. I'd been pacing but sat down on the sofa, my legs in front of me and across the coffee table.

I told her my grandmother told me about what happened when she and my father were in high school.

"I had your name and I asked her if she knew you and she told me, though she, too, swore me to secrecy."

"I guess you have the right to hear about that little chapter in my life. I liked your grandmother. She came across as if she had a stick up her ass, but in the end, she was there for me, and for your father. I've seen her in town occasionally when I've been visiting my folks. That's probably how I heard about your mother. Again, I'm very sorry. But with that background, you want to know about Andrew. Did you mention him to her, your grandmother?"

"Things are coming at me fast and furious, but I've learned to take them one at a time so I'm keeping certain things secret. Including you and Andrew." This was something of a necessary lie since I had mentioned his name, though no more.

She told me she ran into my father when he was visiting his parents. Based on Andrew's age, I must have been around two and was staying home with my mom. It was one of those running-into-each-other-on-a-sidewalk-in-town things. It was a Saturday, she recalled, and he was taking the train back to New York the following night.

Old friends. One thing led to another. Diane had an apartment near town in those days and they went to bed. It was good, she said, reminding her of how she felt those years before in high school before everything, she said, "got fucked up all because of a broken condom." She gave a curt laugh.

"I shouldn't say this to his daughter, but your father was a good lover. I missed how he felt *in* me. We didn't have any condoms. He offered to pull out before he came, but I just wanted him to come inside me. For old time's sake, I guess. I can still remember it."

Diane seemed to have floated elsewhere and she might have even forgotten I was there as she described the scene. She said he came and at that moment she might well have run off with him had he asked. She recovered, and her voice flattened.

She said she was in between serious relationships with men when it happened; "I married a few years later but got divorced a few years after that. My ex grew tired of having to raise someone else's boy."

"What about my father?"

"Oh, he went home to New York the next day. He called and asked whether it was 'alright' and I told him it was. He called a couple of months later to make sure and I told him I'd had my period and everything was good and I so looked forward to being with him again.

"He said, 'You know that's not possible. It sort of happened and it can't happen again.' He told me about your mother and you when we first ran into each other but...he said something was missing."

"Did he say what?"

"Not then. He just said they weren't as compatible as he hoped. Whether he had other affairs, I don't know. I mean, it was only the one afternoon with an old, intimate friend. I asked whether he told her about it, and he said, 'Are you kidding? It'd kill her.'"

By now I was again walking around my apartment cradling my phone. She was sniffling.

"I didn't tell him about Andrew for several years. I hadn't spoken to him about anything. And, again, I was married. After my divorce, though, when Andrew was about five, I realized he would someday ask about who his father was. I didn't want to lie to him, so I called your father to tell him.

"I did it on the phone. I recall it was a Sunday. A landline, of course. I'd called on Saturday but a woman, who I assume was your mother, answered, and I hung up. Sunday night, though, he answered. He said he couldn't talk right then but would call me from his office the next day. I would be at my office—I work in insurance down here and did back then too—but I could speak.

"On Monday morning, like right after I got in, my office phone rings. No 'hello, how were you?' Straight into, 'Why did you call me at home?' I told him I got the number from the operator, and I didn't know how else to get to him. He asked why I called in the first place, five or six years after our little tryst, and I simply said, 'You have a son.'

"There was a pause. Then, 'You bitch. You said it was okay. No problem. You had your period. Why didn't you just have another abortion?' He sprinkled obscenities in there, by the way. And that's how your father found out about Andrew. Gradually the conversation came down to 'What do you want?' I told him that I didn't want anything. I was only calling to tell him that I would not lie to our child and when Andrew asked, I would tell him who his father was. He asked whether I was 'sure,' and I told him I was. He was the only man I was with in those three months, so it had to be.

"He demanded that I take a paternity test. 'I can't have you ruin my life on a mistake.' And we had the test and it confirmed that he was the father."

"And I am the sister," I said, my first words in a while. I was again sitting on the sofa, my legs stretched across the coffee table.

"And you are his sister. Half-sister."

It was strange to have this intimate a conversation over the phone. I suggested we keep everything *status quo* until I could take the train to Philadelphia on the weekend, and we agreed, after I assured her again that I wouldn't tell a soul about the conversation.

47.

Diane Grayson's apartment was a nice two-bedroom she owned in Center City, Philadelphia. I took a cab from the Amtrak station at about nine-thirty on Saturday. True to my word, no one knew where I was going—not even Kate or Jessie—and they knew enough not to ask.

The apartment was on the fourteenth floor and in a corner, so there were great views to the south and west. She has set up a nice breakfast/brunch spread.

"I thought it would be easier if we just stayed here."

She was pretty and, of course, just a year older than my mom would be if she were alive. I didn't know on the train down how much I would get into about my life and what I learned about my parents. I did decide I would not ask about Andrew unless she opened that door, though I was certain she would.

We exchanged small talk about my trip and generally about what we each did for a living and sat with our plates and our coffees on a right-angled sofa that had a view through the large windows down the Delaware River and over Independence Hall. It was overcast, so we were not blinded by the sun.

Relaxed in our seats, on the sofa perpendicular to one another with the smell of the coffee and a hint of the eggs and a light bit of Mozart in the air, she simply said, "I loved your father for the longest time."

She took a bit of her coffee and I followed suit.

"I was the bad, public-school girl who wore her skirts just long enough not to get suspended, and he was the nerdy jock at the Catholic school. I remember the first day I saw him."

She was with friends and running into a bunch of the Catholic boys at the mall near where they grew up. The summer before senior year. She remembered nothing except for the eyes of the otherwise average-looking one with the somewhat unruly hair, longer than the others. As the groups split, she turned back and caught his eyes watching her walk away. She gave the slightest of waves and the slightest of a smile before turning and resuming her cruising with the other girls, with the slightest of ass-gyration.

From that point, she kept her eye out for him. They saw each other now and then, and he always had the hint of a smile. She told herself it was only for her. She didn't care that it probably wasn't. This dragged on for about a month, she said, into August. One of his friends had a birthday, and his parents were throwing a party for him. A bunch of the "dangerous" public school kids, boys and girls, were invited. The groups didn't mingle particularly as a general proposition, but with a few exceptions were on decent terms with each other. Besides, once word about an August party got around, lots of people were likely to show up, invited or not.

"I was anxious that he would be there, and when I got there, I didn't see him at first. If he wasn't there, I didn't want to be, he being the only reason I went in the first place. The birthday boy's parents were there so there was no openly displayed alcohol, and there wasn't even a pool. It was hot and likely to be boring. I planned that if your father, Steve, didn't show up, I'd just walk home.

"Which was what I was about to do when I felt a hand on my shoulder." She tapped her left shoulder. "Right here. I turn and he's there with this big grin. I mean, we'd only exchanged a few words, hello and goodbye mostly, and now he was there and asking me my name and me telling him my name, and me, I guess the polite word is 'swooning,' before him."

She said they ended up in what they thought was a quiet spot and started making out. "Just like that." She snapped her fingers and said she'd never done anything like that before, but she'd been, and she turned a bit red when she said it, "thinking about him often since I first saw him."

She paused for a second.

"We were interrupted, of course, and I think we were both embarrassed and we separated. Before I left, though, he caught up to me and slipped a piece of paper into my hand. His phone number. He leaned in and said, 'Call me at about ten and we'll talk,' and he rushed away."

She said she went out with him a few times, and then neither was afraid to be seen with the other and they started hanging out. It sort of happened. She was a virgin. He was not, "or so he said." On Labor Day weekend, his folks were away— I have an image of Mr. and Mrs. Locus at the time—"and on Sunday afternoon we went to his room and did it. I know it's horrible to say to his daughter, but I couldn't get enough of him. Or his body."

At this point, she got up to remove the plates—she refused my offer of help—and get more coffee for us, and I stepped to the window for her view. She refilled our coffees and sat. I was still standing.

"So, the...sex with your father became a near regular thing on weekends. We talked about where we wanted to go to college, and I thought I might have the grades and SATs to get into Penn or UVA, and he was the same. We kind of agreed— we were so naïve—that if we both got into Penn, we'd both go.

"But I think both of us wanted to get away from home, so my top choice was UVA and his was Columbia and if not that, Cornell. Then in early October, his condom broke. We both panicked but I thought it would be okay."

She kept telling herself, and him, she said, that she wasn't pregnant and then after missing her period she confronted him.

"I was shocked that he told me we could speak to his mother. My parents? No way. He said his mom would understand and help so the day I met your grandmother was the day I told her I'd been knocked up by her son. She was nicer than I could have imagined. No bullshit. 'It's what's got to be done. For both of you,' she said, and we made an appointment at a clinic, and he came with me with money I assume came from his mom and that was it."

Her voice was flat as she said all of this though I saw that the mug in her hand was shaking slightly. I sat beside her. She sniffled.

"Things were different from then. He, well, found someone else. It was like I had the plague. He avoided gatherings where we public schoolers would be. He essentially drifted away. I only found out he was going to Cornell because someone happened to say so. Sure, people asked about our breaking up, but I just said it didn't work out."

Yes, he'd been her first love but that was gone, and she found herself a boyfriend for the rest of senior year and believed she'd gotten over him. She didn't particularly seek information about him—"Remember, this was the pre-Facebook age"—and saw him in town occasionally when they went to college and after graduation—she went to UVA—enough to wave, say hello, etc. She heard he married my mom. She thinks from one of her high school friends who said it in passing. And that was it until the day they ran into each other in town years later.

We'd circled back to where our telephone conversation ended. She got up and so I did too, and we shared the view down the Delaware, and I strained to understand her words.

"I already told you about our more recent 'one-afternoon stand.' Once I called him and sent him proof of the paternity, he arranged for the creation of a trust for Andrew. I was a single mother working long hours after my divorce, and I got nothing from that. I made enough to keep a nice roof over our heads and to pay for Andrew's tuition but that was about it. It was college I was thinking of, so your father set up a trust to help pay for that. And"—she turned to look back at me—"that was how your Agnes Hall came to get involved."

She sat again and I again mimicked her, and we finished our coffees. The sun was beginning to break through the clouds and there was some glare in the room.

"He funded the trust and had me deal directly with Agnes. He sent me a note." She rose and went to a desk along the right wall of the living room and opened the top drawer.

"I meant to take this out before you got here," she said as she shuffled through papers before pulling something out. It was an envelope, ivory. Probably from his firm. She opened it and handed me the contents. The note was hand-written:

Dear Diane,

    I will always treasure our moments together. But they must, sadly, remain in our past. I wish you and your son the greatest of health and happiness. Please direct all future communications to my secretary, Agnes Hall.

                                Steven Locus

I handed it back to her, and she folded it and carefully returned it to its envelope before slowly walking to the desk and putting it back.

"That was the last I heard from him. I knew where he worked so I knew how to get in touch with Agnes. I spoke to her now and then, but I had the feeling she didn't want your father to know. She was more interested in *my*, not our, son Andrew than he was. Of course, as far as I could tell he had zero interest in our son so this window"—she pointed to it—"had more of an interest in him."

She was back on the sofa.

"It seems like the weather's breaking. Let's walk. I have to get out."

I collected my bag, not expecting to be coming back, and she didn't discourage me as we had an uncomfortable trip down on the elevator. We resumed our talk when we got outside. I told her bits and pieces of my mom's life. She didn't have much interest in that, of course, or in my own history.

We were gone for maybe fifteen minutes when she said, apropos of nothing we were talking about, "Do you want to speak to him?" The elephant in the room.

"After you called, I told him of your existence and of you having contacted me, so this will not come as a total surprise to him."

I nodded. We were coming upon a small green with park benches strewn about among the leafless trees, and we sat on one. She dialed her phone. I was completely unprepared as she simply said, "She's with me" and handed it to me. I was even more unprepared for him to say "Hey, sis."

Diane was watching me.

"Hello...brother."

He laughed. "I'm sorry. I couldn't resist. Ever since my mom called. I admit I've been investigating you. I assume you've done the same."

I was a little embarrassed, sitting next to his mother. "Well," I said, "before I contacted your mom and after I first heard your name, I did some sleuthing."

"'Sleuthing'? Is that what you New Yorkers call it?"

His voice was deep, and I realized I'd never had a conversation of this sort with a man before.

"You're 'Alex,' right?"

"Yeah. That's how I go. And you?"

"Generally, it's 'Andy.' Only my mom calls me 'Andrew.' So why don't you go with that? We're family, after all."

I was embarrassed. "In that case," I said, "It's 'Alexandra' to you."

"Listen, Alexandra. I'm finishing up with finals on Wednesday before taking Amtrak home. Maybe we can get together at last over the break, yeah?"

He was incredibly outgoing and relaxed. I had so many questions but, a, couldn't remember what they were and, b, wanted to ask them in person so I said, "I'd like that. Here's your mom," and I handed her the phone and stood, walking slowly the way we came.

She caught up with me. "Can you come down Christmas week?" Christmas was the Monday after next and I had off, so I told her I would.

"I think that's enough for now. Let's get you a cab to the station and talk."

We found a cab at the corner, and I left her behind, after an awkward handshake, and I was in my apartment before it was dark.

Christmas? That was going to be interesting.

48.

"**Y**ou're kidding me."

During our walk and before I spoke to Andrew, I told Diane that I had two or three people I was trying to find information about my past with and that one was a half-sister I recently discovered. This revelation caused her to stop. She made me repeat it and give her some background, which she punctuated by saying, "You have been on one hell of a journey."

We were quickly away from the little park. I asked her if I could tell my friends about her and, more, about Andrew. "I trust them implicitly and they'd never do anything inappropriate with the info."

With that assurance, and the added one that I would not tell Grandmother Locus about it or mention anything to my dad, she agreed. Back at my place, I called Jessie. I didn't tell her much. I'd do that the next morning, Sunday, when we were having brunch in Cobble Hill.

As I went to meet Kate that night, I felt that things were starting to spin out of anyone's control. Especially mine. As to Diane's folks, they came around to her pregnancy she said well before Andrew was born and were rocks. I asked whether they knew the Locuses, and she said slightly, if at all. I asked whether she told them who the father was, and she said she had, but that she swore them to secrecy, that she was the only one with the right—at least until Andrew was of age—to contact his other grandparents. She told him when she made the arrangement—yes, that word again—with my father and made clear that it was for her and Andrew alone. They abided by her wishes.

I dropped the Andrew bomb to Kate shortly after we'd sat down at one of our favorite restaurants on Amsterdam. I was a little tired from my down-and-back to Philly, and the first sip of Merlot went down *very* smoothly.

"When do I meet him? And is he handsome? Answer the second question first," and Kate laughed and laughed as we settled in at the little hole-in-the-wall place we loved and that was likely to close soon because of the rent.

Andrew was a senior at Boston College. His goal was a finance job in New York. He was doing the full Wall Street interview tour and felt he did well enough at school that he'd get an offer. If all else failed, he could get a job at the bank in Philadelphia where he worked before senior year, when he crashed in his old room at his mom's apartment.

"I think you're gonna need a bigger family tree," she said, only half-jokingly.

"You need to get away from it all. All of it. You can sleep on my sofa and you can get some perspective. I think you should start writing more things down. Your mother wrote. Perhaps it's time that you do, but not vague stories that were a puzzle. Your story. Your mother's story. Your father's story. Just focus on that for a bit to get it under control and organized. You've been going through an awful lot here."

At her place later, though, I didn't put down a word. It was a good idea and I thought it was worth a try, but that night was meant for me to just revert to being a twenty-something on the Upper West Side of Manhattan. A girls' night in.

Since Kate had HBO and I didn't, she gave me first dibs on what movie we'd start with. And the night passed as few had passed in recent weeks. Easily. At about ten-thirty, I told her it was time for me to head home. She tried to convince me to stay so I didn't have to see the damn boxes that seemed to have eyes that followed me everywhere, but I was not comfortable imposing.

"It's no imposition." She went into her bedroom and returned a few minutes later with one of her stories.

"This has nothing to do with anything. It's a sweet, diverting piece, and I'd appreciate your reaction."

I still planned to leave but was drawn in by what she wrote. I looked up a few minutes later, about halfway through, and there she was, carrying some sheets, a blanket, and a pillow into the living room.

"I'll sleep here, and you can crash in the bedroom."

It was somewhat absurd, of course. My apartment was less than seven blocks away. Yet Kate was offering me the chance to be away from it, if only for a night.

"At least take a look at the bed," she said.

I put the still unfinished story down and followed her. The room was small and tidy. A small desk in one corner. A dresser in the other. The bed was between them. It was small, not even big enough for two people romantically inclined, as we were not.

She found a toothbrush still in its packaging, and while I took care of myself, she got me a long t-shirt to wear to bed. I dragged my bones into the bedroom. "Are you sure?"

"Go to bed, sweetie. I'll see you in the morning."

Kate gave me a peck on my forehead, and that's the last thing I remember happening till I woke up early on Sunday morning. The sun was barely up. While it felt strange in some ways to wake up in a place both familiar and strange, I was glad to be there.

She'd left a pair of panties with tags for me in the bathroom and when I was dressed, I discovered her snoring lightly on the sofa, looking very uncomfortable, the blanket half off her. Now I was a voyeur. It was still early so I didn't wake her. Instead, I lifted the story I'd not quite finished and retreated to the bedroom to leave her be. But it wasn't long before she was at the bedroom door, looking adorable and saying "good morning" before turning to the bathroom. I sat to finish the story and was just done when she returned, looking, well, awake.

"Come on. I need coffee," she said, and I followed her.

It was a small kitchen with a small, round metal table and two metal chairs. Stools really. I sat on one since the kitchen was too small to have more than one person moving about unless, again, they were romantically inclined.

She refused my offer to do something.

"I liked it," I told her.

"It?"

"Your story." I waited a moment. "It reminded me of some things my mom wrote."

She was quiet as she filled the coffee maker.

"Cereal?"

I looked and saw three boxes. "Special K, please."

She reached for the box and took two bowls out of a cupboard and poured the cereal in both and put them both on the table, before getting two tablespoons and a container of milk. Once we were set and the milk was back on the counter she said, "Writers sometimes live on osmosis. I've read enough of what she wrote that it has seeped in." She took a spoonful of her Special K.

"Did you like it? Putting aside the thing about your mother."

"I did. It made me feel like I was in that forest, regretting and not regretting having walked away."

The coffee beeped, and she rose.

She knew how I took it, and she handed me my mug. We carried our coffees to the table and after we each took long, initial sips, we resumed eating the cereal and speaking between spoonfuls.

"What did it mean?" I asked.

She laughed. "You of all people should know that it's not what the writer thinks, it's what the reader does."

With our cereal bowls empty and placed in the sink, we adjourned to her living room, sitting at either end of her couch with our coffees.

"I can only write so much," Kate began. "The reader has to connect the dots."

"What if there were a gazillion dots?"

She thought. "You know those pointillist paintings? That Lichtenstein in the building on Seventh? You see nothing but dots if you get too close. You need to step away."

Before I could say anything, she laughed. "Class dismissed."

At which point she sent me home, and after a shower and a complete change of wardrobe, I headed to Brooklyn to meet Jessie and tell her in person the details of what I mentioned to her on the phone the day before.

* * * *

I PULLED OUT MY PHONE and opened Facebook. Andrew and I friended each other shortly after we ended our telephone conversation in the park near Diane's. I handed the phone to Jessie so she could see him.

"He's cute in a nerdy sort of way." I told her to behave. She scrolled through some of his entries. "Seriously, he reminds me of some of the nicer guys in law school."

"Jessie, baby," I said, "right now you have to help me digest all of this information."

"Did you tell him about me?"

"Technically you're not related. But not yet. I only told his mom. She was fascinated by how fucked up my parents were revealing themselves to be."

But Jessie soon understood that I needed to speak of anything other than what I discovered so we bored each other with the details of our upbringings in two suburbs of New York City.

49.

In New York then and now, from Thanksgiving, there's no escaping that Christmas is approaching. And I like it. People set up temporary stalls along the avenues of the Upper West Side with their trees and wreaths and space heaters. I always bought a small tree and dragged it back to my apartment. On Christmas itself, Kate and I'd take the train to Bronxville. It was a tradition, and folks on the bus and subway and MetroNorth would be carrying big bags with presents and food platters and maybe a contribution for the day's dessert.

To TimTim, it was a huge event, and Maggie's folks were usually there. They'd moved to Florida before she and my dad got married. They usually came up a few days before and stayed at the house until into the new year. The Millers usually came down while my mom was alive, but only a few times since. Plus me and my dad.

Kate and I got up to Bronxville early enough so I could go to mass at the WASPy Catholic Church near the station and she could be with her family for services at the big church across from the Village Hall. It was always a quiet and peaceful day in our hometown. While that would still be the case, things in the Locus house were more complicated that year than ever.

I spoke to Dot and Edgar and the Millers. We all agreed it was best not to have them come down just yet. They were together in Paterson for the day, and I planned on heading up there on Wednesday with Kate and Jessie and Peter.

Thursday would be Amtrak down to see Diane and Andrew. Whether I'd head up the Main Line to see the Locuses afterward was another question, largely dependent on how it went with the Graysons. I mean, if I weren't going to mention them, how would I explain to my grandparents why I happened to be in Philadelphia? So, I didn't tell them I was coming down.

Christmas came. It was chilly but not cold and, well, everyone was tense and as on Thanksgiving we spoke only of the most mundane things and dedicated our effort to keeping TimTim entertained till he crashed in the early afternoon. Then loaded with wine and turkey, it was me who crashed on the comforter on the bed in my old room, and I was (somehow) able to take the train back to the city in the morning.

50.

"**I**'ve never met him."

I looked at Andrew Grayson's mother, and she nodded.

"To be fair, it was something of a mutual decision. If he wasn't willing to commit to Andrew, he wasn't willing to commit to Andrew."

"Nothing?" I asked.

"Your father"—and this she addressed to both of his children in the room—"wanted to somehow make himself into Andrew's dad. Your mother"—now addressing me—"didn't know about Andrew and your dad wanted to keep it that way. The only person who knew was Agnes Hall."

We were sitting in a restaurant a few blocks from Diane's place. It was on the ground floor of an apartment building and fairly large, but the normal lunchtime crowd was sharply diminished by it being Christmas week, and we had a quiet table in one of the corners. Both Diane and I wore dark pants and light blouses, and the restaurant was toasty enough that we didn't need our sweaters. Andrew wore jeans and a polo, but Diane got him to put on a blue blazer and made him shave so he looked pretty good.

The conversation was, I daresay, more intense than the usual for lunch in this place, but we were keeping our voices down. The meat of it began when we had our drinks and the waitress had our orders.

He was a good-looking man, was Andrew Grayson. He played lacrosse for BC and from the moment he came to meet me in his mother's apartment I could see he was an athlete. He did have a goodly share of my father's features. He got a job as an analyst at a midtown Manhattan investment house, though his mother said she still hoped he come to his senses and get himself a nice bank in Philadelphia to work for. He insisted that "Face it, Mom, no great banking career ever began in Philadelphia," and she shook her head and backed off, for what I was sure wasn't the first time on the issue.

"He's found a place somewhere in Brooklyn with some classmates, and I'm supposed to be happy he's spending all that money on rent and will only let me see him once in a blue moon."

Andrew rolled his eyes, and Diane said, "I'm sorry, honey"—which did nothing to lessen her son's embarrassment—"I'll behave."

He chewed on the bread he grabbed when this encounter began.

"It's just the way it is," Andrew said, returning, I realized, to our father. "I'm used to it. I don't remember my stepdad. I was too young. But him? It's like he's de—"

He stopped, but I finished the thought, "Like he's dead," and he nodded.

I felt a bit of a jerk being sorry for missing out on having just a single parent only since I was fourteen and he'd never really had a father.

"Yeah," he said. "But it's okay. It is what it is."

I asked if he tracked down information about him.

"Well, you couldn't do that when I was a kid," he said. "Mom told me a fair share about him, but she didn't know too much. I've Googled him once or twice, but there's not much there except his lawyer stuff."

He grabbed another slice of bread and buttered it.

"I did look you up, of course, after my mom told me I had a sister."

It was a good lunch that mostly focused on Andrew. When it was over and he was in the men's room, Diane asked about his grandparents. With his having met me, might he meet them?

This was something that was out there, but it had no clear answer. Down the road, I thought it important, especially given the complete alteration of how I viewed Grandmother Locus. I knew she'd be happy to know him.

Things were still very rocky, though. I told her that I hoped there'd come a time to introduce them but not just yet. And that's where things stood when he came back to the table and Diane picked up the check, and we parted ways and I took a cab to the 30th Street Station for the train home. I never mentioned the trip to my grandparents.

51.

From the episode in Kate's basement on Thanksgiving Friday night and its aftermath, everything seemed irrevocably altered about my father. We spoke once or twice a week but I couldn't be honest. I couldn't tell him what I was doing or what I'd found. I always gave him an excuse or outright lied. My trip to Philly? Meeting a friend from Nova. A Paterson trip, when he pressed me about it, was to see the Millers. Before this saga began, I went up to the house every three or four Sundays. Sometimes the three of us, four counting TimTim, went for a drive up to some favored places to the north or over in Connecticut. We'd share cooking duties and eat in the dining room on the good stuff, especially my dad's good wine, and I'd stagger to the station late to get home. Sometimes, I brought work clothes with me and stayed over Sunday night and took the train in with him on Monday morning.

Now, when he asked about things, I was telling him that I was too busy. Something from work. A long-lost friend. It was way too cold to even leave my place.

I was surprised, then, when he said it was him when I answered the buzz for my building around noon on the Sunday after I met with Andrew and Diane. It was New Year's Eve. I let him up. Before he got to my door, I did a quick check to see if any "incriminating" evidence was in sight. There were the boxes, of course. He knew about the ones from Bronxville but not those from Paterson, so I managed to get those three into the closet while he came up the stairs. The things from Nancy were safely away in my bedroom.

That done, I opened the door for him. He was just reaching my landing.

"I was in the neighborhood," he said as he pulled his coat off. I told him he could just drape it across a chair by the door. "Just wanted to see how you were since you don't come up so much," he said as he rubbed his hands together after dropping his coat and closing the door.

"You know, I've been crazy at work, and I was just up for Christmas."

He looked at the boxes. We were both standing.

"And these." He nodded in their direction. "How are things going with your mother's things? I can take them back if you want. The car's not far."

I thanked him but told him that I was slowly working my way through—my own lie to match his about "just being in the neighborhood."

In the old days, including when my mom was alive, I was comfortable with him. Now I just wasn't. This began the last few times we were together, and I felt it more strongly then, when he was in my apartment.

It was early afternoon.

"Hey," he said in an unusually chipper voice and clapping his hands. "Have you eaten? Let me take you to brunch."

We bundled up and walked to Columbus and had no problem getting a table.

"Why are you doing this?"

I wasn't prepared for this and all I could say was, "Doing what?"

We'd just placed our orders and had our coffees. He took some of his.

"I may not be perfect, Alex. But I'm still and always will be your father. I know you've had it tough since your mom died. Don't you think I haven't? But I thought you'd moved on."

He spread his hands before using his right to lift his cup.

"I had moved on. I was happy. We were a family. We still are. I am just trying to piece things together about Mom."

"And about me?"

"What do you mean?"

"Agnes Hall came into my office about a week after I got back from Chicago. She closed the door, which she never does. She said you were asking questions and, well, she admitted she told you things she had no right to tell you. No right. I trusted that woman and—"

His face tightened with each word towards the end before I interrupted him.

"You trusted her to what? To hide the existence of a brother from me?"

I didn't mean to raise my voice, and a couple at the table behind him looked over.

"I'm sorry. But how could you keep that from me? I could understand while Mom was alive. But she's not. I have a brother and you don't tell me?"

"Okay. I have a son. I've been paying for a single accident for over twenty years." Both of our voices recovered, with some difficulty, a conversational tone.

Then: "You've met him, haven't you? That bitch."

Before I could respond, I was up and my napkin was hitting the table: "Who is the bitch? Agnes Hall or Diane Grayson."

And with that, I was gone and on Columbus and I'm sure the entire restaurant stared. I was a block away when he caught me. His right arm was on my right shoulder, and he pulled me around.

"Alex. I'm sorry. I didn't mean it that way."

"Of course you did," I said. "We both know it. Now leave me be," and I turned to get to my apartment, hoping he wasn't following me. He wasn't. I knew that even though I didn't look back. As I approached my building, I kept walking to the park, and when I was through the entrance, I called Diane Grayson. I told her about the encounter.

"Maybe it was not such a great idea for us to get together," she said.

"Bullshit," I said. "I was out trying to get at the truth, and I will never, ever regret learning that I have a brother."

Saying this calmed me. I hadn't thought of it quite that way. That I had a brother. A kid soon to be out of college and coming to New York. How I'd meld it in with Jessie, I couldn't say. But I had a brother.

I
Had
A
Brother

52.

It was all too much. I'd been delving into the past so deeply and encountering so many different significant thoughts and ideas and dreams that I imagined torching the boxes and the memories and going back to who I was before that damn book reading. Which I knew I couldn't do. And the worst, of course, was *My Walls*. There was pain in so much my mom wrote. All centered around her and her perceived inadequacies and fears. Now this with my father.

I cannot say how I got through New Year's Day (and Eve, which I only made it with Kate's help at her place after I marginally recovered from my father's visit) and for that week. Nancy and Kate offered to come over Friday night, but I told them both I just needed time, a couple of days. Saturday morning came, and I needed more time.

Alone time.

It was brutally cold with a wind coming from the north and a blindingly blue sky. Just what I needed. I bundled up and walked to the park. There were, as always, the intrepid runners and cyclists in their tights whose crystalized breaths shot from their mouths. Strollers bundled up, as I was, with only the eyes exposed in faces otherwise covered by a scarf like walking mummies. I suddenly thought of the scene in *The Love of My Life* about the shirtless men and sports bra-wearing women on that hot day in Central Park when Nancy came to help my mom and the contrast in so many ways to this frigid January morning.

It wasn't long before I started questioning the wisdom of this little walk I was taking and after about a mile, I was on a path near the frozen boat pond—near where I'd sat with Kate in the rain long before—and I decided to turn north and go to the Met. It'd be nice and toasty. I climbed the steps to the entrance on Fifth Avenue. I only had ten dollars, but since the contribution for New Yorkers is whatever one wants to pay, that's what I gave. Of course, having given all my money away, I couldn't check my coat. I was sweating and draped it, with my hat in one of its pockets and my scarf in one of its sleeves, over my arm.

The grand museum was crowded but I worked my way around without a particular plan and occasionally looking at a map on a wall. I still do not know how it happened, but I found myself in a particular gallery. The one where Monet's "Bridge over a Pond of Water Lilies" hung. There was the bridge and there were the lilies in the water, floating contentedly with their bits of yellow popping up.

Maybe it was the sudden heat or Monet's Bridge or that photo in Nancy's bedroom—probably some combination of the three—but I swooned and somehow found a spot on one of the leather benches placed around the room. Before I knew it, a woman from the museum was beside me. She wouldn't let me leave alone and asked me to open my phone so she could call my ICE. I had the presence of mind to realize that was the last thing I wanted her to do; it was still my dad.

Instead, I opened it and dialed Nancy while she watched. "A friend on West 94th," I said.

I was helped to a small room down a corridor and given a cup of water while I waited, with someone popping her head in periodically to check on me. At one point, a nurse took my vitals. I explained that I must have overheated from my walk, and she nodded and said I should be fine but that I shouldn't be alone for a few hours, and I think she was satisfied when I told her a friend was coming to collect me.

Before she left, she signed a paper that she'd put my vitals on and approved my leaving, after I promised I wouldn't go until my friend appeared. Almost as soon as the nurse left, an out-of-breath Nancy in her black cashmere coat came through the door with a museum staffer.

"Sweetie. What happened?"

"I think it was the heat. I'd overdressed and nearly fainted. I feel fine now."

She stood above me, staring. The staffer was by the door, and Nancy leaned in.

"You can be so much like your mother. I'm taking you home."

My coat was on a small table on one side, and she grabbed it and told me to follow her. We both thanked the staffer and the nurse, who we ran into in the hall, and as we left the grand building, Nancy handed my scarf to me and after I had that around my neck I turned as she held my coat and I put my arms through its sleeves and turned towards her and buttoned it up and she nodded and paused for just a moment and I then followed her to the sidewalk and when it was our turn her arm shot up and a cab pulled over and soon we were crossing the park at 79th Street and then getting out in front of 34 West 94th Street.

She treated me like a baby or a puppy, and I hate to say that I kind of liked it. I was directed to her sofa.

"Have you eaten?" she called from the kitchen.

"Just cereal and coffee."

Her head popped out and I had to turn my own to see her.

"I'm making you a grilled cheese and some coffee," and she disappeared again and I could smell the butter melting in a pan. I heard the microwave ring, and she came with a cup of canned minestrone soup with a couple of packs of saltine crackers she'd had for who knew how long.

"Start with this," she said, and I turned to sit up and leaned forward and the first sip was an elixir and I hadn't realized how hungry I was. She was jabbering about something as she made the sandwiches—one for her—and she had my coffee in a "Sag Harbor" mug on a tray just as I was finishing the soup, and she took the bowl with her to the kitchen. Before I had more than a couple of sips of the coffee, she came with the sandwiches and her own coffee. She put them on the coffee table and pulled a chair over so she could sit opposite me.

And I told her about the Monet.

53.

It was late afternoon and already dark when we finished. She said I could spend the night, that she'd make dinner, but I said I'd feel more comfortable in my little cubbyhole. She insisted that she walk with me when we finished, and we proceeded with my arm through hers, saying nothing. At the corner of West 85th, I thought someone was on my stoop. She agreed and said she'd see if it was who I think we both suspected it was.

She walked on the south side of the street, opposite my brownstone, and I watched from next to the large apartment building on the corner of Central Park West. She pulled something from her pocket and put it back after playing with it and then crossed the street. The man on my stoop stood. I inched closer, still out of his sight. He was the far more animated of the two, making gestures and sidling back and forth. It was cold, as I say, and both of their breaths sparkled in the streetlight's beams. Without realizing it, I was almost halfway between the corner and my building.

Nancy looked to be calmly taking something from her coat pocket and he slapped her. Hard. Loud enough to reach me even though it was muffled by his glove and just as the sound died, he turned towards Columbus Avenue and disappeared.

With him gone, I rushed to Nancy. She was trying to alternately control her tears and control her rage.

"That bastard struck me," she said, and I told her I saw it and asked if she was okay.

"I will be. Take me upstairs."

I wrangled my keys from my bag, and we were quickly into my small lobby and up the two flights to my apartment. I struggled to get the right keys, and we were in. I got her water while she stood in my living room.

"Anything stronger?" she asked. I pulled a bottle of gin from the freezer and some tonic water from the fridge and poured her a gin-and-tonic, and one for myself.

She was sitting on the sofa. Her coat was in a pile beside her. The radiator heat was its typical brutal self, and I opened my windows to get some cool air in, and we could hear the traffic that comes down the block, cars and people.

"What happened?"

She hesitated a moment and reached into her coat pocket and pulled out her phone. She found an app and hit play.

It was all muffled noise at first but then I could just make out the voices. Hers was first.

"What do you want?"

"Excuse me?"

"I asked what you wanted?"

"I'm sorry, do I know you? Do you live here?"

"No. I live on West 94th."

There was a pause and I wondered if that was it. I looked at her and she raised a finger and I suddenly heard him. The voice was almost not my dad's. He'd lost the big city lawyer tone.

"I know you. You're the fucking bitch who ruined my wife and is trying to ruin my daughter."

"I'm Nancy Penchant and I loved your wife and I love your daughter."

"Are you—?"

"I love your daughter like a mother. No more. No less."

"Just stay away from her. I swear, stay away."

"Don't threaten me. When Alexandra is ready to see or speak to you, she'll do it. Don't force the issue or you may never see or speak to her again."

"Now are you threatening *me*?"

"I'm just telling you the reality here. She's going through things that she needs to work through."

"Fuck you, you dyke skank."

It was quiet. Then I heard the crack of his gloved hand on her bare face. Then he said, "Fuck you" a second time and then nothing more from him. Nancy murmured, "Oh my God," and the recording ended.

She looked at me. "That's what I said to him and that's what he said to me. Shall I delete it?"

I knew I should have told her to, but I couldn't.

"No. And send me a copy."

She opened her arms, and I lean for her embrace, with my head on her shoulder.

"Did you mean it?" I asked.

She paused then kisses the top of my head.

"I thought you were smart enough to know how much I love you."

I dug my head a little deeper. We savored our G-and-Ts and then had seconds before she said it was time for her to leave. I don't know when I'd last drunk hard liquor, and the gin was in my freezer for a long time. But we both deserved one—or two—that night.

I assured her that I'd be okay, that I might give Kate a call to come over, and with a final hug, Nancy was gone.

* * * *

KATE APPEARED ABOUT twenty minutes later. We stayed in the living room and sat beside each other on the sofa. I'd switched to red, and our wine glasses were cradled in our hands and our feet were on the coffee table, and *Kind of Blue* played on the speakers Bluetoothed from my laptop.

We sat there like that for, oh, five or six minutes, occasionally taking sips, and Kate said nothing.

"I'm scared," I said to the wall across. I'll admit to being a bit lightheaded from the booze, but I knew exactly what I was saying even if I was unsure what I was thinking. The knot in my stomach was getting tighter and tighter since he—my dad—came by and that night's encounter he had with Nancy made it almost unbearable. Kate reached over for my hand

and she, also speaking to the wall, said she I'd always have her and Nancy and Jessie and Dot and who knew who else and I wasn't so scared anymore.

54.

I was in no position to object to being ambushed—having been Jessie's ambusher—when I left my office for lunch but thank God it was Maggie. Each day when I left for lunch or to head home, I scanned the sidewalk, but my father was never there.

It was the second week of January, entering the long, cold spell that seems endless each year. I spotted her immediately, standing near the curb watching people as they went through the revolving door until that person was me.

I would've gone the other way if my father tried this. I'd not thought of what to do if it was Maggie. Before I could decide, she'd crossed the sidewalk to me and I, frankly, was pleased to see her. She—and TimTim—were a loose end.

"Can we talk?" she asked. Though it was cold, it wasn't frigid. "Please?"

I nodded, and we headed a couple of blocks away to where we could get tables and some privacy. There are a million places to eat in midtown, but it's amazing how difficult it can be to come up with a spot that has tables and privacy.

We got our soups and coffees and carried them to a small table with two rickety wooden chairs against one wall. We both well knew the drill and once our things were on the table and our coats on the backs of our chairs, I waited.

"At this point, I love you both and am just trying to find out what is going on and what you and he are thinking."

I didn't know what to say, not having thought this particular thing through.

"Right now," she said, "I just want to talk to you about *you*. Your father told me what happened, but that's him. I'm not trying to do anything at this point as to the two of you. Just tell me, Alex, what's going on?"

I hesitated a moment and took a breath. Before I knew it, all my discoveries came out, starting with my mom. What I read in what she wrote about her life. Little hints here and there about her and her life. That again and again I found her concerns about losing a child, and that I always thought that child was me.

I described beginning with my friend Kate to explore further and going to my grandparents in Paterson and learning more and more about her from her diaries. Her loneliness. Her fears. Then learning that she had a baby she gave up for adoption.

Maggie was listening, saying nothing, until this. I knew I would have to tell her, so I included it in the background. At the mention of the daughter, Maggie's hand shot across the little table and gripped my wrist and her eyes got big. She leaned closer to me and lowered her voice even below where it had been for our entire conversation.

"She gave up a baby?"

I nodded. I told her about the letter her parents received years after she died. How I tracked down that daughter and met with her.

This completely overwhelmed Maggie. I've no idea how my dad didn't tell her this. I told her about Jessie, as much as I could. Meeting her. Speaking regularly with her. How she has become part of *my* family.

"This is all, well, shocking," she said, "but I don't know how it affects your father. Did he know about this baby?"

"I don't think he did. Obviously, my grandparents knew but if my mom didn't say anything, why would they? And after she was gone, there was no reason to. Only when I was digging did they think the time was right for them to tell me."

I took a deep breath.

"There's more. My grandparents are not really my grandparents."

"Your mom's folks?"

I nodded. "My mom was given up for adoption. Taken, more accurately. Her mother, who I've also met, had a very hard time. She was unmarried and her parents were killed in a car crash. She turned to drugs and prostitution and they took my mom away when she was four and gave her to the Millers."

"Oh, honey," Maggie said, as she again reached for my hand. "I'm so sorry."

I was able to control my emotions here since I'd been living with this for so long. I told her it was alright.

At this point, our soups were cold, but she insisted we eat, so I did the best I could. In the sudden change of pace, we spoke in a way we never did before.

"You must miss her horribly."

"I do. But you want to know about my father."

"That's what I *need* to know."

I took a breath and dabbed bread into my black-bean soup and took a bite.

"My mom essentially died while making love to a woman with whom she had a long-term affair."

I said this flatly, not wanting her to interrupt. I couldn't tell from her reaction if he'd told her this.

"My father discovered the affair, and he tolerated it on the condition that she tolerate his own dalliances. An open marriage, as it were. I won't get into what I learned about what he did except for two things.

"First, he used me as leverage to control my mother and he made her think that she was evil because she cheated on him when he cheated on her well before she did anything with anyone but him. I know it's true. I've met the women."

This she clearly did not know. She was shocked, and I soldiered on.

"Second, he forced himself on my mother as part of the arrangement they had. I can't say how often he did this, but he did.

"So, Maggie, I don't know what he told you about what happened between us. But that's it. He…Well, he did things to my mother he shouldn't have, horrible things, and now I don't know when or if I will have anything to do with him again. I'm sorry. You wanted the truth. That is the truth."

She sat there trying to process what I said.

I stood and put my coat on. The one last piece had to be said.

"Has he mentioned an Andrew Grayson to you?"

Her look said she had no idea what I was talking about.

"I'm so sorry, Maggie, but you have to ask him about that."

I picked up my tray and put my bowl on it and, with a last look at her and a light tap on her shoulder, I left. I felt like a shit. There was no alternative. In high school a teacher told us what a Hobson's Choice was. No choice at all, and that's what this was. I was sure of it. Whatever my father told her was not the complete truth. Still, she didn't deserve what I did to her in that little soup-and-salad place near my office.

But I had. I took a final look at my stepmother as I reached the door. She hadn't moved. And I felt the cold but not frigid air when I was back on the sidewalk.

EPILOGUE

1.

I shouldn't be nervous, but I am. Kate's in the bathroom, and Nancy's finishing up in her bedroom. I'm in the living room near the photo of my mom and Nancy at the Met that once was in the bedroom but now is in a prominent place on the mantel next to a quite similar one of Nancy and me before the Monet, this one taken by Kate. Nancy's phone buzzes, and she calls out, "The car's downstairs." I look out and see the huge black Escalade double parked.

She flows into the living room with a slight twirl and gives me a final look of assurance, followed by Kate leaning to me and kissing my cheek and whispering in my ear, "You look great," and with that the three of us troop down and out front. The driver jumps out when he sees three overdressed women—Kate and me in summer dresses in blue (Kate) and yellow (me) with short sleeves and (in her case) a floral pattern dancing about and Nancy in white pants over black flats and a red blouse and those pearls of hers (the origins of which she's yet to reveal to me)—emerging from 34 West 94th Street late on a warm, mid-June morning. The three of us climbed into the backseat, with me in the middle, for our trip to Westchester.

In all that went on and though they had that calm phone conversation when I was beside myself in anger, Kate didn't actually meet Nancy until about two weeks after I had that lunch with cold soup—if you can call it that—with Maggie. This wasn't intentional. It was because I was always rushing here and rushing there and to one or the other of them and their paths didn't happen to cross.

That changed when we all sat at a very nice place on Columbus, just the three of us, on a Saturday night. Since they both got along with strangers in a way that I've never been able to and since by then they were not really strangers, it was a grand dinner on Nancy's dime.

Back to now. The Caddy SUV's not going to Bronxville. We're heading to a similarly upscale village to the east, on Long Island Sound itself. For the most part, the others engage in chit-chat as we cross the Triborough Bridge (which has a formal name nobody uses) and through the Bronx and into Westchester. I watch the unfamiliar scenes on either side of the Interstate. Jessie and Peter's house is in Larchmont, a couple of miles from Exit 16 of I-95, and once we're on the local streets my nerves begin bubbling again, and the others, perhaps sensing it, quiet and each holds one of my I'm afraid sweaty hands and while they pretend to ignore me each gives the one she holds a squeeze every once in a while.

Waze gets us to the house. It's a Dutch colonial on a slight hill fenced in by some hedges. The front door is open, and when we're through, Peter says Jessie will be right down, after she gets baby Emily asleep, and even as the words are uttered our hostess appears in a holy-shit-I-can't-believe-you-just-had-a-baby fire-engine red dress and there are hugs and kisses all around.

Most of the others are here, wandering around the living room or in the patio out back beyond the French doors. My grandpa and grandma—the Millers—seem cozy on the living room couch, with Dot on one end and Edgar in an armchair. They came down together this morning from upstate and are speaking comfortably with one another. More than anything, Edgar brought the two couples together in Hudson, and it was not long since we had a family party in the Millers' backyard just when spring broke through.

Shortly after we met her, Dot gave Jessie and me the name of our grandfather, but the last record we found of him was a brief funeral notice in the online archives in *The San Francisco Chronicle* that, assuming it was him, said he died of an overdose in 1976. We told Dot after discussing it with Edgar, and we did it in person. She heard and nodded and went up to her room and he told us it was best that we leave, and nothing more was said of our grandfather.

The search for Jessie's father was a dead-end, though for him there simply were *no* records and for all we hoped he might still be alive. Same for his parents. Jessie periodically has an agency do a search for all of them.

The "Nancy Question" was also delicate. Maybe the most delicate of all. It was necessary that Dot be told. Nancy agreed. She was such a part of Emily's life and so important to Emily—and Emily was such a part of hers—that she had to know at least of the woman Dot's daughter loved even if they might never meet.

Again, I called Edgar. Again, he said that she was stronger than she sometimes looked. He offered to tell her that Emily loved a woman, but I said it was for me to do.

On a Saturday in mid-April when spring was beginning to appear, Jessie picked Kate, Nancy, and me up and we drove to Hudson. They got out, and I drove to the Davises'. I spoke to Edgar that morning, and as I pulled up in the light blue Volvo he was quickly through the door.

"She's as ready as she's going to be."

She was thrilled to see me but a bit suspicious, especially after I asked her to sit beside me on the sofa, with Edgar on one of the armchairs opposite.

"What is it, dearie?" she asked in the sweet voice I knew hid her steeliness.

"I need to tell you something about my mom," I said.

She'd moved from looking suspicious to looking, well, alarmed.

"It's nothing bad, I promise you. It's just something about her that I found out only recently but I think it's something very special about her."

Dot looked across to Edgar, and I saw him give her a smile and a nod.

"Yes, I told Edgar. He said you'd be fine with it."

"It?" she asked.

I took a long breath.

"Mom was pregnant with me and met someone, a woman and after I was born, they got...close."

"Close?"

"They became lovers."

"Did your father know?"

"He found out. I can't say anything more. I just want you to know that Mom fell in love with this woman and—"

"How do you know she fell in love? This sounds very strange. She was married with a baby and she had an...affair. Is that what you're telling me? That my Emily was a...cheater?"

I began to panic. It was going very, very badly. Before I knew it, though, Edgar was beside her, half on the sofa, half on the floor and holding her hands.

"Dot. Emily loved this woman. That's what Alex is saying. She just wants you to know that. That there is someone you don't know who was very, very important to Emily."

Again, thank God for him. Dot had been asking about meeting my dad, but I kept putting it off. She was looking at Edgar, and he was nodding and smiling at her as I studied her profile until she turned back.

"We've come this far, Alex. Tell me."

And I told her. I softened some of the details but she seemed grateful for each word of truth about her daughter and when I told her that there were some "issues" between my mom and my dad, she understood and didn't require details and accepted it when I said, "I just can't deal with him just yet."

Edgar had by then gotten back into his armchair, and when I was finally done, Dot asked whether she could meet "this woman Emily was so fond of." I looked at Edgar yet again and he nodded and in half-an-hour we were all—"all" being Dot, Edgar, Jessie, Kate, and, of course, Nancy and me— at that restaurant on Warren Street in Hudson where the

Davises met the Millers and I swear that Dot seemed to see a bit of her Emily in Nancy.

They sat beside each other, and Dot couldn't get enough of the stories Nancy had to tell of her adventures with Emily in the city and I was so glad I told Dot.

Things went well enough that we crossed the final border and drove to Paterson and the Millers and in the end Grandma told Nancy that she was glad that Emily found someone she truly loved.

I'm not worried, then, about awkwardness concerning Nancy, who's in Jessie's kitchen. As Kate and I go into the living room, Edgar jumps up, displaying a short-order cook's dexterity with the crystal tumbler in his right hand, and I signal for him to sit back down as I move from Jessie to the four of them. Edgar squeezes my hand, telling me—as he always does—that I look great but "not as great as my Dot," which is always punctuated with that delightful wink of his, and Dot tells him to behave—as she always does. The tenseness that appeared when I brought my mom's birth and adoptive parents together on Hudson's Warren Street is long gone, and they quickly fall back into whatever they are talking about as I walk out to the patio. Kate brings a glass of white for me and one for herself.

Andrew's with a woman I've never seen before, with his arm around her waist with what looks like a Bloody Mary in his free hand, holding court with several people I don't recognize. He's in a tan suit, with a white shirt whose cuffs are held together by a pair of gold links his mom got him as a graduation present, a pastel tie, and shiny black loafers. He looks like I imagine my father did when he was first in law school at Andrew's age. His arm around a young woman also in a lovely summer dress in a floral pattern and I can't help but think of what my parents looked like when they went to a party long ago, though Andrew's date looks nothing like my mother.

The thought flashes through me as I look to them, and he waves us over. I whisper to Kate that he's off-limits but I'm pretty sure she's going to ignore me.

As we reach him, he says, "Hold on a sec," and calls to Jessie, who is just coming out herself. He turns to the others when Jessie reaches us.

"You've all met our host, and my half-sister Jessie," and they nod, "and this is today's honoree, my other half-sister, Alexandra Locus, and the sweet Kate."

He introduces his date, someone he knew vaguely at BC but ran into and decided to know more specifically at an unofficial BC reunion near her place on the Upper East Side. Her name is Shirley Evans and a glance from her makes it clear to Kate—at least it does to me—that he is decidedly attached even if he doesn't know it yet.

Before he can introduce the other two in his group, Jessie says they're neighbors who, like her, recently moved up, in their case, from the East Side, and after Andrew tells me his mom is somewhere inside, I leave to check up on her and on Nancy, and Kate says she'll be in shortly.

I find Nancy and Diane in the kitchen, doing various assembling fortified by periodic sips of their wines. I arranged for Diane to meet the others when she came up just about a year earlier to see how Andrew was doing after his first month of living in Williamsburg, Brooklyn and working in midtown, and Andrew and Kate bonded right off the bat, though it didn't go anywhere romantically at first and in the end I think both Kate and I knew it never would. But they can't resist a bit of flirting with one another.

A few months after that trip, Diane came up. She didn't have to. My mom was not part of her family but she was a major part of mine. She and Andrew joined almost everyone else for a trip up to the cemetery in Valhalla where my mom is buried on the tenth anniversary of her death. That was a Saturday, and with Nancy's help I arranged a suite of rooms for us all—my now *six* grandparents, Diane and Andrew,

Jessie and Peter, Nancy, Kate, and me—in a nice hotel in White Plains for that night and we reminisced about Emily Locus at a large table in the top floor restaurant with its view to Manhattan to the south.

And now I find Nancy and Diane, contemporaries, in the kitchen. They spoke, Nancy said, every couple of months and sometimes exchanged Twitter memes. They refuse my offer of help. "You're the guest of honor," Nancy says.

It's my first time in the house, so I wander, cradling my wine. Jessie sees me and takes me to say hello to her folks and then asks me to go upstairs with her. She leads me to Emily's room. I hadn't seen the baby since her christening three months before, and I lean in to look at her on her back, asleep with a bit of spittle sliding from her mouth.

"I get it now," Jessie says.

I grip her hand. "She is so beautiful. I see how you would," and then put my arm around my sister as we look at my niece and I daresay both think of the other adoptee in our blood. I hope to get to the baby stage one of these days, but for now I'm still finding it hard to get past the three-or-four date mark with anyone and go home too often than I'd like to admit with one of those non-Goldman guys I run into at Teddy's, where I still go with Kate most Thursday nights. All of which I put out there to explain why I don't have anyone to bring to this little party where I'm the "guest of honor."

My moment with Little Emily is too brief when Peter calls up to Jessie, and she, wiping a slight tear, whispers "I love you," and I say, "Me too," as she calls down to Peter that she's coming. I stay with Little E a few moments more, thinking again of the woman for whom she is named, until I hear Jessie call me to join them. The house's stairs lead to a small landing at the back of the house, between the kitchen and the living room. I don't see anyone until I reach the bottom and turn right and then I'm surprised to see my stepmom.

Technically, I don't know if Maggie is still my stepmother. She moved out shortly after our cold soups that frigid afternoon she ambushed me as I stepped from my building. She found a small two-bedroom apartment in Yonkers, just across the Bronxville border. Much as I tried to keep in touch, though, she withdrew and after a while I stopped leaving messages. She doesn't want anything to do with my family— by which I mean the Locuses—and is getting a divorce. I've no idea what the status of the proceeding is or whether it's been finalized and what the deal is with TimTim.

What I do know about Maggie I learned from a couple of people in town with whom I sometimes speak but mostly from Kate's mom. Had Nancy not been around, I might have taken Mrs. Winslow up on her offer about filling something I'd lost when my mom died, but we were both, as was Kate, more than content about her slipping into the role of a favorite aunt. I don't go see her in Bronxville, lest I encounter my own Voldemort, but she comes into Manhattan maybe once every month or so and takes Kate and me to dinner when she does And we spent several days with her and Mr. Winslow at their rental in East Hampton just this past August.

As to everyone else in Bronxville, they are completely in the dark as to how what everyone thought was a perfect marriage had so quickly gone south.

I miss Maggie now and then (and TimTim more often than not). I understand why she did what she did. Sympathize with her. Now she's standing in the foyer of Jessie and Peter's new house in Larchmont. I don't know who invited her, but that doesn't matter. I race to her and am crying before my body hits her with far more velocity than I expect.

I don't know for how long I hold her, but however long it is, it is not enough. I don't realize how much I missed her, how much I loved her, until those moments.

"I'm so proud of you," she says. "It's your day and an adults' party so I found a babysitter for TimTim but tell me you'll come up to visit?"

I of course tell her I will, and then I escort her around the room and introduce her. The most difficult introduction is Diane and Andrew. Before I go to them, I ask what she knows of them. She says my father confessed the whole story when she asked about it after our lunch. It was another shoe that dropped but she says she hasn't spoken to, met with, or written to either of them. She's happy, though, to meet Andrew and his mom, and he helps smooth things out among the three of them off to the side of the O'Toole/Alpert living room.

It's nearing one, and we are getting hungry when a couple I have no idea is coming are through the door. I'm in regular contact with my Locus grandparents. They are careful about maintaining a wall. They know I'll only speak of my father, if ever, when I'm ready to. So, they never mention him. Our agreement is a reason I know so little about what is going on between my father and Maggie.

I decided five or six months after meeting Andrew, though, that he should know these grandparents. In a call with Grandmother Locus—"Lydie"—I spat it out. "That boy you saw with Diane Grayson? He's your grandson."

It took a moment, but she recovered and after I gave some details, she understood, at least in broad strokes.

"Does your father know?" she asked.

"That's how I found out. Not from him. From his secretary. His name is Andrew and, well, he's never met his father. It's complicated, but he'd like to meet you and grandfather."

Everyone wanted to meet everyone, and that's how that happened, with Andrew taking Amtrak with me to Philly where we met with Diane and the three of us drove out to the Locuses, and, all things considered it went, well.

The wall between the Graysons and my father, though, remains. Neither Diane nor Andrew has spoken to him, and, as far as I can tell, he's made no effort to contact them.

I'm afraid the meeting between the Locuses and the Millers did not go so well as the one with the Graysons. The two couples hadn't seen each other since my graduation from Villanova. They were uncomfortable then and they're uncomfortable now. Whether they will ever get along remains a mystery, but I'm well past allowing their tensions to affect my (separate) relationships with either of them.

I'm glad the Locuses made the trip and am with them near the door when Peter clinks his glass with a fork in the living room. Those outside scurry in.

"Thank you all for coming to Jessie's and Emily's and my new house. We're so glad to have you. Enough about me. My wife wants to say a few words about our guest of honor, my sister-in-law, Alexandra Locus."

There is a smattering of applause as Jessie steps beside her husband, who puts his free arm around her waist.

"Most of you, I know, are aware of the genesis of Alex's book project. It was her discovery of materials that our mother wrote over the years, before her tragic death, which happened before I got the chance to meet her."

She almost...almost lost her composure but Peter pulled her closer and she put her hand up to stop me from coming to her as she regained her lawyerly control.

"Emily Locus had a facility with words and with telling stories. I am proud to have played a slight role in helping Alex organize those words and those stories.

"Were it not for a serendipitous—if that's the right word—book reading at Barnes & Noble almost two years ago when a young woman named Karen Adams read from her book and when Alex met Nancy and that meeting began Alex's journey to find the truth about our mother, I would never have known all of the wonderful family I have. And part of that journey found me as her half-sister and Dot Davis as our mother's birth mother, our grandma."

She lifts her glass in Dot's direction and others follow suit as Edgar smiles, gives her forehead a kiss, and tightens his grip around her.

"I never met my mom," Jessie continues, "when she was alive but came to know so much about her from meeting Alex on a sidewalk outside my office and from reading my mom's words and stories. They're put together in this book," and she lifts a copy handed to her by Peter for all to see, "and I know everyone here is thrilled to have met Alex and to have learned about our mother.

"So, everyone. To Alex."

And the toast is made and "to Alex" is echoed and people again congratulate me, and we all head to the dining room for some food.

2.

"**I** am Alex Locus."

I stand at the same podium with the same Barnes & Noble logo and mic to which Karen Adams stepped two years before, my hands gripping its sides as hers did. I'm pleased Karen's sitting in the crowd, next to Nancy. And I end up mimicking some of her nervousness that night. As she did, I lift and sip from a water bottle and dampen my mouth. *Words of My Life* is in my left hand. I cough and look down at my notes and proceed to ignore what I prepared.

"It's normal, as I understand it in these readings, for the author to explain a bit about who she is and how she came to write the book she is trying to sell. She'll then read an excerpt, and the excerpt will be just enough to get you interested enough to want to buy her book and then you'll tell your friends and before you know it Emma Watson is playing her in the movie.

"But I'm not this book's author. I am her daughter. *One* of her daughters. I was fourteen when my mother died. Were you to ask me then about her, I would only have been able to say that she was good to me and she drove me to field hockey practice and took care of me when I was sick and I loved her and she loved me.

"That's what all, or at least most I assume, a teenager would say about her mother. Over time, I imagine as in most families, I would grow to know her as an adult and, perhaps, as a friend. And she would be with me as I, too, became an adult and had my own family. Perhaps my own children.

"As I say, though, my mom died when I was fourteen. And I didn't know her at all.

"This book is her story. Or at least part of it. The words and nuances of a woman trying to describe herself. It's not an autobiography or a biography or memoir. It's a collection of her stories, which I discovered some nine years after she died."

As I went through the stories to try to put them in an order for the anthology, I circulated them. Certain of the people involved had veto power but, for example, Nancy was happy to see important portions of *The Love of My Life* included. I showed Grandmother Locus *A Misty Morn* before I showed it to anyone else, and she said she'd be "proud'—she used that word—at its inclusion. Indeed, no one even *asked* about maybe excluding anything, and in the end, it became an issue of what I could put in and not what I couldn't.

Much as Karen Adams had, the more I spoke, the more comfortable I got. A little more water.

"With the help of many, many people—I will not burden the proceedings by naming them all, we don't have time for that, but I talk about each of them in the introduction and explain why my mom meant so much to them and why they mean so much to me—some of whom are here today.

"It was my discovery of these documents that led me to discover who she was. Her loves. Her lies. Her strengths and her weaknesses. Most of all, with the help of several people, the project that led to the book led me to discover a sister and a brother I never knew I had and a grandmother I never knew I had. Families I never dreamed of being a part of.

"Most of all, it led me to discover a mother I never knew. And with this collection, I hope others will get a glimpse of that woman. Faults and all. A woman who was, who *is*, my mom.

"The story I selected to read to you tonight was not one of her best, I'm afraid. But it is, I think, the one that best tells me, at least, who she was. It's historical. Set in 1863 New York.

"To set the stage, the hero, Mary McNeil, is twenty-five. She came to New York with her parents when she was eleven, part of those who abandoned Ireland, or who were abandoned by Ireland, during the Famine or Hunger years.

"Her husband was away at war, a private with the 69th Infantry Regiment. She doesn't know where he is or even if he is still alive. He sends letters every few weeks, but they take a while to reach her. He worked on the docks before being drafted. She works as a domestic in a house of one of the *nouveau riche* Irish. It's there, in that house, that I'll begin."

I drink a little more water in the hope that I won't have to stop midway.

I know before I enter the room that Mrs. O'Rorke will be dismissing me. I don't blame her. I could no longer hide my condition and seeing as my husband has been away for over a year, 'tis no doubt there is a bastard in my womb. Whose it is is of no concern to Mrs. O'Rorke. Much as she liked me in the sixteen months I've worked for her and the O'Rorke clan, I cannot remain.

Nor can she give me a proper testimonial. A proper reference, we both know, would be of no good given the condition of my belly.

The room is darker than usual but as stuffy as it always is. The master's den. I enter it each morning to tidy it and to clean it. It's where the master took me five months before. That is a fact of no relevance I think to anyone but me so I don't mention it to Mrs. O'Rorke. She wouldn't believe me if I did.

The room is dark because she closed the curtains. As if the light would allow her words to be heard throughout the neighborhood and bring shame upon the premises. 'Tis bad enough that over time people who see my belly and talk about where I worked when what happened happened. There can be no suggestion that Mrs. O'Rorke or any member of the family were anything but victims of the loose woman they had the misfortune to employ.

Mrs. O'Rorke is, as always in the morning, wearing a morning gown. She sits in her husband's chair and she directs me to sit opposite her, on the other side of the large, mahogany desk. What she says don't matter. Her actual words are irrelevant. I'm to leave immediately and never to return. Neither she nor anyone in the O'Rorke clan will know me from that moment forward. I receive one week's pay and am grateful.

Without pay, except for the slight portion of my husband's I receive, and without prospects, I don't last long in the tenement apartment I share with five other girls—all of them seamstresses—while my husband is at war. They try to help since we all try to help each other, but they've too little to make a difference and I return to the slightly larger flat of my parents, now empty except for them and my youngest brother. He is just fifteen and works on the docks as my husband did before the draft. My parents pray the war will not last so long that my brother, too, will be drafted.

My parents were good to me when I lost our first baby three years earlier. She—my baby was a girl—came early and was small and sickly when she did. They let me hold her just once before taking her forever from me, telling me that she died in the night. They said it was best that I do not see her frail, lifeless body.

This child, this bastard in me, will not be small and sickly. He or she will arrive and I will hold my second child and I promise I will never let go.

I can make some money scrubbing floors in some of the office buildings off Washington Square and I do. It isn't much and the work is hard. But it is work, and I am not afraid of hard work. My mom, bless her, lost two babies before we left Ireland and one after we arrived. I can only hope I will be more blessed than she was.

I begin my confinement in a dank apartment on Grand Street. I am confined to bed, surviving only by the kindness of my mom and Mrs. Ellison. Mrs. Ellison is a widow. She has four children. Her husband was lost at

Shiloh, and she ekes out survival by scullery maid work. It, too, is hard work—all work is hard work, even for those in domestic service for kind families, as the O'Rorkes are—but it keeps body and soul together.
"I'm going to jump a little."

It is dark and rainy when he comes. He is led into my room, which smells of my piss and my sweat. There's less light than the little there normally is, seeing as the sky is lowered and the winds are pushing the rain against the sides of the building. No, it is dark and rainy, but he comes, his coat across his arm. He somehow finds a clean spot to sit. A gentleman. I fear people will know why he is here and I know he fears that, too. But he is not deterred.

"My mother has sent me. She regrets that I could not come sooner. But I am here now. She asks that I inquire into your condition and the condition of your child."

I put the book down and look out across the room.

"I won't read what happens next and will just say that she has a very difficult time of it but the baby, a girl, is healthy. The story discusses how her mother and Mrs. Ellison get her through. She writes to her husband as they both hope the war, the Civil War, will finally and mercifully be over and how she again gets domestic work in a house a bit off the beaten path, where among her jobs is making sure the house's children are kept occupied.

"She continues."

'Tis a fine enough day for me to take the children to the square in the morning. It's about eleven when we reach the gates. Mr. Aston, the caretaker, gives me a nod as we go in, as he always does. He carries a spade and is smoking a pipe, as he always does.

The children and I complete our first lap when I sense someone approaching from behind. The square is crowded with nurses, governesses, nannies, and entire families so I'm not afraid. The person behind me, a footman, taps me on the shoulder.

"Excuse me, Miss. When you pass the gate again could you spare my mistress a moment?"

I look towards the gate and see the O'Rorke carriage. It is distinctive, what with its neat, green trim against its ebony paint. She is not letting me see her face, but I know she must be watching me, wondering what I will do.

I turn to the footman.

"Tell your mistress that I'd be pleased to see her. But I can't abandon these children. Ask her to meet me at the gate. Then she and I can do a lap."

I know it is forward of me but 'tis true that I can't leave the children alone. It'll be a test of her. Whether she's willing to chance being seen with me.

Her footman doffs his cap and nods. "Thank you, Miss." He walks to the carriage, and I continue the lap with the children. When we're at the far end, I take a second glance to the gate. The carriage is still there, the footman standing by its door. As I near the end of the lap, he opens the door and pulls down the steps. He helps Mrs. O'Rorke descend and closes the door as she walks to the gate.

She does not look well. It's been over a year since I saw her. She is not old—surely not older than her early 50s— but she seems to have suffered gravely since our last encounter. She uses a cane but refuses the footman's offer to assist her.

When I reach the gate, she stands in the middle of the path. I don't know if she planned it, and I rather think that she hasn't, but she reaches her arms to encircle me. I tell the children that it's proper, that she is an "old, dear friend."

She asks if she can accompany us on our third lap, and we continue, slower than before. Now she willingly puts her arm through mine as we resume.

"He confessed. What he did with you." Before I can respond she adds, "To you."

I remain silent. He is a good man, and I expected no less. He took advantage of me in a moment of weakness, for both of us. From the moment I knew I had another chance of life inside me, I was glad of that weakness, however wrong it was. To God. To my husband. To his wife. I knew I would be shut out, as I was. I'm glad, though, especially now that Alexandra Edwina is alive and that there's the hope of being able to provide for her, especially after my husband forgave me and will be home finally when the infernal War ends as it surely must someday.

I can provide, if barely, for my child. My daughter. My second and only daughter.

She has a good heart, does Mrs. O'Rorke. Whether she truly forgives her husband I cannot know. On that day, though, as we are in the third lap of the park and after she tells me that her children are well and healthy and that her youngest son, the one who visited me during my confinement, is recently wed, she brings up what she came to see me about.

"I know it's difficult for you, my dear. I made inquiries and learned that you have safely given birth to a girl."

"Yes. Alexandra Edwina."

"I didn't know the name. So, you named her after her father?"

"Aye. Her father is part of her. I thought she should—"

Her tone chills.

"Do you intend on...telling her about her father? Who her father is?"

"In time, I think I must."

Her fears realized, she becomes rigid and pulls her arm from mine and halts. She turns to face me as the children appear confused.

"If you plan on trying to get—"

I stop her.

"Mrs. O'Rorke. She is my baby. She'll be raised as my baby. The child of my husband and me. Someday she'll ask me about her true father. That can't be helped. She'll understand at some age that my husband cannot be her real father."

My tone is perhaps icier than I meant it to be. But Mrs. O'Rorke turned it into a question of money. That I would want her money.

"I will tell her the truth. She's entitled to know. I can't say what she will do with that truth."

I reach for the children and resume the walk, with Mrs. O'Rorke standing in place. She cannot catch us and I don't look back. Till I hear her plea.

"Mary. Please wait."

The children and I stop. Then I turn.

"I didn't come here to do that, to accuse you of planning to blackmail us," she says.

"Why would asking for a father's help in raising his own daughter be blackmail? And before you ask. He is the father. He's the only man I've...been with like that since my husband left."

"Mary, I don't doubt it. But I came to try to help you, not to accuse you. I am sorry that it went the way that it did. I came to offer you something. For your daughter—"

"Alexandra Edwina."

"Alexandra Edwina. We would be willing to take her from you. To raise her in a way that you could not possibly raise her. To give her things you could not—"

"Stop. You make it sound like a simple transaction. You will 'take' my child. You will 'raise' my child."

I try to control my anger. I know, or hope, that she means well. That she'd spoken to Alexandra Edwina's father about it. I know she is a good woman, at heart, and that she would provide more than I possibly could. That

my daughter might rise in society, as a member of the
O'Rorke clan. That my daughter might become a lady.

I close the book and reach for a legal pad that I'd placed on the podium.

"It's a conventional story. I would like to be able to tell you that you can find out how it ends by buying the book. But I can't."

I lift the pad and flip its pages to the audience. They see that about halfway through the pages become blank.

"What I read was what my mom wrote in this pad. It's the seventh pad she filled with the story of Mary and Alexandra Edwina. It ends where I stopped. We don't know when my mom wrote this. We don't know why she stopped. How long it sat around. Whether she looked at it at times and thought about what would happen to Alexandra Edwina. The only time she used my name. Was this her *Edwin Drood*? Her *Sanditon*?"

I take a long, final drink of water. I reach to the table and lift my copy of *Scream*.

"One of those most instrumental in my discoveries, perhaps *the* most instrumental, was Nancy Penchant and this"—I hold *Scream* up and nod to it—"is in some senses my mother's story, told through the eyes of her lover. I hope I can fill some of the gap my mother left when she passed as she has filled some of mine."

Nancy not only agreed that I could but encouraged me to say this.

"The truth can sometimes set one free. In my case, though, that freedom has come at a cost. My mother, as her tales make clear, doubted whether she could be an adequate or capable mother. Perhaps while she was alive my own shortcomings might have reinforced that view, for which I will always bear a large share of the responsibility. But if I had one wish, it would be for her to be looking down on me today and understand how wonderful she was, how wonderful she still is to me and to many others, and that she'd be proud of this daughter as I know she would be proud of the other daughter"—I point in Jessie's general direction and fight through my emotions—"who she never knew."

3.

When I finished the reading and in the glow of a nice round of applause, I was pleased that I'd managed to hold it together. Nancy and Jessie came to me, and I sat between them as a stream of people, several of them strangers, thanked me for the reading and had me sign the book as if it contained my words.

It was more than I expected or was ready for, though. Nancy had booked a large table at a restaurant on the northeast corner of Broadway and 84th, but as we were getting ready to leave, I began to tell her I was not up to it. She leaned to me and said she understood and that I deserved some alone time and with a hug she whispered "goodbye" and "I love you" and I left her to explain my disappearance to the others and with a wave I headed for that long down-escalator.

And now, here I am again on Broadway outside the bookstore on a Thursday night in the summertime. I don't know where to go, where I can walk and clear my head. It was light when I went in but it now is dark, or as dark as it gets on Broadway, and the steady north and south stream of walkers and strollers and those hurrying for a date pass by and I turn left and join the flow to the north.

It's not long until I cross Broadway and then Amsterdam and Columbus. I make it a point not to go down my block but cut across 86th Street to Central Park West. I find a bench on the park side of that avenue, but not the one where I had that second encounter with Nancy, the one where I didn't sit but left her with what was then my only copy of *The Love of My Life.*

The bench is where 94th Street begins, at CPW, at the northernmost of the two crosswalks. It's a beautiful night. The afternoon heat is gone. I hear activity in the park behind me, the noise carrying well in the clear air.

Past the large apartment buildings that frame the street and just through the small trees in full bloom that dot blocks in the city, I can make out number 34. It's too far for me to really *see* it. But I know it's there.

I sit on the bench with my bag in my lap as the buses go up and down the avenue and people, alone or in couples, head to or from the park with their big or little or medium-sized dogs and others hurry past to get a late run in now that the heat has broken.

I imagine—again it's too far to see and I don't dare get closer—my mother going up the stoop to apartment 3F. Going into her refuge. I can't think of her leaving without seeing the EMTs hurrying down with her on a gurney and rushing her into the back of their ambulance, its siren wailing as it heads east and turns north right in front of where I sit to where she will officially die, though she was already gone.

I choose to imagine her going in. How wonderful it would be for me to take those steps two-at-a-time carrying flowers from a stall on Columbus for a Sunday brunch that Emily Locus and her famous author wife would hold once or twice a month.

Nancy still has brunch now and again where she tells us—usually several from her book world, including Karen Adams—of her latest project and I sometimes return the favor. But...it's not the same as it *could* have been. *Should* be.

I don't do it often enough. This sitting and thinking. My family. Now around some large table over on Broadway and talking about me and, I expect, my mother. Saying how glad they are that I undertook my quest. It was for them, too, a way to make things a little better for all of us.

Slight as it might have been, it's enough.

I get up and tidying my light blue blouse and white linen pants and a pair of diamond stud earrings that were my mother's and sat unnoticed in the back of one of my drawers for years—a bit of Nancy's style having seeped into me—and putting my bag over my right shoulder, I turn to the south. I decide to go to Broadway itself and not straight home. The door of this restaurant (like that of the since-departed bistro where I bought lunch for Agnes Hall) has its Zagat's stickers, and I go in.

The bar area to the left is crowded with people much like me—that is, on the prowl for a night or a life with someone much like me—and the din of a New York City Thursday night wafts across.

As the hostess, tall, blonde, and in black pants, a white tuxedo shirt, and sensible black flats, approaches, I wave for her to stop.

"I see them," I tell her. There's an empty chair; Nancy hadn't bothered to ask that it be taken away. There's laughing and cups and saucers and desserts and more than a few wine glasses and two wine bottles—a white and a red—on the large round table in a corner by the open window looking out onto Broadway and onto the tables set on the sidewalk for *al fresco* dining.

I stand beside the hostess. "Sometimes they embarrass me," I say.

"One of Tolstoy's happy families?" she asks as the cacophony rises and falls from the group and across the half-empty floor above the Broadway noise.

I smile. "I've never thought of it that way, but, yeah, a happy family."

They haven't yet noticed me. Before I start across the room, I turn to the pretty woman. "I think, though, that we're not quite the same as any other. And wouldn't give this one up for the world."

She nods, and I leave her to wind my way through the tables to claim my seat.

THE END

ACKNOWLEDGEMENTS

As always, I thank those who read early versions of this book and gave helpful comments. The list includes my sisters Clio Garland and Liz Sauer and my brother Jimmy Garland as well as my cousin Dawn Brady. Cassandra Felice provided editing services, for which I am grateful. Fellow author (and editor) Renée Gendron (@ReneeGendron) provided comments in the very early stages and in the very late ones. GL Robinson (@GL_Robinson) provided late comments.

Any errors in the book are entirely my own.

ABOUT THE AUTHOR

Joseph P. Garland is a native New Yorker. He grew up in Tuckahoe, New York, less than half-a-mile from the fictional home of Alex Locus. He lived on West 85th Street while and for years after he attended Columbia Law School. It is the same block on which Alex Locus lives in the story. He is a lawyer, now living in Westchester County.

He has written *Róisín Campbell: An Irishwoman in New York* and *A Studio on Bleecker Street*. They are both literary novels set in the 1870s, chiefly in New York City and have intersecting stories, with *Róisín Campbell* being the first of them. He also wrote *Bridget and Joseph in 1918*, a mixture of fact and fiction about his father's parents, set on Manhattan's Lower East Side, as well as a number of romances under the name J.P. Garland. They are available in paperback and email from Amazon and other retailers.

His books/stories are listed at DermodyHouse.com/stories

ADOPTION

In this story, Jessica Alpert learns who her birthmother (Emily) is through a New York State Registry. It requires that both parties register.

On January 15, 2020, New York State adopted the Clean Bill of Adoptee Rights Act. It grants adoptees who are at least eighteen the right to obtain copies of their original birth certificates.

A DIFFERENT PERSPECTIVE

Originally, this book had a
second prologue. Here is the
story of how Karen Adams was
discovered by Nancy Penchant
and her view of that first reading
at the B&N on Broadway.

KAREN'S STORY

1.

It's a small college in New Hampshire but there are those who love it and Karen Adams was among them. A western Massachusetts native, in 2014 she was a Dartmouth sophomore majoring in economics who dabbled in story-writing. *Lonesome*, a piece she wrote about a middle-aged woman losing a friend, was published in the college's literary magazine. Though it was well received, she was surprised when she received a call on a Thursday in early April from the magazine's editor-in-chief, Michael Devers.

An hour later, Karen, in an outfit she threw together—the cleanest of the three dresses that hung in her closet, pantyhose from the bottom of the middle drawer of her dresser, and a pair of flats that were sufficiently broken in to be comfortable—and her hair well-brushed, was sitting in a comfortable chair in the English Department lounge beside Nancy Penchant. Nancy was a novelist who'd been a finalist for an American Book Award for her novel *Scream*. Devers introduced them to each other and promptly disappeared.

Nancy Penchant was about forty-five and striking. She was perhaps five-seven or five-eight, about Karen's height, and while it was clear that Karen struggled to make herself presentable, Nancy Penchant had the look of a woman who could roll out of bed and onto a runway.

She wasn't particularly or at least conventionally pretty. "Striking" was the word. They both had the same slim figure and the same dark-brown hair—Karen's was long, Nancy's was kept a few inches below her shoulders—and Karen wore none and Nancy just a little make-up. Nancy was in black pants and wore a cream-colored blouse with white buttons and black shoes with two-inch heels and only the slightest of gold jewelry in the form of a small gold heart necklace. She did not wear a wedding band.

As they shared tea in the time-honored Ivy League tradition (at least until four), Nancy told Karen how much she enjoyed *Lonesome* and more to the point that it was selected for the Emily Locus Award. Karen had no idea what the Emily Locus Award was. Karen had no idea who Emily Locus was. There was a $2,000 stipend, Nancy Penchant explained, and *Lonesome* would be published in a national literary magazine and that, she said, could lead to all manner of opportunities.

Karen thanked the older writer who, when she rose, gave the student a hug and said, "It was very nice to get the chance to meet you. You'll be hearing from us and, again, congratulations." She turned towards the door, but Karen rushed to walk her out.

A black sedan was parked on the street near the entrance to the English Department. The driver jumped out when he saw the women. He opened the back door for Nancy Penchant. Before she got in, though, the author smiled, handed a card to Karen, and said, very softly, "When you get to New York, and of course you will, please call me. I can tell you who Emily Locus was" and then she was in the car and the driver closed the door and raced around and before she knew it Karen Adams was watching it leaving the campus.

2016

In late August 2016, Karen Adams was enjoying dinner with her parents in a new restaurant on Railroad Street by the movie theater in Great Barrington, Massachusetts. A family friend stopped by to congratulate her on graduating with honors. In two weeks, the Wednesday before Labor Day, she'd be moving to New York to begin work as an analyst at an investment house in midtown Manhattan. She would be living in a studio apartment on the seventh floor of a large building in the mid-Eighties near Broadway, only a block or so from a subway station and a few from Riverside Park.

As the friend was about to leave, Karen's mother put a hand on the girl's arm and said that her daughter had won a writing prize in college. The Emily Locus Award, she said, and the friend congratulated her again and was gone.

"Mother. Stop doing that. It was just a little thing," Karen said. She lost track of how often she repeated this to her mom, but this admonition never did any good and they both knew it and Karen said it as a matter of for-the-record principle.

On the Tuesday after Labor Day, Karen sat with the four or five other new analysts at her firm in a drab windowless conference room with a Danish on a small plate and a black coffee in a mug stenciled with the institution's name watching a PowerPoint presentation about the bank's work-assignment and record-keeping protocols. She'd been in her apartment for a week and it was finally becoming "home." All but a few of the boxes were unpacked and she was getting comfortable there and in the City. She'd even walked the three plus miles home a couple of times.

In her second week at the bank, Karen went to lunch in one of those pocket parks that dot midtown with Denise Elms, the only other woman among the new analysts. About halfway through their salads, Karen looked at Denise and said, "Just spit it out."

Denise, after assuring Karen that Karen was not her "type" and getting a promise of secrecy, came out to her friend. She wanted, she told Karen, to visit a lesbian bar but was afraid to go alone. She'd found one in the West Village and asked Karen to be her "wingwoman"?

"You don't have to do anything," Denise said. "I'll be forever grateful if you're just there. My treat." She smiled and nodded and Karen couldn't say no since she had absolutely nothing else to do, and on Friday night, the pair met in front of Ethel's, a lesbian bar in the West Village off Hudson Street. Denise got there about ten minutes before the appointed hour, and when Karen arrived, Denise said a couple of the woman going in "checked me out and smiled" and maybe things might actually work out for her.

Once inside, it took a minute to get used to the dark interior and the pounding music. A hostess came to them and, well, checked them out before leading them to a small table off to the back and to the side of a small dancefloor.

She proofed them before taking their order of beers and finger food. Karen asked, when they were alone, "What happens now?" and Denise said, "I have no idea." Denise had been to gay bars before but only with three or four others up in Boston where she went to school. That was toe-tipping. This was body-diving.

Two women, maybe twenty-five, approached and asked them to dance. Starting to panic, Karen said, "I'm just helping my friend out," the shorter of the two said, "we're going to dance, not get married," and Karen hopped up and forgot where she was and with whom she was dancing and against all expectations enjoyed herself. It was clear that Denise was enjoying herself even more.

About forty-five minutes later and on their second beers, with Denise's on the table while she danced with yet another stranger, Karen said "Oh shit." She said it aloud, though no one heard.

The source of this was walking in with two other women, Nancy Penchant. Recognized by her manner and, strangely enough, her hair (a little longer than normal for a woman her age but incredibly beautiful on her).

Why the "Oh shit"? Karen was in New York and hadn't called. She hadn't even thought of calling and had no idea whether she still had the number, let alone where it could be.

But it didn't take long for Karen to realize how ridiculous her reaction was. It was years ago. Gallons and gallons had gone under the bridge. The older woman would have forgotten all about her and Karen relaxed as Nancy went to a large round table to the side and near the front, where she sat and held court for her guests and several others who clustered around to say hello.

Denise was still on the dancefloor with yet another someone else when, ten minutes after she walked into the bar, Nancy Penchant said something to the people with her and left her table and start walking in the direction of the ladies' room, which happened to be in the direction of Karen's table.

Karen grabbed a drinks menu that was between salt and pepper shakers and a red plastic bottle of some type of hot sauce and pretended to study it.

"Anything interesting?" Karen looked up. "May I sit?" she heard. Trying to look surprised by seeing Nancy Penchant again. Before Karen could answer, Nancy was in Denise's chair. Karen dropped the menu back.

"Aren't you ordering anything?" Nancy said, and Karen recalled the slightly husky but wholly enticing voice. She coughed.

"No. I'm fine, thanks."

Still, Karen had a flash that in truth since Nancy surely hadn't recognized her, she was trying to...pick her up. She was sitting alone in a lesbian bar after all. She might as well have posted a large "Pick Me Up" sign with an arrow on the wall behind her. She started panicking. *What would she do?*

The flash didn't last long.

"Karen Adams, isn't it? Small world, but I'm not surprised to see you here."

"I'm just helping out a friend," Karen said, to which Nancy just smiled and nodded. She'd heard that at this very table more than once but it was no matter. This was Karen Adams, and Karen Adams was a damn good writer, and Nancy Penchant never forgot her talent from the first time she read *Lonesome* in the DARTMOUTH QUARTERLY. Such a sad but vibrant piece. Nancy was anxious about what Karen wrote after that.

The waitress came to see if Nancy wanted anything, but the author waved her off. She grabbed some of the nuts in the little wooden bowl. Put a few in her mouth and ate them. She wiped her hands on a paper napkin she lifted from the table and then squeezed into a ball when she was finished. Looking across to Karen the whole time, and sufficient time having been bought she asked, "Have you ever wondered about Emily Locus?"

Karen was relieved by the question and by the fact that Nancy Penchant didn't appear pissed that she hadn't looked her up when she got to New York. She had, though, deposited the $2,000 check, and the emblazoned certificate that accompanied it was in some box still up in the house in the Berkshires and though she was forever telling her mom that it was no big deal, it meant the world to her and she hoped Nancy Penchant would ask her about her writing because she knew exactly where the printed drafts of a dozen stories and the initial rumblings of an actual novel were.

First, though, Nancy said, "My book *Scream* is about her. About us, in a way." Karen had read and liked *Scream* and if she'd known that it had something to do with Emily Locus she would have taken an interest in the namesake for the award.

As Denise neared, Nancy held Karen's hand on the top of the table for a moment and stood to give up her seat. She reached into her bag for a card and handed it to Karen. "Please, please call me this time. Promise?"

Karen looked at the card and back up and she promised to call.

Nancy nodded at Denise and without being introduced was gone. Denise asked who that was, and Karen told her, that she was an author who she met when she got a writing award in college. Studying Nancy's return to her group, Denise half-jokingly said, "I wish you'd introduced me," and with that the two finished their beers and the nuts, and Karen said it was time to leave and Denise....Well Denise asked if Karen would mind Denise staying a bit longer and so Karen took her cab alone to her studio apartment on the Upper West Side.

2.

Karen did well at the investment house, but the price was having to work longer and longer hours. In by eight-thirty and rarely done before half-past-seven. Lunch at her desk. The pay was good and the work had its interesting moments and it pretty well was as good a job as anyone in her shoes could expect.

It was made tolerable because of her weekends. Not that she spent them slumming and barhopping and hooking-up for no-commitment sex. Denise, who did all three and was well past the point of needing a wingwoman when she did, made a point of asking Karen each Monday, "So what'd you do this weekend, *Miss* Adams," and Karen's unvaried reply was that she wrote.

It was true. She wrote. She was content in her studio apartment near Broadway and walked most Saturday and Sunday mornings up and down Riverside Park. She always carried a spiral notebook with her. She'd gotten a package of five, each with a different color cover, and two sets of blue, red, and green pens in see-through plastic pockets at a dollar store on Broadway and 98th. If it weren't raining, she carried her notebooks and pens in one of those small green heavy-cloth Army bags with a long strap and would find a bench facing out towards the Hudson and along the stretch where there was an ever-changing community garden. Where she wrote.

Equally important was that she kept her promise to Nancy Penchant. Within a week of meeting her again at Ethel's, she called and they met for brunch on the Saturday at a restaurant on 84th and Broadway where Nancy told Karen who Emily Locus was and why Emily Locus was so important to her.

And every few months, more often in the spring and fall, the two met at the Soldiers and Sailors Memorial on

Riverside Drive and 89th and walked down into the park and sat at one of the benches Karen liked and spoke about what Karen was working on. Just talking about ideas and holes in the young woman's stories and whether Karen might get them published.

They spoke, too, of what Nancy was working on, and after a bit Karen was free with her opinions, though, in truth, they were mostly and honestly positive.

She finally thought they were ready to be examined by someone who knew quite a bit about the medium, Karen asked Nancy to read and comment on her stories. And Nancy was genuinely and professionally impressed, as she had been with *Lonesome*, and Nancy's agent became Karen's agent and Nancy's publisher published Karen's collection and efforts were afoot to premiere it at a reading, maybe even at the Barnes & Noble a few blocks from Karen's place.

Which is what happened.

3.

At about 8:05 on a mid-September Thursday evening in 2017, Karen Adams stood at a lectern at the Barnes & Noble on Broadway and 82nd Street. She was introduced as "a fine new storyteller from Massachusetts," and now she was in front of mostly strangers. She sipped her water and struggled at first with the book, *her* book, itself—she had the hardcover edition—and then she struggled with saying what she planned on saying. There was a false start or two before the young storyteller overcame her nerves and began reading the first paragraph of *Lonesome*:

> *The Lake was its usual calm on the late-July afternoon. Michelle and Audrey rowed across it as they had each day since their arrival while their husbands were in the City. Except for the two days when it rained and the one on which Audrey's daughter Dawn fell off her bike and was rushed to the hospital in Great Barrington for some stitches.*

She continued with her description of the boat and of Michelle and Audrey. How the sky was blue with speckles of clouds across the western horizon. And then she got to the point where a pair of other wives on their own daily row called across to them, reminding them of the dinner the four couples were due to have on the weekend and, most importantly, that Michelle was to bring the wine. Not long after the two rowboats were no longer within hailing distance of one another, a dark sky appeared across the slight hills to the west. And the wind. How the wind just came up, rushing over the treetops and dropping to skim the surface of the lake. How the rain joined that wind and pummeled those who were still on the lake, Michelle and Audrey most of all since they were the farthest from shore.

Audrey is suddenly in the water and struggling to get back to and into the boat and Michelle is trying to control her own panic and grab her friend as the rain if anything increases in its fury.

Karen closed the book, told the crowd of twenty-five or thirty that they would have to buy it to find out what happens, and found a bookmark and opened the book to the appropriate page and began a second, much lighter story about some clueless college kids, which she didn't finish either.

Before she took questions, Nancy Penchant was introduced by Molly, the B&N staffer helping with the reading. She, Nancy, rose to the podium with Karen looking embarrassed beside her. She spoke kindly of Karen, finishing by noting that the young woman was the first recipient of the Emily Locus Award.

Nancy moved slightly so the attention would fall on Karen, who smiled and nodded and began to redden as she took in the crowd's applause. At that moment, Karen was drawn to the sight of a woman not much older than herself and stylishly if plainly dressed in black pants and a burgundy blouse getting up from the left side towards the back and rushing off down the hall to the ladies' room. She paid it little mind—something she ate probably—and took questions.

Asked the source of *Lonesome*, Karen still had no truly honest answer. It was the question asked of her most often, but she was never able to tell anyone whence it came.

"My folks told stories of summer trips to the lake with their parents and how the mothers and kids would spend a month while the fathers went to work. I heard about Saranac Lake and Googled it and the story flowed and I set it not far from where I was raised, where there was another small lake where my friends and I sometimes went for a swim and sometimes even went out on a rowboat."

It was the answer she always gave, and it always satisfied those who heard it.

There were three or four more questions before Molly stood and Karen again thanked everyone for coming and sat down to sign copies of her collection, with Nancy and Molly giving their moral support from behind her. Nearly everyone who sat through the reading bought one, some two. It was a good night.

She and Nancy helped Molly load the unsold copies into a box and then headed to the escalator. They had reservations for dinner at that place on Broadway and 84th where they met for brunch the year before.

At the bottom of the long escalator, Karen turned, and Nancy was behind her. She was staring at a stranger, though, behind her, holding the rubber rail to keep from falling. From her outfit, Karen recognized the stranger as the woman who'd jumped up and rushed away at the end of the reading. She was three or four people behind Nancy.

Nancy reached her and pulled Karen to the side to get out of the way and, it was clear, waiting for this stranger. As soon as the stranger got to the ground floor, Nancy pulled her to the side too. She asked if she was "Alexandra Locus," and after the girl said she was and Nancy gave her a hug and asked her to join them for dinner, the girl raced out onto Broadway, and was gone.

Nancy was shaking. Karen had never seen Nancy shake. She couldn't imagine Nancy Penchant shaking. She put her hand on Nancy's right shoulder and the two watched the woman pass by the large plate-glass window of the bookstore.

Nancy sighed, and her hand reached up to touch Karen's.

"I never imagined," she chortled, "ever seeing a piece of Emily again, and now she's gone."

She got control. "That was Alex Locus, Emily's daughter. The true love of Emily's life." Karen had, by then, figured out who Alexandra Locus was, but to see the never non-plussed author react as she did came as a complete surprise. Karen just watched Nancy as she ran her wrist beneath her nose to control her sob and after taking a deep breath, she smiled.

"I'm sorry...I'm just an old, cold bitch suddenly thrown into her past. This is your night. I'll be fine after I get some liquor in me."

Karen doubted that, but she walked with her arm through the "old bitch's" as they went the block and a half to the restaurant on Broadway where they had their reservation and where there was in fact more than enough liquor for the pair of them.

This is a bit of short fiction I wrote, a perspective on Karen Adams's story

Lonesome

Bliss. To be floating lazily with my best friend—Audrey and I met as Holyoke freshmen—on this last afternoon alone. The husbands were coming up later and staying till Labor Day. The kids were at camp.

One last afternoon spent on the small lake in the small canoe that came with the house. There were others, also from the city, rowing. Conversations carried across the placid water. You could listen to the gossip without listening for the gossip. Like at dinner parties.

Heaven. Especially after two humid days. The sky was rocket blue unmarred by a cloud, and Audrey and I sat on either end with our wide-brimmed hats warding off the sun.

"Don't forget you're bringing the wine," Susie called about Saturday's party at her house as she and Alison rowed past, and I promised I wouldn't.

My right hand was dragging along the water's crust when Audrey said, "Shit." I turned. A cloud bank was racing over the hills on the New York border. "We'd better get in." The other couples were doing that, though we were a bit farther out.

We struggled to get the oars back in place and I moved to row. Audrey sat at the stern facing me. There was a sudden wind, and a sheet of rain came from nowhere drenching us. She started laughing at my awkwardness as I tried to get a rhythm. We'd barely moved. Suddenly an oar came out, and the boat rocked and began to flip.

When I got it under control, she was gone. Then she was off to the left and I tried to grab her and I reached the oar to her but she couldn't get a hold of it and after bobbing up and flailing three times above the surface, Audrey disappeared forever.